英语学习金典丛书

Essay Translations
with Comments

英汉散文
名篇选译

刘士聪 编著

外文出版社
FOREIGN LANGUAGES PRESS

图书在版编目（CIP）数据

英汉散文名篇选译 / 刘士聪编著. -- 北京 ：外文
出版社, 2023.7
ISBN 978-7-119-13674-5

Ⅰ．①英… Ⅱ．①刘… Ⅲ．①散文集－世界－英、汉
Ⅳ．①I16

中国国家版本馆CIP数据核字(2023)第091187号

出版策划：胡　敏
责任编辑：焦雅楠
特约编辑：张艳茹
封面设计：彭振威设计事务所
印制监制：王　争

英汉散文名篇选译

刘士聪　编著

© 外文出版社有限责任公司
出 版 人：胡开敏
出版发行：外文出版社有限责任公司
地　　址：中国北京西城区百万庄大街 24 号　　**邮政编码：**100037
网　　址：http://www.flp.com.cn　　**电子邮箱：**flp@cipg.org.cn
电　　话：008610-68320579（总编室）　　008610-68996181（编辑部）
　　　　　　008610-68995852（发行部）　　008610-68996183（投稿电话）
印　　刷：清淞永业（天津）印刷有限公司
经　　销：新华书店 / 外文书店
开　　本：889mm × 1194mm　1/32　　**印　张：**8.5　**字　数：**203 千字
装　　别：平装
版　　次：2023 年 7 月第 1 版第 1 次印刷
书　　号：ISBN 978-7-119-13674-5
定　　价：58.00 元

总 序

语言学习是人生必修课，男女老幼、古今中外，莫不如此。语言是人类特有的重要功能，是人区分于其他动物的重要标志。语言使人们能传情达意，相互沟通；语言使人得以思考，并因此而创造；语言储存民族文化，积淀思想精华，使之流芳百世。

因此，学习和掌握好语言，会让人阅读无数，交流无碍，受益无穷。

但是外语的学习看似却非必需，也远不像学习母语那么天然和顺利。

一个人生而习得母语，足以应付日常生活和劳作，为何还要学习外语？我想，是为了融通，为了求知，为了发展，为了译介。

掌握一门外语，会使人发现，天地因之开阔，交流因之扩大。

外语是域外民族思想文化存放之处，是他人的精神家园。我们习之，会更多地吸收不一样的人生养分，陶冶性情，培育心智，并理解他人，使民心相通。

习近平总书记在出访时，曾多次谈到他青少年时期多么喜欢阅读莎士比亚、狄更斯、歌德、巴尔扎克、托尔斯泰、普希金等外国文豪的作品。可见，通过译作间接地接触域外精神食粮，就已经让人受益良多了。

年轻的周树人1902年东渡日本求学求知，凭借所学日语、英语等外语，博览群书，大开眼界，我们始有后来的鲁迅，以及《摩罗诗力说》等纵评外国文学的宏文和《狂人日记》等带来新启迪的名作。

无数事例说明，外语学习，使我们可以更好地与人沟通，开阔眼界，育心育智，审己知人，自身自然就得到更大更好的发展。

同时，我们还能借助所学外语，特别是英语，向域外汲取新的文学、思想、学术养分，并将其翻译成本国语言，惠及子孙后代。

当今世界，75%以上的传媒使用英语，90%以上的主要国际刊物使用英语，这个数字还在增长中。这意味着英语储存着最广博的新知，孕育着众多的人才，产生出巨大的能量，也连通着最广泛的地域。

可以说，学习外语，尤其是学习英语，能够带来巨大的文化红利。

新航道国际教育集团董事长胡敏先生，早年学习英语，后来成为优秀的英语教师，对英美文学有很深的研究和领悟，对英语的教与学都有自己独到的认识。他深知"让英语点亮人生"的意义。他为年轻一代英语学习者着想，提出将经过时间检验的英语学习辅导书籍重新修订出版，并亲力亲为与专家协商挑选"英语学习金典"，精心组织团队编辑出版，于是我们面前便有了这套印制精美、令人欣喜的丛书。

一本好书，是值得一辈子阅读的。一本好的学习辅导书，则可以让几代人从中受益。"英语学习金典"丛书是各位作者的心血之作，而这些作者都是知名学府的资深教授。书中蕴含着他们数十年英教学、翻译教学之所得，因而普受欢迎，历久不衰。

例如南开大学刘士聪教授编写的《英汉散文名篇选译》，收录作者精心挑选的 30 篇中文和英文散文名篇，及其相应的译文和评鉴，既有助于学习者欣赏原作和译作，也很适合翻译课教师做教学辅导材料或补充读物。

上海对外经贸大学黄源深教授编写的《英汉散文比较赏析二十讲》，与上述刘士聪教授的著作有异曲同工之妙。他用明快的行文撰写英语和汉语的名家散文赏析，并按主题分类，方便读者对中英散文进行比较、体会和学习。

云南师范大学刘守兰教授的《英美名诗课》是别具一格的诗歌赏析读本。它对一首首英文诗歌名篇的解读，为读者朋友呈现了一堂堂精美的文学素养课，英语爱好者，特别是英语写作者和翻译工作者，都会有极大的兴趣阅读这本英美诗歌赏析，增添自己英文写作与翻译的文学色彩。

北京大学王逢鑫教授和北京外国语大学陈德彰教授分别编写的《汉译英常见错误解析》和《英汉互译常见错误解析》，更是有针对性地将中国的英语学习者和翻译学习者容易出现的问题，即 100 个在汉译英或英译汉中常见的差错和误解，进行细致的分门别类的点评，加以词汇、语法、搭配等方面问题的分析，以及英汉语言背后文化差异的讲解，对学习者特别有指导意义。

此次出版，这些书籍得到原作者再度修订和充实，相信会给读者带来更多的收获。让我们致敬英语界、翻译界的前辈学者、知名教授，是他们留下传世之作，惠及莘莘学子；也期待青年读者们开卷受益，学好英语，学好翻译，走出亮丽的人生之路。

王克非

北京外国语大学

2023 年 4 月 1 日

序

从 20 世纪 80 年代中期开始，我边教学边学习做翻译，虽然所译屈指可数，比较满意的篇目寥寥无几，也略微积累了一些材料。关于翻译是什么、如何做翻译，虽有些认识，也很肤浅。

翻译的历史很久远，人们研究翻译的时间也很长。把对翻译的研究作一门学问，一门学科，人们也已摸索、探讨了一段时间，朝着这个方向的努力也已取得很大进步，有了很多成果。随着时间的推移，关于翻译的一些理论问题，会越来越明朗。我对翻译理论知之甚少，更无所谓创见，只有些微实践，随之而产生的关于翻译的一些想法也不过是些感性认识，在这里提出来与读者共勉。

如果从文本转换的意义上，即从一种文字的文本转换到另一种文字的文本的意义上看翻译，我认为，翻译，这里指文学作品的翻译，是语言艺术，其至高境界是再现原文的韵味。译作的"韵味"就是原作的艺术内涵通过译文准确而富有文采的语言表达时所蕴含的艺术感染力，这种艺术感染力能引起读者的美感共鸣。作者因心有所感，把自己的精神境界、思想情操和审美志趣，以语言为媒介，倾注于作品之中，使作品产生一种审美韵味。译者经过阅读和分析原文，感悟到作者的精神境界、思想情操和审美志趣，产生与作者类似的审美感受和审美愉悦，然后用另外一种语言将其表达出来，传达给译文读者。译文的韵味是原文作者和译者共同创造的产物，而译文读者在阅读译文时继续了这一创造活动。

文章的韵味，尤其是散文的韵味，主要表现在三个方面。

一、声响与节奏

凡文学作品，不论是小说、散文或诗词，写在纸上是文字，读出来就是声音。一切文学作品都可以朗诵，而文学作品的朗诵本身就是艺术。作者通过写景、抒情、叙事、论证或创造形象传达他的意图，同时，作品的审美价值通过语言的声响和节奏表达出来。因此，语言的声响和节奏是文学作品审美价值的标志之一。这种声响和节奏在传统诗词里表现最为突出，格律也最为严谨。有声语言是自然界里的一种运动形式，广义的散文的语言，和自然界其他运动形式一样，是有节律的。这种节律虽不规则，但唯其随意，唯其自然而妙不可言。清桐城散文家刘大櫆说："凡行文字句短长抑扬高下，无一定之律，而有一定之妙。"桐城另一作家姚姬传说："文章之精妙不出字句声色之间，舍此便无可窥寻。"他们都认识到行文的声响和节律之"妙"。朱光潜说："声音节奏在科学文里可不深究，在文学文里却是一个最主要的成分，因为文学须表现情趣，而情趣就大半要靠声音节奏来表现……"他们所谈都只限于汉语文学作品。其实，别的语言也一样，以声响节奏形式所表现出来的语言的审美特征是普遍存在的。比如英语，朗读起来其轻重缓急、抑扬高下的节奏感特别强。

美国散文家 E. B. 怀特（E. B. White）说："我们谈到菲茨杰拉德（F. S. Fitzgerald）的语言风格时，不是指他掌握关系代词的能力，而是指他的文字在纸上所发出的声音。"

文学作品里语言的声响与节奏，特别是语言的节奏感，要在翻译里体现出来，这是保持和再现文学作品语言审美价值的一个不可忽略的方面。

二、意境和氛围

一般来说，任何形式的文学作品都有一种意境与氛围，这种意境与氛围通过作者在作品里所表达的精神气质、思想情操、审美志趣以及他所创造的形象营造出来，并构成作品审美价值的核心。孙犁说："状景抒情，成为散文的意境。意境有高下，正如作者修养有高下，胸襟有广狭，志趣有崇卑，不可勉强……范仲淹先忧后乐之明言，并非一时乘兴创作出来，乃是久萦于心的素志，触景生情而出。"作者的"修养""胸襟"和"志趣"，反映在他所创造的情景或形象里，对读者产生艺术感染力。关于氛围，冯骥才写过一篇文章叫《阐释五大道》，是写在天津市区五条街道上遗留下来的殖民地时期的建筑的。他说："历史留给我们的绝不是一幢幢房子，还有它迷人的氛围。而这又不只是一种建筑氛围，更是一种历史人文的气息。"这种氛围或气息在文学作品里同样存在。

文学翻译只有保持和再现原文的这种意境和氛围，才能使译文具有和原文类似的审美韵味。我们说文学翻译是再创作，主要是在这个意义上说它是再创作。

三、个性化的话语方式

每一个作家都以他独特的方式表达自己，因此，他所使用的语言是属于他自己的，也就形成了他自己的语言风格。汪曾祺说："语言决定于作家的气质。'气以实志，志以定言，吐纳英华，莫非情性。'（《文心雕龙·体性》）鲁迅有鲁迅的语言，废名有废名的语言，沈从文有沈从文的语言，孙犁有孙犁的语言，何立伟有何立伟的语言，阿城有阿城的语言。"汪曾祺把语言看作是作家气质的表现，这非常重要。就是说，当我们翻译一个作家的作品时，通过翻译他的语言可以再现他的气质。这对一个有艺术责任心的译者来说，是不可回避的，当然，做起来也是非常困难的。要把不同作家的语言特色用另外一种语言表达出来，把他的语言风格用另外一种语言再现出来，译者不能不通过作品研究作者，研究作者的精神气质、思想情操和审美志趣。单纯研究翻译技巧是远远不够的，从根本上弄清作者的话语方式，对译者是非常重要的。

总之，文学作品的翻译应把传达原文的审美韵味作为至高的追求。虽然传统美学认为，文学作品的韵味有它"不可言传"的内涵，但具体分析起来，也有它可操作的成分。这可操作的成分主要是语言的"声响与节奏"，作品的"意境和氛围"，以及作者"个性化的话语方式"。这样看来，传达韵味对译者来说要求是很高的，但只要加强语言、文化和审美方面的修养，这个目标是可以逐步达到的。

我的朋友们与我合作翻译了本书的部分篇章或对本书的部分篇章做了解释，他们是：靳梅琳、王宏印、张保红、温秀颖、高巍、任东升、余东、段钨金、丁连普、马会娟、马红军等，在此一并表示感谢。

刘士聪

2023 年 4 月

出版前言

《英汉散文名篇选译》与读者见面，顺便做一点说明。

书中所收文章多在过去 30 余年的研究生翻译教学中使用过，学生们建议将其结成集子，我也有类似的想法。于是着手翻阅整理原有文稿，经过反复的修改加工，在朋友和学生们的热情帮助下，书稿终于成形。本书曾于 2010 年由译林出版社出版，书名为《英汉·汉英美文翻译与鉴赏》（新编版）。现作为新英汉"英语学习金典"系列丛书之一，由外文出版社重新出版，与广大读者再次见面。为简洁起见，书名也随之更改为《英汉散文名篇选译》。

本书分上、下两篇。上篇为散文汉译，选了 10 篇英美现当代作家的作品，写了赏析文字，并附汉语译文和翻译提示；下篇为散文英译，选了 20 篇中国现当代作家的文章，每篇文章附有英语译文和翻译提示。所有篇目均以英汉对照的形式呈现，便于读者对照赏析。

所选皆为篇幅小、文字好的优秀散文，用来学习和研究翻译很适合，也可作为文学作品阅读与鉴赏。

对于译文，不同译者会有不同译法，译文也各有特色，这就是所谓原文的唯一性与译文的多样性。因此，本书提供的译文仅供读者参考。读者在阅读译文时应有批评的眼光，对译文的优劣、正误、雅俗有自己的判断，必要时或可自行对译文进行处理，正所谓批判的阅读。

若论散文之美，可从三个方面看：一、好的散文有实在内容，不论是叙事的还是抒情的，总是言之有物；二、好的散文感情真挚，有了真挚的感情便有了艺术的真实；三、好的散文语言朴素、自然，而朴素、自然是审美语言的属性。

学习翻译，从散文入手效果比较好，因为散文体的文字是各种文体的基础。小说、戏剧的语言，社会科学、自然科学文献的语言，应用文体的语言，都具有散文语言的特点，甚至连诗歌语言也是在散文语言的基础上升华而成。有了翻译散文的经验，可为翻译其他文体的作品提供借鉴。

书中所选文章皆为名篇，值得反复学习和研究，不可泛泛而读，阅读时应随时关注以下三个环节：字词、搭配、句子。

第一，我们初学英语时是从一个词一个词开始的，那时比较重视字词；后来，慢慢对字词便不够重视了，这主要是指对字词在写作或翻译中所占的重要位置和所起的重要作用认识不足，重视不够。其实，学好字词是学好写作和翻译的一个重要环节。美国散文家怀特（E. B. White）称自己是"word man"，他对字词尤为重视，写作时反复推敲，所以，他的文章，不论是针砭时弊，还是描写风情，都具有震撼的力量，因此，他的文章历来受到普遍欢迎。我们做翻译也是一样，不厌其烦地推敲字词，在恰当的地方使用恰当的字词，是做好翻译的一个重要环节。

第二，搭配是英语中的一个重要语言现象，也是一个重要表达手段。两个或几个单词搭配在一起可以表达非常的概念，产生非常的效果。比如，本书原版中所选文章"Roses, Roses, All the Way"（该篇由于版权问题，很遗憾在新版本中未能展示，读者可上网自行搜索），讲述英国前首相撒切尔夫人于 1958 年 32 岁时竞选议员成功进入英国权力机构，文章里有这样一句话：

She **parried her way** through the complacent, mail-dominated councils of power—no woman had ever **roiled those waters**.

此处有两个搭配，一个是 parried her way，关于动词 parry，英语词典这样解释：to defend yourself against sb who is attacking you，说明作为一个女人，撒切尔夫人经过左挡右闪、奋力拼搏，才得以成功进入男人主宰的权力机构，这很不容易。另一个搭配是 roiled those waters，这个搭配是说，那些权力机构的水很深，在她之前从来没有女人到那里去折腾。这两个搭配里的单词意思都很简单，但它们结合起来所表达的意思就很有内涵。好句子一般都有好的搭配，好的搭配是构成好句子的必要成分。

第三，句子是表达意义的基本单位，句子可以表达一个完整的概念，所以，不论是汉语还是英语，历来作家在句子的写作上都下了很多功夫。书中我们选了英国作家查尔斯·爱德华·蒙塔格（Charles Edward Montague）的一篇散文，《感知快乐的天赋》（"The Faculty of Delight"），其中有一个句子：

A child in the full health of his mind will put his hand flat on the summer turf, feel it, and **give a little shiver of private glee** at the elastic firmness of the globe.

如果我们仔细观察一下，构成这个句子的成分都是一些简单的单词，还有几个妙用的搭配，如 in the full health of his mind、put his hand flat、private glee 等，作者把这些成分组织在一起，用一个完整的句子，便将小孩如何在大自然中感知到快乐的情景写活了。

学习翻译，也同样需要关注前面提到的三个方面：字词、搭配、句子。不论是汉译英还是英译汉，通过两种文字的对比，发现它们各自在表达方式上的优长，特别要关注它们之间的差异。汉英两种语言在表达方式上有很多相同之处，但在表达同一个概念时，两种语言的表达方式有时差异很大，而且这种现象很多。在考察书中的译文时，注意这一点很重要，是我们学习地道英语的重要一环。

正如前面所说，本书也可以作为文学作品阅读与鉴赏。比如，书中选了英国作家米尔恩（A. A. Milne）的"Golden Fruit"一文，其中有这样一段文字：

The fact is that **there is an honesty about the orange** which appeals to all of us. If it is going to be bad—for the best of us are bad sometimes—it begins to be bad from the outside, not from the inside. How many a pear which presents a blooming face to the world is rotten at the core. How many an innocent-looking apple is harbouring a worm in the bud. But the orange has no secret faults. **Its outside is a mirror of its inside...**

文章赞扬柑橘表里如一的诚实品质，柑橘坏了，从表面开始，让人一目了然；不像鸭梨，表面光鲜，内核已经烂了，也不像苹果，表面好好的，心里却生了虫子。作者通过对水果品性的描写来影射人的品行，赞扬表里如一，针砭用光鲜表面遮掩内在腐败的假象。仔细观察它的表达方式时，我们发现，用词简单易懂，行文简洁明朗，却又含蓄地把文章的寓意表达得清清楚楚。

书中还选了许地山的《落花生》，这是一篇传之甚广的文章，其中有一段文字是这样说的：

花生的用处固然很多；但有一样是很可贵的，这小小的豆不像那好看的苹果、桃子、石榴，把它们的果实悬在枝上，鲜红嫩绿的颜色，令人一望而发生羡慕的心。它只把果子埋在地底，等到成熟，才容人把它挖出来。

这段文字也告诉人们，做人要低调，不要炫耀自己。同样，这里的文字也简单易懂。当我们读懂了作者用这样简单的文字表达深奥的寓意时，感觉受到教益，也欣赏他们的文字，此时我们心里会有一种愉悦之感，会有一种审美的感受，这可能就是艺术的魅力。

学习翻译者，或翻译实践者，需要具备一定的翻译理论知识，但要提高翻译水平，增强翻译能力，重要的是读书，读经典文学，读报纸杂志，读好的文章，长期读，坚持不懈地读。

阅读的目的不单单是为了读懂，只求读懂远远不够；更深一层的追求是读出文字或文章的美感。凡作家写文章，包括社科文章甚至应用文章，都讲究审美，都有审美追求。比如，多年前，曾经在一家英文报纸上看见一则为德国奔驰汽车作的广告：

Mercedes Benz is the car by which other cars are judged.

这则广告写得好，连车名在内一共 10 个词，或者 11 个词，很简洁，所占篇幅很小，但它的宣传效果很好。它告诉买家或读者，奔驰汽车是最好的，别的汽车如何，要用奔驰的标准来衡量。写这则广告的人一定动了脑筋，要以最简洁的文字取得最好的宣传效果。好的作家追求简洁，因为简洁的文字有美感。如果我们朗读一下这个句子，会发现它有很强的节奏感，这种节奏感也是文字美感的一种表现。

广告是这样，其他文字，特别是属于文学范畴的散文更是如此，更讲究文字之美。

中国留学生先驱容闳（Yung Wing，1828—1912）写过一本书，*My Life in China and America*，书中谈到他在考入美国耶鲁大学之前曾在马萨诸塞州的孟松预备学校（Monson Academy）补习英语，关于他的英语老师是如何教授英语的，他有以下的回忆：

He had the faculty of inspiring his pupils with the love of the beautiful, both in ancient and modern literature. In our daily recitations, **he laid a greater stress on pointing out the beauties of a sentence and its construction**, than he did on grammatical rules, moods and tenses.

这位英语老师有一种能力，能激励学生热爱古典文学和当代文学中美好的东西。在每天的朗读课上，比起讲语法规则、动词语气或动词时态等，他更强调句子之美和句子结构。

这位老师所强调的句子之美和句子结构，给了我们启发。如果我们阅读时不只是停留在语法上，而是上升到语言的审美层次，阅读将给我们带来艺术享受。

希望本书对于翻译工作者、翻译爱好者，对于高校英语翻译专业的学生，以及准备报考翻译专业的考生，能够有所启发，有所补益。对于书中的不足之处，或者谬误之处，也希望得到各方人士的批评和指正，编者将不胜感激。

刘士聪
2023 年 4 月

目 录
Contents

下编　散文英译

上 编

散文汉译
CHINESE TRANSLATIONS
OF PROSE

1

The Cardinal Virtue of Prose

Arthur Clutton-Brock（1868—1924），英国散文家，文艺批评家。
"The Cardinal Virtue of Prose" 选自 *The Oxford Book of English Prose*，
以散文语言讨论文学理论，有文采。

Prose of its very nature is longer than verse, and the virtues peculiar to it manifest themselves gradually. If the cardinal virtue of poetry is love, the cardinal virtue of prose is justice; and, whereas love makes you act and speak on the spur of the moment, justice needs inquiry, patience, and a control even of the noblest passions. By justice here I do not mean justice only to particular people or ideas, but a habit of justice in all the processes of thought, a style tranquillized and a form moulded by that habit. The master of prose is not cold, but he will not let any word or image inflame him with a heat irrelevant to his purpose. Unhasting, unresting, he pursues it, subduing all the riches of his mind to it, rejecting all beauties that are not germane to it; making his own beauty out of the very accomplishment of it, out of the whole work and its proportions, so that you must read to the end before you know that it is beautiful. But he has his reward, for he is trusted and convinces, as those who are at the mercy of their own eloquence do not; and he gives a pleasure all the greater for being hardly noticed. In the best prose, whether narrative or argument, we are so led on as we read, that we do not stop to applaud the writer, nor do we stop to question him.

原文赏析

《散文最重要的品质》（"The Cardinal Virtue of Prose"）是关于散文的一篇短论。

这篇文章只有一个段落，240多个词，但论述的是一个大题目。

文章从散文本身、作者、读者三个角度谈散文的品质。全文共七句话，前三句讲散文本身，中间三句讲作者，最后一句讲读者。讲散文时由 Prose 起始，讲作者时由 The master of prose 起始，讲读者时由 In the best prose...we 起始。从形式到内容，这三部分的衔接与连贯都是内在的。在它们之间没有连接词，也没有使用文字说明它们的关系或顺序，可见作者运用文字的简练和写作手法的老练。

开始，作者从三个方面论述散文的性质。首先说 the cardinal virtue of prose is justice，所谓 justice，是指"真实""合理"地反映思想、感情和事物；接着说 justice needs inquiry, patience, and a control even of the noblest passions，是指这种"真实"和"合理"需要"调查""耐心"和"清醒的头脑"；最后，作者进一步明确这是一种习惯、一种文风和一种形式（a habit of justice in all the processes of thought, a style tranquillized and a form moulded by that habit），所谓 justice，是指思想过程中"真实"和"合理"的习惯，以及由此习惯所形成的沉稳的文风和由此习惯所造就的形式。

作为论说文，这篇文章还有以下特征：

1. 多用具有确定意义的动词和句式，如 love **makes** you **act** and **speak**、he **pursues** it 和"By justice here I **do not mean…but…**"等。

2. 多用具有实义的名词，而少用意义伸缩性较大的形容词和副词，如 habit、style、form、beauty、reward、accomplishment 等。

3. 为使行文简洁，作者使用了：(1) 介词短语，如 **of** its very nature、**out of** the whole work and its proportions、**By** justice；(2) 起修饰作用的形容词短语，如 and the virtues **peculiar** to it、with a heat **irrelevant** to his purpose、a pleasure **all the greater** for being hardly noticed；(3) 起限定作用的过去分词短语，如 a style **tranquillized** and a form **moulded by** that habit；(4) 作状语的现在分词短语，如 **subduing** all the riches、**rejecting** all beauties 等。

4. 为增强文章的说服力，作者使用了一些带对偶性质的句子，如"If the cardinal virtue of poetry is love, the cardinal virtue of prose is justice…""…we do not stop to applaud the writer, nor do we stop to question him."。

5. 为说理透彻周密，作者使用了较长、较复杂的句式，最长的57 个词，最短的也有18 个之多，平均每句话35 个词；多是主从句和复合句，没有简单句。

作者能够以简短的篇幅、简洁的语言论述在形式上不太好规范的散文，从散文本身、作者和读者三个不同的角度抓住散文的本质特征，文章虽短，但论述准确，对英语写作很有启示。

散文最重要的品质

阿瑟·克拉顿—布罗克

散文，就其本质而言，比韵文篇幅长。而且，其特有的品质是逐渐展现出来的。如果说诗最重要的品质是爱，那么散文最重要的品质是合理；并且，尽管"爱"使你因一时冲动而行动、而抒发，"合理"则需要调查，需要耐心，需要控制即使是最崇高的激情。关于合理，我不是指只针对具体人或具体思想的合理，而是指在思想的全过程中的一种合理的习惯，一种由此习惯所形成的沉稳的文风和由此习惯所造就的形式。散文大师并不冷漠，但他也不允许那些满含激情，但又与他的初衷毫不相干的词语或形象来激发他的感情。他不慌不忙、永不停止地追求着，克制着脑子里丰富的思想活动，摒弃所有与之无关的美，从完成的作品之中、从作品的整体和各部分之间和谐的关系里，去创造自己的美。因此，你必须把作品读完，才能知道它是美的。可是，他享有自己的报偿，因为他取得人们的信任，他令人信服，正像那些单靠显弄雄辩的人们得不到这一报偿，道理是一样的。而且，他不露声色，这反而能给人更大的愉悦。我们在阅读最好的散文时，无论是叙事的还是说理的，是在情不自禁地一直读下去，而不会停下来向作者欢呼，也不会停下来向作者发问。

| 翻译提示 |

这篇文章一是短小，二是讨论的问题很大。因此，文章的凝聚力和说服力是作者运思的要点，也是译者要考虑的要点。所谓文章

的"凝聚力"和"说服力"，就论说文而言，就是经过作者周密的构思和合理的组织以后，文章对读者产生的震撼和影响；作者的目的是要以自己的观点说服读者。这篇文章的"凝聚力"和"说服力"通过三个重要的行文手段得以实现。

一是层次清楚，主题突出；二是上下文衔接紧密，发展线索清晰；三是词义准确，行文畅达。下面分别来看：

一、层次清楚，主题突出

文章讨论散文的品质从三个视角入手：散文的本质、作者的写作和读者的感觉。讲散文的本质时以 Prose 起始，讲作者的写作时以 The master of prose 起始，讲读者的感觉时以 In the best prose...we 起始。这种将主题词放在句首的写法暗示了也突出了作者从三个不同视角讨论散文的用心。译者意识到这一点很重要，译文也将"散文""散文大师"和"我们"三个主题词放在句首，也相应地暗示、突出了作者本来的意图。这种有意的安排可以加强文章的凝聚力和说服力。

二、上下文衔接紧密，发展线索清晰

本文上下文的衔接分篇章的连贯和句子的衔接两种情况。篇章的连贯主要是通过内在的联系体现出来，作者没有也无须使用连接词，如前面讨论过的三个层次问题。读者清楚，每个层次自然构成整个篇章的一个部分，而三个部分的聚合又指向文章的核心问题——散文最重要的品质。这多少是属于对文本宏观方面的关照，需予以特别的注意。句子的衔接多靠连接词，如：具有并列功能的连接词 and，具有转折功能的连接词 but、whereas，还有同样起到连接作用的介词短语 By justice、In the best prose 等。翻译这些连接词本身并不难，但如何翻译才能起到好的连接作用却是一个需要仔细思考的问题。

三、词义准确，行文畅达

翻译时，文字的准确不只是指单个字词的准确，在短语和句子层面上，依据译入语语言特征的要求，准确、充分地表达原文的意思，是同样重要的。请看下面两个译例：

［原文］ ...justice needs inquiry, patience, and a control even of the noblest passions.

［译文］ "合理"则需要调查，需要耐心，需要控制即使是最崇高的激情。

原文中，needs 带三个并列的名词作宾语（inquiry, patience, and a control...），needs 不重复使用，重复了听起来反而累赘、臃肿。但在汉语里，这个动词却要重复。

［原文］ But he has his reward, for he is trusted and convinces, as those who are at the mercy of their own eloquence do not...

［译文］ 可是，他享有自己的报偿，因为他取得人们的信任，他令人信服，正像那些单靠显弄雄辩的人们得不到这一报偿，道理是一样的……

翻译这句话里的从句时需要斟酌，其中 do not 是英语里特有的一种很好的省略形式，在这个上下文里，需要将省略的部分翻译出来。在这里，do not 是指 they do not have their own rewards。

2

A School Portrait

Robert Bridges（1844—1930），英国诗人，剧作家。1913 年获桂冠诗人称号。1929 年，85 岁时，发表哲理诗 *The Testament of Beauty*，被认为是他最伟大的作品。"A School Portrait"选自 *The Oxford Book of English Prose*，文字朴素无华，真实感人。

I had not visited Eton for many years, when one day passing from the Fellows' Library into the Gallery I caught sight of the portrait of my school-friend Digby Dolben hanging just without the door among our most distinguished contemporaries. I was wholly arrested, and as I stood gazing on it, my companion asked me if I knew who it was. I was thinking that, beyond a few whom I could name, I must be almost the only person who would know. Far memories of my boyhood were crowding freshly upon me: he was standing again beside me in the eager promise of his youth; I could hear his voice; nothing of him was changed; while I, wrapt from him in a confused mist of time, was wondering what he would think, could he know that at this actual moment he would have been dead thirty years, and that his memory would be thus preserved and honoured in the beloved school, where his delicate spirit had been so strangely troubled.

This portrait-gallery of old Etonians is very select: preeminent distinction of birth or merit may win you a place there, or again official connection with the school, which rightly loves to keep up an unbroken panorama of its teachers, and to vivify its annals with the faces and figures of the personalities who carried on its traditions. But how came Dolben there? It was because he was a poet, —that I knew; —and yet his poems were not known; they were jealously guarded by his family and a few friends: indeed such of his poems as could have come to the eyes of the authorities who sanctioned this memorial would not justify it. There was another reason; and the portrait bears its own credentials; for though you might not perhaps divine the poet in it, you can see the saint, the soul rapt in contemplation, the habit of stainless life, of devotion, of enthusiasm for high ideals. Such a being must have stood out conspicuously among his fellows; the facts of his life would have been the ground of the faith in his genius; and when his early death endeared and sanctified his memory, loving grief would generously grant him the laurels which he had never worn.

原文赏析

《一张肖像》（"A School Portrait"）是一篇回忆往昔朋友的文章，讲作者罗伯特·布里吉斯回母校伊顿公学访问，在校园里看见已故三十年的老同学迪格比·多尔宾的肖像和当今名人的肖像挂在一起时的瞬间感慨。

文章分两段，很像中国词的上、下两阕，上阕写景（这里是人文景观），描写作者在校园里看见多尔宾的肖像之后引起回忆；下阕抒情（抒发对朋友的崇敬和爱慕之情），分析多尔宾之所以能和当今名人并论，是因为他有圣人的品格。

文章的一个突出特点是：由于内在的逻辑性强，不求形式上的联系。第一段四句，第二段五句，句与句之间不用连接词，段与段之间也没有字面上的转承。

文章的又一个特点是：文笔简练，既不修饰，也不用典，用朴实的文字表达真挚的感情。好的文章常常是这样。

清桐城派散文家刘大櫆主张"文贵简"。"简"是一种美，这种美不仅表现在字词、句子和修辞的选择上，或句与句、段与段的组织上，更表现在文章整体的艺术境界上。

文章整体的艺术效果来自作者、题材和表现手段。作者，是指作者的思想情操、个人气质和审美倾向，这些都自然地渗透到作品的字里行间；题材，是指作者赖以发现美的客观素材，从中着力挖掘其美学内涵；表现手段，是指作者运筹文字的谋略。这三者是互动的。作者是主观因素，题材是客观因素，主、客观因素的结合是文章美学的源泉；文字是媒介，是表现美的手段。文章的美学价值主要是通过文字表现出来的，但要体会由文字所创造出来的艺术境界，更全面、更深刻地把握文章的美学价值，需要把作者和题材考虑进来。艺术境界是作者的精神气质和所描写的素材在文字内外散发出来的美的光芒。作者用简朴的文字对多尔宾的崇高品格做了深刻的分析和诚挚的评价，这篇文章的艺术境界也由此体现出来。作者所表达的全部思想和情感，归结到最后两句话。以 There was another reason 为开始的一句，是对多尔宾的正面评价，在他的肖像里，you can see the saint, the soul rapt in contemplation, the habit of stainless life, of devotion, of enthusiasm for high ideals。最后一句，从三个与多尔宾相联系的客观方面出发，赞美多尔宾：1) Such a being must have stood out conspicuously among his fellows; 2) the facts of his life would have been the ground of the faith in his genius; 3) and when his early death endeared and sanctified his memory, loving grief would generously grant him the laurels which he had never worn。

| 译 文 |

一张肖像

罗伯特·布里吉斯

　　我多年没回伊顿了。一天，在从研究员图书馆去画廊的路上，我看见学生时代的朋友迪格比·多尔宾的肖像和当代杰出名人肖像一起挂在门外。我被吸引住了，正在我停下来盯着画像出神的时候，我的同伴问我是否知道那是谁。我在想，除了几个我可以叫出名字的人以外，我差不多是唯一认识他的人了。遥远童年时代的记忆鲜活地涌进我的脑海：他又重新站在我的身边，焕发着青春的风采；我能听见他说话的声音，他没有一点变化；同时，我在寻思着，因为与他之间相隔一段宛若迷雾的年月，假如他知道在这一时刻他已经死了三十年，他可爱的母校在以这样的方式纪念他，给他这样高的荣誉，而他上学时，他脆弱的心灵曾经莫名其妙地烦恼过，他会做怎样的感想呢？

　　这个为昔日的伊顿校友建立的肖像画廊在决定入选的人选时是很慎重的：出身显赫或表现突出有可能得到一个位置，或者与校方有正式的联系，而校方也希望完整地再现教师队伍的全貌，使那些保持了学校传统的名人形象构成的校史有生气，学校这样做是完全正确的。但是，多尔宾是怎么来到这里的呢？因为他是一个诗人——这我很清楚；然而，他的诗并不为人所知，他的诗是由他的家人和几个朋友精心保管着；要说只凭学校当局见到的几首诗就同意以这种方式纪念他，理由还不太充分。还有另外一个理由：他的肖像本身就是证明；虽然你也许不能从肖像里看出他是诗人，但你看见的是圣人，是沉浸在沉思默想之中的灵魂，是一生无瑕的、执着和热烈地追求崇高理想的气质。这样的人在他的同时代人当中一定是出类拔萃的；他生活的现实与经历足以使我们相信他是天才；当他的英年早逝使我们对他的怀念变得亲切而神圣时，出于对他的爱而产生的悲哀便赋予了他生前未曾享受过的诗人的桂冠。

| 翻 译 提 示 |

我们在"原文赏析"里提到，这篇文章的一个特点是：文笔简练，既不修饰，也不用典，用朴实的文字表达真挚的感情。在叙事风格上是直叙的语气，这就为译文的风格定了调子，即译文也应该是直叙的语气。运用直叙的语气来翻译比较短、结构上比较简单的句子还好处理；翻译比较长、结构比较复杂的句子时，则需要首先理顺原文句子里各个部分和成分之间的关系，在译文句子里做相应的安排。翻译好这样的句子对保持和再现文章风格的统一至关重要。如：

…while I, wrapt from him in a confused mist of time, was wondering what he would think, could he know that at this actual moment he would have been dead thirty years, and that his memory would be thus preserved and honoured in the beloved school, where his delicate spirit had been so strangely troubled.

这个句子比较长，结构也比较复杂，如何用朴实的文字和直叙的语气将这句话翻译出来，以保持文章整体风格的统一，这一点需要译者认真考虑，慎重处理。首先，这不是一个独立完整的句子，而是一个长句里的半句话，因此，译文要考虑与前半句的衔接。译文是这样的：

……同时，我在寻思着，因为与他之间相隔一段宛若迷雾的年月，假如他知道在这一时刻他已经死了三十年，他可爱的母校在以这样的方式纪念他，给他这样高的荣誉，而他上学时，他脆弱的心灵曾经莫名其妙地烦恼过，他会做怎样的感想呢？

因为原文里有连接词 while，译文便以"同时"开始，一方面与前半句联系起来，一方面引导出下面的文字。原文中，I...was wondering 和它的宾语从句 what he would think 是连在一起的，后面的（虚拟）条件从句很长，但这是英语的表达习惯，即使条件从句很长，句子的意思也清楚。汉语多是把谓语动词和宾语从句分开的，前者放在句首，后者放在句尾，其间插进条件从句，这符合汉语的表达习惯。如上面的译文所示。再如：

There was another reason; and the portrait bears its own credentials; for though you might not perhaps divine the poet in it, you can see the saint, the soul rapt in contemplation, the habit of stainless life, of devotion, of enthusiasm for high ideals.

翻译这句话时，要确定什么是 you can see 的宾语，宾语有三个：the saint，the soul 和 the habit。habit 译成"习性"或"气质"符合这句话的含义。三个宾语若直译成汉语的三个宾语也不太好安排，这里做了变通。译文如下：

还有另外一个理由：他的肖像本身就是证明；虽然你也许不能从肖像里看出他是诗人，但你看见的是圣人，是沉浸在沉思默想之中的灵魂，是一生无瑕的、执着和热烈地追求崇高理想的气质。

3

Golden Fruit

A(lan) A(lexander) Milne（1882—1956），英国作家，著有长篇小说、短篇小说、诗歌和散文。一战后开始剧本创作，主要有 *Mr. Pim Passes By*、*The Truth about Blayds*、*The Dove Rood* 等。散文"Golden Fruit"文笔轻巧，诙谐幽默。

Of the fruits of the year I give my vote to the orange.

In the first place it is a perennial—if not in actual fact, at least in the greengrocer's shop. On the days when dessert is a name given to a handful of chocolates and a little preserved ginger, when macedoine de fruits is the title bestowed on two prunes and a piece of rhubarbs, then the orange, however sour, comes nobly to the rescue; and on those other days of plenty when cherries and strawberries and raspberries and gooseberries riot together upon the table, the orange, sweeter than ever, is still there to hold its own. Bread and butter, beef and mutton, eggs and bacon, are not more necessary to an ordered existence than the orange.

It is well that the commonest fruit should be also the best. Of the virtues of the orange I have not room fully to speak. It has properties of health giving, as that it cures influenza and establishes the complexion. It is clean, for whoever handles it on its way to your table, but handles its outer covering, its top coat, which is left in the hall. It is round, and forms an excellent substitute with the young for a cricket ball. The pip can be flicked at your enemies, and quite a small piece of peel makes a slide for an old gentleman.

But all this would count nothing had not the orange such delightful qualities of taste. I dare not let myself go upon this subject. I am a slave to its sweetness. I grudge every marriage in that it means a fresh supply of orange blossom, the promise of so much golden fruit cut short. However, the world must go on.

…

With the orange we do live year in and year out. That speaks well for the orange. The fact is that there is an honesty about the orange which appeals to all of us. If it is going to be bad—for the best of us are bad sometimes—it begins to be bad from the outside, not from the inside. How many a pear which presents a blooming face to the world is rotten at the core. How many an innocent-looking apple is harbouring a worm in the bud. But the orange has no secret faults. Its outside is a mirror of its inside, and if you are quick you can tell the shopman so before he slips it into the bag.

我们有时用"精粹"形容短而好的文章,《柑橘》("Golden Fruit")就是一篇"精粹"。

全文四百多个词,五个段落,联系紧密,是一个连贯的篇章。

第一段"Of the fruits of the year I give my vote to the orange."是一个强调句。因其以 Of 开头,就很自然地把文章的中心词 orange 放在了句尾强调的位置上,这是很巧妙的手法。

第二段有一个对应的排比句,以分号为界,结构很有章法:

On the days when…when… 对 and on those other days of plenty when; then the orange 对 the orange; however sour 对 sweeter than ever; comes nobly to the rescue 对 is still there to hold its own。这种大体对称的形式给人以美感。

第三段在谈柑橘的用途的同时,又以幽默的口吻顺便谈及柑橘的其他"功能":

It is round, and forms an excellent substitute with the young for a cricket ball. The pip can be flicked at your enemies, and quite a small piece of peel makes a slide for an old gentleman.

这是真正的幽默。作者的幽默感在第四段和第五段里继续:

I grudge every marriage in that it means a fresh supply of orange blossom, the promise of so much golden fruit cut short. **However, the world must go on.**

…and if you are quick **you can tell the shopman so before he slips it into the bag**.

作者地道的表达方式赋予了英语应有的韵味。

如第一段里"I **give my vote** to the orange",第二段里"the orange…comes **nobly** to the rescue; …when cherries and strawberries and

raspberries and gooseberries **riot** together upon the table…",第三段里
"**It is well** that…",都能看出作者运用英语的轻巧和娴熟。第四
段里"…it means a fresh supply of orange blossom, **the promise of so
much golden fruit cut shorts**.",这句话里的名词短语用得好,特别
是 the promise of so much golden fruit,后面又有一个分词短语 cut
short,读到这里,cut 里短促的元音和 short 里轻辅音 /t/ 的戛然而
止,真给人以"夭折"之感。第五段里 inside 和 outside 两字的循环
出现,从"…it begins to be bad from the outside, not from the inside."
到"Its outside is a mirror of its inside…",其间的几个表达方法,虽
然没有重复这两个字,但可以视其为 outside 或 inside 的同义语,如
a blooming face (outside)、an innocent-looking apple (outside)、rotten at
the core (inside)、a worm in the bud (inside)、no secret faults (inside)。这
一部分从 outside 和 inside 开始,中间用了几个同义语过渡,最后以
"Its outside is a mirror of its inside…"终结,用对比和比喻道出柑橘的
品质,一切都很自然,没有刻意雕琢。

这篇文章还有一个特点,由于内在逻辑严密,因此省略了很多
过渡性的语言和形式上的联系。

(与靳梅琳合写)

| 译文 |

柑橘

A. A. 米尔恩

一年四季的水果里,我最推崇柑橘。

首先,柑橘常年都有——即使不是在树上,至少也是在水果店
里。有的时候,只用几块巧克力和一点蜜饯生姜充当餐后的甜点,

两块李子干加一片大黄便被冠以蔬果什锦美名时，这时仍带酸味的柑橘便前来慷慨救驾；其他时候，水果丰盈，樱桃、草莓、木莓、醋栗在餐桌上相互争艳时，此时比往日更加甜美的柑橘依然能坚守自己的岗位。对于人们的日常生活，面包和黄油，牛肉和羊肉，鸡蛋和咸肉，都未必像柑橘那样不可或缺。很幸运，这种最普通的水果恰恰是最好的水果。论其优点，难尽其详，柑橘有益于健康，比如，可以治疗流感，滋养皮肤。柑橘清洁干净，不管是谁把它端上桌，也只触到它的表皮，亦即它的外衣，吃完后橘皮便被留在餐厅里。柑橘是圆的，给孩子当板球玩是再好不过了。柑橘核可用来弹射你的敌人，一小片橘皮也能让一个老者滑个趔趄。

但是，如若不是柑橘的味道甜美可口，上述的一切便都不足取。我真不敢纵谈柑橘的美味。我为它的美味所倾倒。每当有人结婚我便心生怨意，因为那就意味着一束鲜橘花——未来金黄果实的夭折。然而，人类总得继续繁衍。

……

我们年复一年地吃着柑橘生活，这就是对它有力的辩护。事实上，是柑橘诚实的品格吸引了我们。假如它要开始腐败的话——因为我们之中的优秀者有时也会腐败的——它是从外表而不是从内里开始的。有多少梨子在向世人展示其鲜嫩的容光时，内里已经腐烂。有多少看上去纯美无瑕的苹果，刚刚发芽就已经包藏蛀虫。而柑橘从不隐藏瑕疵。它的外表是它内心的镜子，那么，如果你反应快，不等售货员把它丢进纸袋儿，你就能告诉他这是一个坏橘子。

（与靳梅琳合译）

| 翻译提示 |

这篇文章虽短，若就翻译来谈，可讨论的问题还是很多。比

如，短小文章的翻译如何再现其凝练的语言特征，幽默话语该如何翻译等等。这里只就尊重原文的语言形式和几个文字上的细节问题说一说。

先说尊重原文语言形式的问题。翻译主要是翻译意义，同时也要注意到与意义相适应的语言形式。应将这二者都充分地表现出来，这是一个不可忽略的问题。

文章开头的这个句子"Of the fruits of the year I give my vote to the orange."是简单句，但作者为了强调主题词 orange 而将其放在句子的最后，这也算是一个尾重句（periodic sentence）。译成汉语时，也应加强中心词"柑橘"："一年四季的水果里，我最推崇柑橘。"

第二段里有一个很长的句子，是一个以分号为界的排比句：

On the days when dessert is a name given to a handful of chocolates and a little preserved ginger, when macedoine de fruits is the title bestowed on two prunes and a piece of rhubarbs, then the orange, however sour, comes nobly to the rescue; and on those other days of plenty when cherries and strawberries and raspberries and gooseberries riot together upon the table, the orange, sweeter than ever, is still there to hold its own.

分号前后几乎所有的成分都是平行对应的，使这个句子呈现一种形式上的对称美，也突出了柑橘常年为人享用的特别之处。先看一看句子各个成分对称的情况，如 On the days when 对 and on those other days of plenty when，then the orange 对 the orange，however sour 对 sweeter than ever，comes nobly to the rescue 对 is still there to hold its own。翻译时注意到这个句子的修辞特点，可以取得与原文相似的效果：

有的时候，只用几块巧克力和一点蜜饯生姜充当餐后的甜点，两块李子干加一片大黄便被冠以蔬果什锦美名时，这时仍带酸味的柑橘便前来慷慨救驾；其他时候，水果丰盈，樱桃、草莓、木莓、醋栗在餐桌上相互争艳时，此时比往日更加甜美的柑橘依然能坚守自己的岗位。

文章里一些具体字词的翻译也值得注意。如第二段里的 then the orange, however sour, comes nobly to the rescue，这里的 nobly 一词翻译起来很费思索。根据原文可以体会出它的意思，但用汉语的哪一个词来翻译它却是个问题。"高尚地"，"崇高地"，其基本的意思是可以的，但放在上下文里习惯上不这么说。《朗文医学大辞典》里有一个解释很有启发：deserving praise and admiration because of unselfishness and high moral quality，根据这一解释可以将其译成"慷慨"，含义是恰当的，放在上下文里也符合汉语的习惯。由此便有了下面的译文，"这时仍带酸味的柑橘便前来慷慨救驾"。

第三段里有 The pip can be flicked at your enemies，这里的 enemies 译成什么好呢？考虑到这段文字诙谐的语气，还是将其直译成"敌人"好。于是译为"柑橘核可用来弹射你的敌人"。

最后一段 Its outside is a mirror of its inside 中的 mirror 也不必变通，就翻译成"镜子"好。这是在汉英两种语言里通用的隐喻，不妨直译："它的外表是它内心的镜子"。

4

The Clipper

John Masefield（1878—1967），英国作家，作品有诗集 *Collected Poems*，小说 *The Bird of Dawning*、*Dead Ned Live* 等。1933 年被誉为英国桂冠诗人，1935 年荣获英国功绩勋章 OM (Order of Merit)。"The Clipper" 选自 *The Oxford Book of English Prose*，文笔绚丽如画。

When I saw her first there was a smoke of mist about her as high as her foreyard. Her topsails and flying kites had a faint glow upon them where the dawn caught them. Then the mist rolled away from her, so that we could see her hull and the glimmer of the red sidelight as it was hoisted inboard. She was rolling slightly, tracing an arc against the heaven, and as I watched her the glow upon her deepened, till every sail she wore burned rosily like an opal turned to the sun, like a fiery jewel. She was radiant, she was of an immortal beauty, that swaying, delicate clipper. Coming as she came, out of the mist into the dawn, she was like a spirit, like an intellectual presence. Her hull glowed, her rails glowed; there was colour upon the boats and tackling. She was a lofty ship (with skysails and royal staysails), and it was wonderful to watch her, blushing in the sun, swaying and curveting. She was alive with a more than mortal life. One thought that she would speak in some strange language or break out into a music which would express the sea and that great flower in the sky. She came trembling down to us, rising up high and plunging; showing the red lead below her water-line; then diving down till the smother bubbled over her hawseholes. She bowed and curveted; the light caught the skylights on the poop; she gleamed and sparkled; she shook the sea from her as she rose. There was no man aboard of us but was filled with the beauty of that ship. I think they would have cheered her had she been a little nearer to us; but, as it was, we ran up our flags in answer to her, adding our position and comparing our chronometers, then dipping our ensigns and standing away. For some minutes I watched her, as I made up the flags before putting them back in their cupboard. The old mate limped up to me, and spat, and swore. "That's one of the beautiful sights of the world," he said. "That, and a cornfield, and a woman with her child. It's beauty and strength. How would you like to have one of them skysails round your neck?" I gave him some answer, and continued to watch her, till the beautiful, precise hull, with all its lovely detail, had become blurred to leeward, where the sun was now marching in triumph, the helm of a golden warrior plumed in cirrus.

朱光潜在谈到艺术与自然的关系时说："艺术根据自然，加以熔铸雕琢，选择安排，结果乃是一种超自然的世界。换句话说，自然须通过作者的心灵，在里面经过一番意匠经营，才变成艺术……我们要了解情与辞的道理，必先了解这一点艺术与自然的道理。情是自然，融情于思，达之于辞，才是文学的艺术。在文学的艺术中，情感需经过意象化和文辞化，才算得到表现。"（《谈文学》，第112 页）他的意思是，只有情感是不够的，情感的自然流露还不足以产生文学作品。情感必须经过思想的"熔铸"，然后通过具体的"意象"和适合的语言才能得以表现。

如果对《快帆船》（"The Clipper"）做一分析，我们对朱光潜所说的"情感""意象"和"文辞"三者的关系会有一个清晰的印象。

本文以第一人称"我"的视角出发，即"我"之所观，"我"之所感，构成文章的焦点和脉络。一开始，作者描写"我"最初看见帆船时（When I **saw** her first）的情景；在第4—7句，又以 and as I **watched** her 起始，进一步描写帆船行进的情景及其色彩的变换，此间使用了明喻（simile），将帆船比作有生命、有思想的生灵（like a spirit, like an intellectual presence）；在第8—14句，从描写帆船的状貌进而描写它的内蕴（She was a lofty ship），也是以 and it was wonderful to **watch** her 起始来对帆船做深化的描绘；第15—20句以 For some minutes I **watched** her 开始，正当"我"凝神注视帆船时，老水手一瘸一拐地走过来，吐了一口唾沫之后大发感慨。这一部分最生动、最精彩。当老水手问"我"是否愿意摘下一面天帆作围巾时，"我"好歹应了一声，又继续注视着帆船（I gave him some answer, and continued to **watch** her...），直到远去的帆船又模糊起来，只有舵轮在阳光照耀下激起一片烟雾。

作者"即景生情"，对情感的描写条理清晰、步步深入、比喻精湛，显然是经过回味的。I saw her、I watched her、to watch her 等类似句式的重复使用，"我"的情感的步步深化，也是语篇衔接与连贯的需要。

关于本篇文章的语言，有三点应当提及，即色彩词、动作词和比喻的运用。

色彩词汇的运用是这篇文章的一个特色。帆船在阳光的照耀下，形成一幅斑斓的图画。作者使用一系列鲜明的色彩词，使读者几乎可以凭视觉看见船体折射出来的不断变换的色彩和光亮，如 a faint glow、the glimmer of the red sidelight、burned rosily like an opal turned to the sun、radiant、the red lead、gleamed and sparkled 等。如果读者把这些绚丽的色彩放在雾霭蒙蒙的海面和冉冉升起的太阳的背景之下去想象，那是十分壮丽的景观。

动作词汇的运用也是这篇文章的一个特色。作者观察细致，对行进的船做了生动的描绘，一句话是一个画面。读者不仅可以看见帆船正在行进的姿态，甚至可以听见它在行进时激打海水的声音。

暗喻（metaphor）和拟人法（personification）的运用赋予了帆船以生命和灵感，如"She was alive with a more than mortal life. One thought that she would speak in some strange language or break out into a music…"。老水手具有很高的审美修养，他的想象很奇特："That, and a cornfield, and a woman with her child. It's beauty and strength. How would you like to have one of them skysails round your neck?"。他发现了帆船的 beauty and strength，他看出了"That's one of the beautiful sights of the world…"。

作者约翰·梅斯菲尔德用文字编织的这一色彩斑斓、无比壮观的图画，感染了读者，使我们对帆船产生敬意，甚至使我们相信，她肩负着一个神圣的使命。

快帆船

约翰·梅斯菲尔德

我初看见她时，她前帆下桁以下的部分全笼罩在大雾里。上桅帆和迎风飘动的轻帆映着晨曦的微光。然后雾霭从她身边慢慢弥散开去，我们这才看见船身和刚刚挂起的舱内红色的舷灯发出的微弱的光。她轻轻地起伏着，在天穹之下画着一个个的弧。我看着她，船身上晨光的颜色渐渐加深，直到船上的风帆好像面向阳光的蛋白石一样透着玫瑰色，像火红的宝石。她灿烂绚丽，美若天仙，那只款款而动、体态轻盈的快帆船呀！她一路驶来，出迷雾，入熹微，她好像一个魂灵，一个智慧女神。她浑身泛着光，船帆泛着光；她携带的小船及索具都染上了颜色。她亭亭而立（张着天帆和豪华的索帆），看着她在阳光里泛着红晕，轻轻摆动着，上下颠浮着，令人心旷神怡。她是一只有生命的活船，比世间的生命更具生命力的活船。人们以为，她就要用一种陌生的语言开口说话，或演奏一首乐曲来抒发对大海的依恋，歌唱太阳的温情。她飘然而至，时而随浪涌起，时而随浪而下，一会儿露出吃水线下面的测深铅锤，然后又潜入水中，让水雾淹没锚链孔。她俯首前行，接着又昂然跳跃；阳光照进船楼的天井；船身闪烁着光芒；当她涌起的时候，便抖掉全身的海水。船上的人们没有一个不为快帆船的美而感慨。我想，假如快帆船距离再近一点，他们一定会为她而欢呼；可是，事实上，我们升起船旗来对她做出回应，我们确定了位置，核准经纬仪，降下各色彩旗，然后站开。有好几分钟的时间，我一边整理着降下的旗子，准备把它们放回旗柜，一边看着她。这时老水手一瘸一拐地走过来，吐了一口唾沫，斩钉截铁地说：“这真是世上美景之一。那个，还有玉米地，还有抱着孩子的女人。这是'美'和'力'的化身。摘下一个天帆扎在你的脖子上，怎么样？”我好歹应了一声，继续看着她，直至她那美丽的、棱角分明的船身，连同她精美的细部变得模糊时，太阳正照着她的下风处，从那里凯旋而上，身披金甲的勇士般的舵轮拨打起羽状的水云。

| 翻 译 提 示 |

这篇文章的翻译有几点需要提及。一是文学语言的审美特征，二是常用词的翻译，三是行文速度与节奏。

一、文学语言的审美特征

张保红在《文学语言的审美性与翻译》里谈道：

文学语言的特性既有指义的特性，又有审美的特性。……文学翻译不只是作品语言指义性的翻译，更为重要的还是作品语言审美性的翻译。文学翻译研究与批评既要在其指义性下进行，更要在其审美性中予以审视。

在结合《快帆船》的翻译时，他又说：

作者实处写的是快帆船，而虚处呈现的是一位美女的形象（这从作者选词用字上可得到证明），实乃曲笔传情，"言在此而意在彼"，且彼此之间又颇能和谐浸染、回环映照。鉴于此，翻译中我们在再现快帆船的物理美之时，还应译出"这位美女"阴柔的形象美与作者对她一见倾心的深情美。

张保红在此提出一个文学作品"语言审美性的翻译"问题，切中要害。在语言的选择上如果只注意了它的"指义的特性"，而忽

略了它的"审美的特性",文学形象就会受到损害或歪曲。如以下诸句的翻译都值得推敲:

1) She was radiant, she was of an immortal beauty, that swaying, delicate clipper.

2) She was a lofty ship…and it was wonderful to watch her, blushing in the sun, swaying and curveting.

3) One thought that she would…or break out into a music which would express the sea and that great flower in the sky.

4) She came trembling down to us, rising up high and plunging; showing the red lead below her water-line; then diving down till…

（以上几句的翻译请见译文）

二、常用词的翻译

我们在"原文赏析"里说过,这是一篇描写快帆船在大海上航行场景的文章,作者用了较多的比喻,用了色彩和动感很强的词汇,但所使用的多是普通的词汇,而且使用得当。这些句子用的都是很普通的词,但所创造的形象给读者留下既具体又生动的印象。用普通的词汇,有时借助比喻,对具体事物做具体、贴切的叙述和描写,以此来创造形象,这可能是当今英语的一个特点。也即用常用的词汇搭配短语和组织句子,进而创造可感可触的形象。翻译时,能否在字词的选择、短语的搭配和句子的组织等特点上与原文的风格保持一致,这是一个值得思考的问题。

三、行文速度与节奏

英语的行文速度与节奏主要表现在轻重音节的安排上。这可以通过在文字上做符号标注出来,也可以通过朗读听出来。比如"One thought that she would speak in some strange language or break out into a music which would express the sea and that great flower in the sky.",译成汉语:"人们以为,她就要用一种陌生的语言开口说话,或演奏一首乐曲来抒发对大海的依恋,歌唱太阳的温情。"通过对译语的合理安排,可以使译文取得一些节奏感。

5

The Faculty of Delight

Charles Edward Montague（1867—1928），英国作家，诗人，主要著作有 *A Hind Let Loose*、*The Morning's War*。"The Faculty of Delight" 选自 *The Oxford Book of English Prose*，语言清新优雅。

Among the mind's powers is one that comes of itself to many children and artists. It need not be lost, to the end of his days, by any one who has ever had it. This is the power of taking delight in a thing, or rather in anything, everything, not as a means to some other end, but just because it is what it is, as the lover dotes on whatever may be the traits of the beloved object. A child in the full health of his mind will put his hand flat on the summer turf, feel it, and give a little shiver of private glee at the elastic firmness of the globe. He is not thinking how well it will do for some game or to feed sheep upon. That would be the way of the wooer whose mind runs on his mistress's money. The child's is sheer affection, the true ecstatic sense of the thing's inherent characteristics. No matter what the things may be, no matter what they are good or no good for, there they are, each with a thrilling unique look and feel of its own, like a face; the iron astringently cool under its paint, the painted wood familiarly warmer, the clod crumbling enchantingly down in the hands, with its little dry smell of the sun and of hot nettles; each common thing a personality marked by delicious differences.

The joy of an Adam new to the garden and just looking round is brought by the normal child to the things that he does as well as those that he sees. To be suffered to do some plain work with the real spade used by mankind can give him a mystical exaltation: to come home with his legs, as the French say, re-entering his body from the fatigue of helping the gardener to weed beds sends him to sleep in the glow of a beatitude that is an end in itself…

The right education, if we could find it, would work up this creative faculty of delight into all its branching possibilities of knowledge, wisdom, and nobility. Of all three it is the beginning, condition, or raw material.

| 原文赏析 |

在这篇短文里，作者讨论了关于人的天性的一个方面，也以一个教育家的眼光指出，正确的教育可以将这种天赋引向"知识""智慧"和"高尚的情操"的发展方向。作者只用了不足四百词的篇幅，讨论了有关"人"和"人的培养"这样大的题目，可见其语言修养之深，文字功力之厚。从本文的写作来看，有以下几个地方值得提出：

一、叙事视角的变化

因为是讲人的"感知快乐的天赋"，文章便以人的心理能力（the mind's powers）为出发点，解释这种天赋的本质特征；接着转向孩子（A child），讲具有这种天赋的孩子的表现，他不是受某种功利的驱使，而完全是出于喜爱（sheer affection），是事物内在的特质（the true ecstatic sense of the thing's inherent characteristics）让他有一种欣喜若狂的感觉；然后转向事物（the things），每一个事物都有其独特的、使人激动的面容和感觉（a thrilling unique look and feel），比如 the iron、the painted wood、the clod 等；然后讲快乐（The joy），人与物相接触以后，便产生一种快乐，一个孩子在他所做及所见的事物里所感觉到的快乐和亚当初来伊甸园时所感受到的快乐一样；最后落到教育对于这种天赋的启迪作用（The right education…would work up this creative faculty…）。而这几个不同的视角都是指向这个"心理能力"的，使文章围绕着一个焦点搭建起来。我们阅读时会感受到文章的美和力。除了语言本身之外，还与这种严密的结构有直接的关系。

特别是文章的第一句"Among the mind's powers is one that comes of itself to many children and artists."以介词开始，最后一句"Of all three it is the beginning, condition, or raw material."也以介词开始，这是为了强调、突出句子中的主语，而这两句话的主语所指又是相同的。这种形式上的首尾照应和意义上的前后一致及深化，使文章形成一个文气贯通的整体。

二、句子开始方式（opening）的变化

这篇文章共有 12 个句子，其中以普通名词开始的有 4 句，以人称代词开始的有两句，以指示代词开始的有两句，以介词短语开

始的有两句，以不定式开始的有一句，以状语从句开始的有一句。在一篇短文章里，有如此多样的句子开始方式，再加上字词和短语的巧妙运用，使文章读起来生动活泼，韵味十足。

三、被动语态

如第一段的第二句"It need not be lost, to the end of his days, by any one who has ever had it." 和第二段的第一句"The joy of an Adam new to the garden and just looking round is brought by the normal child to the things that he does as well as those that he sees." 都是被动语态的句子。我们说汉语的人若用英语来表达或翻译这样的意思时，可能不会用这样的句式。这是因为汉语的思维方式和表达方式与英语之间存在差异，有时也和叙事视角有关。在汉语里，多以行为的主体为主语，但在英语里，常有以行为的客体为主语的情况发生。对于这种情况，以英语为母语的作者或读者都不会有异样的感觉。但在汉语里，这句话的意思习惯上是用主动句式表达的。

| 译文 |

感知快乐的天赋

查尔斯·爱德华·蒙塔格

在人的心理能力中，有一种是很多孩子和艺术家自然就有的。不论是谁，一旦有了这种能力，直到他生命的最后一天也不一定会丢失。这就是从某一事物，或任一事物，每一事物，都能感受快乐的能力，不是为了某一目的，只是因为它就是这样。这好比一个人喜爱一样东西，不论它有什么特征他都喜爱。一个心理健全的孩子会把他的手掌平放在夏天的草皮上，抚摩它，在他感觉到具有弹性又很坚实的地球表面时，他心里便产生一种快乐的冲动。他不是在想，要是在上面做游戏或放羊什么的该有多好哇。那岂不是就像求婚者一心只想着女友的钱财一样吗？而孩子则完全是因为喜爱，是事物内在的特质真正让他有一种欣喜若狂的感觉。不论是什么事物，也不论它们有没有用途，它们就在那里，每一样东西都像一张脸孔，都有其独特的使人激动的面容和感觉；上过油漆的铁器使人感觉冷峻，而上过油漆的木器则让人感觉温和而亲切，当土块在手里松动而散发出阳光和热荨麻的微干的气味时，简直让人陶醉；每一样普通的东西都有它自己的"性格"，而这"性格"都有其不同的怡人的特征。

一个像亚当那样的人初次来到伊甸园举目四望时所感到的那种快乐，一个正常孩子在其所做及所见的事物里都可以感觉到。在他被允许使用人类常用的铁锹去做一些简单的体力劳动时，他会感到一种神奇的兴奋：他拖着双腿回到家，就像法国人常说的那样，从帮助园丁在花坛里锄草而产生的疲劳中恢复过来，使他在一种幸福感的光辉里进入梦乡，这本身就是目的……

正确的教育，如果我们能够发现它，可以调动这一带有创造性的快乐的天赋，使其纳入所有可能的各个方面——知识，智慧和高尚的情操。对于这三者，这种心理能力是开始，是条件，或是原始材料。

| 翻 译 提 示 |

下面就几个具体句子的译法做点说明：

[原文] The Faculty of Delight
[译文] 感知快乐的天赋

这个标题按字面可译成"快乐的天赋",这种译法有歧义,没有把原文的意思准确地翻译出来。应该是"感知快乐的天赋"。

[原文] It need not be lost, to the end of his days, by any one who has ever had it.

[译文] 不论是谁,一旦有了这种能力,直到他生命的最后一天也不一定会丢失。

这里的 need 是一个情态动词,It need not be lost 带有 not necessarily 的含义,因此,特意将其译作"……不一定会丢失"。

[原文] The child's is sheer affection, the true ecstatic sense of the thing's inherent characteristics.

[译文] 而孩子则完全是因为喜爱,是事物内在的特质真正让他有一种欣喜若狂的感觉。

这里的 the true ecstatic sense 是说人对事物的感觉。

[原文] ...each common thing a personality marked by delicious differences.

[译文] ……每一样普通的东西都有它自己的"性格",而这"性格"都有其不同的怡人的特征。

这里的 differences 是一个巧妙的用法,实义为"不同之处",或"不同的特征";而 delicious differences 更是富有新意的搭配。

[原文] The joy of an Adam new to the garden and just looking round is brought by the normal child to the things that he does as well as those that he sees.

［译文］　一个像亚当那样的人初次来到伊甸园举目四望时所感到的那种快乐，一个正常孩子在其所做及所见的事物里都可以感觉到。

　　这个英语句子的基本构架是 The joy…is brought…to the things，这种由客体格作主语的情况在英语里很多，而且十分灵活自如；这个意思在汉语里是不这样说的，重要的是抓住这句话的意思，用汉语习惯的表达方式说出来即可。在对原文和译文做比较时，看出其在表达方式上的差异，对汉译英尤其有启发。

［原文］　Of all three it is the beginning, condition, or raw material.

［译文］　对于这三者，这种心理能力是开始，是条件，或是原始材料。

　　这是一个倒置句，其正常语序应该是"It is the beginning, condition, or raw material of all three."。作者将语序倒置产生两个效果，一是与前面 knowledge, wisdom, and nobility 衔接，二是将 the beginning, condition, or raw material 放在句尾表示强调：教育若能达到传授"知识"、发展"智慧"和培养"高尚的情操"的目标，这种感知快乐的能力"是开始，是条件，或是原始材料"。

6

Nature and Art

James Whistler（1834—1903），美国画家，代表画作为 *Nocturnes*，有论辩文集 *The Gentle Art of Making Enemies*。"Nature and Art" 选自 *The Oxford Book of English Prose*，文笔优雅雄辩。

Nature contains the elements, in colour and form, of all pictures, as the keyboard contains the notes of all music.

But the artist is born to pick, and choose, and group with science, these elements, that the result may be beautiful—as the musician gathers his notes, and forms his chords, until he brings forth from chaos glorious harmony.

To say to the painter, that Nature is to be taken as she is, is to say to the player, that he may sit on the piano…

The dignity of the snow-capped mountain is lost in distinctness, but the joy of the tourist is to recognize the traveller on the top. The desire to see, for the sake of seeing, is, with the mass, alone the one to be gratified, hence the delight in detail.

And when the evening mist clothes the riverside with poetry, as with a veil, and the poor buildings lose themselves in the dim sky, and the tall chimneys become campanile, and the warehouses are palaces in the night, and the whole city hangs in the heavens, and fairy-land is before us—then the wayfarer hastens home; the working man and the cultured one, the wise man and the one of pleasure, cease to understand, as they have ceased to see, and Nature, who, for once, has sung in tune, sings her exquisite song to the artist alone, her son and her master—her son in that he loves her, her master in that he knows her.

To him her secrets are unfolded, to him her lessons have become gradually clear. He looks at her flower, not with the enlarging lens, that he may gather facts for the botanist, but with the light of the one who sees in her choice selection of brilliant tones and delicate tints, suggestions of future harmonies.

He does not confine himself to purposeless copying, without thought, each blade of grass, as commended by the inconsequent, but, in the long curve of the narrow leaf, corrected by the straight tall stem, he learns how grace is wedded to dignity, how strength enhances sweetness, that elegance shall be the result.

In the citron wing of the pale butterfly, with its dainty spots of orange, he sees before him the stately halls of fair gold, with their slender saffron pillars, and is taught how the delicate drawing high upon the walls shall be traced in tender tones of orpiment, and repeated by the base in notes of graver hue.

In all that is dainty and lovable he finds hints for his own combinations, and thus is Nature ever his resource and always at his service, and to him is naught refused.

Through his brain, as through the last alembic, is distilled the refined essence of that thought which began with the Gods, and which they left him to carry out.

Set apart by them to complete their works, he produces that wondrous thing called the masterpiece, which surpasses in perfection all that they have contrived in what is called Nature; and the Gods stand by and marvel, and perceive how far away more beautiful is the Venus of Melos than was their own Eve.

原文赏析

《自然与艺术》（"Nature and Art"）讲述了一个画论问题——自然、艺术与艺术家的关系。文章前三段用三个比喻说明艺术和自然的关系：艺术家的创作基于自然；但艺术创作又不是照搬自然。第四、五、六段说艺术家是自然的骄子，是自然的主人。第七、八、九、十段说自然是艺术创作的源泉，但它只有经过艺术家的创作才能成为艺术。最后一段说艺术家的创作比自然更美。

这篇文章运用了一系列修辞手法，值得学习：

一、比喻（simile or metaphor）。仅前三段就是三个比喻：

1) Nature contains the elements, in colour and form, of all pictures, as the keyboard contains the notes of all music.

2) But the artist is born to pick, and choose, and group with science, these elements, that the result may be beautiful—as the musician gathers his notes, and forms his chords, until he brings forth

from chaos glorious harmony.

3) To say to the painter, that Nature is to be taken as she is, is to say to the player, that he may sit on the piano…

二、省略句式（fragmentary or elliptical sentences）。如：

1) The desire to see, for the sake of seeing, is, with the mass, alone the one to be gratified, **hence the delight in detail**.

2) …and Nature, who, for once, has sung in tune, sings her exquisite song to the artist alone, **her son and her master—her son in that he loves her, her master in that he knows her**.

这种省略句式使句子显得简洁，节奏加快。

三、排比句式（parallelism）。例如，在第七、八、九三个段落里，作者有意重复一个相同的句式：

1) …but, in the long curve of the narrow leaf…**he learns**…

2) In the citron wing of the pale butterfly…**he sees**…

3) In all that is dainty and lovable, **he finds**…

这几个段落间的排比强调自然是艺术创作的源泉，艺术家在自然中发现美。

四、拟人（personification）。文章里有好几处使用了拟人的修辞手法：

1) …and Nature…**sings her** exquisite song to the artist alone…

2) He looks at **her** flower…

五、连词叠用（polysyndeton）。文章使用了连词 and 的叠用，如第五段开头有这样一句：

And when the evening mist clothes the riverside with poetry, as with a veil, **and** the poor buildings lose themselves in the dim sky, **and** the tall chimneys become campanile, **and** the warehouses are palaces in the night, **and** the whole city hangs in the heavens, **and** fairy-land is before us...

金岳霖在他的《论翻译》中提道："有一位英国文学家说'And the Lord said'这几个词神妙到不可言状。"这几个词的"神妙"之处和 And 的运用有密切关系。本句一共连用了六个 and，不仅将六个从句连接起来，产生环境描写的渐增效果（cumulative effect），而且为全句创造了十分优美平和的节奏和意境。

这篇文章所讨论的虽然是自然、艺术和艺术家的关系，但是对写作和翻译也很有启示。因为文学和文学翻译都属于艺术范畴，也存在语言、语言艺术和语言艺术家的关系问题。如果说 "Nature contains the elements, in colour and form, of all pictures...", 对于语言艺术我们也可以说 "A language contains the elements, in words and expressions, of all writings.", 因为词语和表达方式是文学作品的基本元素，它们与语言的关系就像自然元素与大自然的关系一样；如果说 "...the artist is born to pick, and choose, and group with science, these elements, that the result may be beautiful...", 我们也可以针对语言艺术家说 "The writer or translator is born to pick, and choose, and group with science and art, these elements, that the result may be beautiful.". 作家或翻译家所要做的是在语言这个大自然中选择他所需要的词语和表达方式，再科学地、艺术地将它们组成文章；这文章就是艺术品，应该是美的。

自然和艺术

詹姆斯·惠斯勒

大自然，就色彩和形状而论，包含所有图画的元素，就像键盘包含所有音乐的音符一样。

艺术家的天职就是对这些元素进行选择，将它们科学地组织起来，结果可能是一幅美丽的图画——就像音乐家用声音谱成和音，从混乱无序的声音中创作出动人和谐的乐曲一样。

如果对画家说他可以照大自然本来的样子作画，就等于对演奏家说他可以一屁股坐在钢琴的键盘上……

白雪皑皑的高山若是变得清晰可见就失去了它的威严，但观光者却因为能看见山顶上的游客而喜形于色。大多数人是为了看见而要看见，只是为了使这个愿望得到满足而已，因此，他们以能看见细节而感到快乐。

当傍晚的迷雾以其柔纱般的诗意笼罩着河边，破旧的建筑消失在朦胧的天空，高高的烟囱变成一座座孤立的钟楼，大大小小的仓库恍如夜间的宫殿，整个城市悬在了空中，宛若仙境展现在我们眼前，那时候，路上的人们匆匆赶路回家；劳动者和文化人，智者和浪子，因为他们熟视无睹，他们也就不能理解，而只在此时才开始歌唱的大自然便把自己美妙的歌唱给艺术家——她的儿子和她的主人；说他是儿子是因为他爱她，说他是主人是因为他理解她。

只有对他，她才展示她的秘密，只有对他，她的教诲才逐渐变得清晰。他观察着她的花朵，不是用为植物学家采集实据的放大镜，而是用一种眼光，她用这种眼光在她精选的灿烂色调和精妙色彩中看见孕育和谐的迹象。

他并非不假思索地描摹每一片草叶，如同那些微不足道的人们所赞扬的那样，而是在又高又直的茎干上的细长叶弯里，他发现，优雅和尊严融为一体，力量使它更加温柔，而后才产生了高雅。

在蝴蝶那淡淡的香橼色并布满雅致的橘黄斑点的翅膀上，他看见庄严的金色大厅就在眼前，还有又细又高的金黄顶柱，他懂得了那高墙上精巧的图画要用轻柔的雄黄色调来描绘，并要以更加庄重的色调为底色将其绘制下来。

在所有这些雅致和可爱的元素里，他得到如何进行融合的启示，这样，大自然成了他取之不尽的源泉，随时为他服务，对他从不拒绝。

通过他的大脑，如同通过最后一道蒸馏器一样，那发端于诸神，并由诸神托付他去实现的思想精髓得以净化。

由于受到诸神的青睐去完成他们的作品，他创作了被称之为杰作的绝妙之作，它的完美超出诸神在大自然里所创造的一切；他们站在一旁，惊叹不已，发现米洛斯岛上的维纳斯雕像比他们自己创造的夏娃要美丽得多。

| 翻 译 提 示 |

这篇文章里的修辞很多，如比喻、省略、排比、拟人等。这里仅以第五段为例，讨论一下英语长句的翻译，顺便也谈一谈连接词and 的叠用问题。

第五段是一句话，很长，将近 120 个词。翻译之前弄清它的意思，理清它的句法关系，这是第一步。然后在译文里把句子各成分的关系摆顺，把意思说清楚，这是第二步。然后将修辞方面的美学特征体现出来，这是第三步。

句子从 And 开始，直到 before us 为止，是六个从句，后面是主句，分两个部分：

1. then the wayfarer hastens home 此后直至 as they have ceased to see，可以看作是对 wayfarer 的进一步说明；

2. and Nature, who, for once, has sung in tune, sings her exquisite song to the artist alone，后面的成分是 artist 的同位语（appositive）。这句话讲明了普通人和艺术家的区别，普通人看不见，因而也不理解大自然的美；唯有艺术家能够听见大自然对他所唱的美妙的歌。

理清原文的句法关系为翻译铺平了道路，译文大致不会出现句法错误。但作为文学作品的散文有其鲜明的超出句法之上的美学特质。这种美学特质首先来自作者对整个句子所描写的自然景象的感受，作为译者，读了这个句子以后，也应产生与作者大致相同的感悟。这个感悟是前提。其次是要体会其修辞特征所产生的艺术效果，这里主要指由 and 的叠用而产生的行文的优美节奏和静谧意境。第三是在词语的选择上要有与原文相应的文采和文气。这三者亦虚亦实，结合了语言的审美感受和翻译技巧。

7

The Weather in His Soul

George Santayana（1863—1952），西班牙裔美国人，哈佛大学哲学教授，后移居欧洲。主要哲学著作有 *The Life of Reason* 和四卷本的 *Realms of Being*，散文集 *Soliloquies in England*，也写诗歌和小说。"The Weather in His Soul" 选自 *The Oxford Book of English Prose*，文笔潇洒，善用比喻。

Let me come to the point boldly; what governs the Englishman is his inner atmosphere, the weather in his soul. It is nothing particularly spiritual or mysterious. When he has taken his exercise and is drinking his tea or his beer and lighting his pipe; when, in his garden or by his fire, he sprawls in an aggressively comfortable chair; when well-washed and well-brushed, he resolutely turns in church to the east and recites the Creed (with genuflexions, if he likes genuflexions) without in the least implying that he believes one word of it; when he hears or sings the most crudely sentimental and thinnest of popular songs, unmoved but not disgusted; when he makes up his mind who is his best friend or his favourite poet; when he adopts a party or a sweetheart; when he is hunting or shooting or boating, or striding through the fields; when he is choosing his clothes or his profession—never is it a precise reason, or purpose, or outer fact that determines him; it is always the atmosphere of his inner man.

To say that this atmosphere was simply a sense of physical well-being, of coursing blood and a prosperous digestion, would be far too gross; for while psychic weather is all that, it is also a witness to some settled disposition, some ripening inclination for this or that, deeply rooted in the soul. It gives a sense of direction in life which is virtually a code of ethics, and a religion behind religion. On the other hand, to say it was the vision of any ideal or allegiance to any principle would be making it far too articulate and abstract. The inner atmosphere, when compelled to condense into words, may precipitate some curt maxim or over-simple theory as a sort of war-cry; but its puerile language does it injustice, because it broods at a much deeper level than language or even thought. It is a mass of dumb instincts and allegiances, the love of a certain quality of life, to be maintained manfully. It is pregnant with many a stubborn assertion and rejection. It fights under its trivial fluttering opinions like a smoking battleship under its flags and signals; you must consider, not what they are, but why they have been hoisted and will not be lowered. One is tempted at times to turn away, in despair from the most delightful acquaintance—the picture of manliness, grace, simplicity, and honour, apparently rich in knowledge and humour— because of some enormous platitude he reverts to, some hopelessly stupid little dogma from which one knows that nothing can ever liberate him. The reformer must give him up; but why should one wish to reform a person so much better than oneself? He is like a thoroughbred horse, satisfying to the trained eye, docile to the light touch, and coursing in most wonderful unison with you through the open world. What do you care what words he uses? Are you impatient with the lark because he sings rather than talks? And if he could talk, would you be irritated by his curious opinions? Of course, if any one positively asserts what is contrary to fact, there is an error, though the error may be harmless; and most divergencies between men should interest us rather than offend us, because they are effects of perspective, or of legitimate diversity in experience and interests. Trust the man who hesitates in his speech and is quick and steady in action, but beware of long arguments and long beards. Jupiter decided the most intricate questions with a nod, and a very few words and no gestures suffice for the Englishman to make his inner mind felt most unequivocally when occasion requires.

Instinctively the Englishman is no missionary, no conqueror. He prefers the country to the town, and home to foreign parts. He is rather glad and relieved if only natives will remain natives and strangers strangers, and at a comfortable distance from himself. Yet outwardly he is most hospitable and accepts almost anybody for the time being; he travels and conquers without a settled design, because he has the instinct of exploration. His adventures are all external; they change him so little that he is not afraid of them. He carries his English weather in his heart wherever he goes, and it becomes a cool spot in the desert, and a steady and sane oracle amongst all the deliriums of mankind. Never since the heroic days of Greece has the world had such a sweet, just, boyish master. It will be a black day for the human race when scientific blackguards, conspirators, churls, and fanatics manage to supplant him.

原文赏析

《英国人灵魂的气象》("The Weather in His Soul")的作者是哲学家也是诗人，文章既有哲学家思想的深邃，又有诗人语言的灵妙。

这篇文章写英国人的"内在的情调"和"心灵里的气象"。这是一个超乎精神层面的"气质"和"心理倾向"的问题，近乎人的某种天性的东西。它是"本能和忠诚的结合体，是对某种生活品质的爱"，"它孕育在比语言，甚至比思想还要深得多的层次上"。虽说它并不神秘，但用语言也难以将其表述清楚，于是作者用了一系列比喻。说它是"在各种旗帜和信号的指挥之下进行战斗"的"战舰"，说它是"沙漠里一个清凉的处所，人类谵妄之中一个稳固而明智的圣堂"等等。

《新哥伦比亚百科全书》中说："桑塔雅那全部的哲学著作展示出一种特有的富丽丰润的风格。"（The whole of Santayana's philosophic writing displays a characteristic richness of style.）

这篇文章突出的特点是雄伟的气势。它谈的虽是人的气质和心理倾向的问题，但作者渊博的知识、深邃的见解和肯定语势的话语使得文章如江河直下，自有一股不可阻挡之势。

作家兼学者的唐弢说："古文家有所谓文气，也叫作气势……然则究竟什么是文气呢？我们知道，一句句子的构成，或长或短，或张或弛，彼此是并不一律的，因此读起来的时候，我们从这些句子所得到的感觉以及读出来的声音，也就有高低，有强弱，有缓急，抑扬顿挫，这就是所谓文气了。"（《文章修养》，第 159 页）这是从语言的声响节奏上说。此外，文章的气势还应考虑它论说的雄辩力和叙事抒情的感染力。作为文学作品，任何体裁或形式的文章都表现出一种力（strength）和美（beauty）的特质。所谓"力"是指文章的说服力，感染力。这取决于作者对所论事物有独到、深刻、合乎情理的见识，他的分析发人深省，令人信服，因而说理是有力的。当然，这也涉及文章的组织。所谓文章之"美"所包含的内容要多一层，除了题材即话题方面的内容以外，更有语言方面的因素，表现在作者对于语言的运用和选择上。从这个角度看，它是作者美学信仰和美学修养的反映。作者在选择语言时，他的取舍标准是很严格的，除了表达意义时文字的准确和简洁以外，还要文字的美和雅。在这篇文章里，三个方面集中体现了"力"与"美"。

一、行文方式

1. 直截了当的语气，如"Let me come to the point boldly…"。

2. 肯定的语势，如：

1) …what governs the Englishman is his inner atmosphere, the weather in his soul.

2) …it is always the atmosphere of his inner man.

3) It will be a black day for the human race when scientific blackguards, conspirators, churls, and fanatics manage to supplant him.

3. 反面排除与正面论述，如：

1) To say that this atmosphere was simply a sense of physical well-being, of coursing blood and a prosperous digestion, would be far too gross; for…

2) On the other hand, to say it was the vision of any ideal or allegiance to any principle would be making it far too articulate and abstract. The inner atmosphere…

二、修辞手段

1. 比喻，如 "He is like a thoroughbred horse…"。

2. 拟人和反问，如：

1) Are you impatient with the lark because he sings rather than talks?

2) And if he could talk, would you be irritated by his curious opinions?

三、声音效果

在诗歌里，特别是在古典诗词里，声音效果往往是用心安排的；在散文里，多数情况下应是自然产生的。对声音效果可做微观分析，也可做宏观分析，在宏观层次上其声音效果主要体现在行文语气上。在这篇文章里，作者以他深邃的见识对英国人的气质和心理倾向做正面论述，读者可以体会出他的行文语气里充满了信心和勇气。不论是开始的命题，中间的论述，或结尾时的终结语，其论断和语气都是斩钉截铁的，表现出一种宏大的气势，因而具有很强的说服力。

| 译 文 |

英国人灵魂的气象

乔治·桑塔雅那

让我直接进入正题吧：左右英国人的是他内在的情调，心灵里的气象。这绝不是什么精神层面的或神秘的东西。设想在他运动之余品茶或喝酒，并且点着烟斗；或在花园里或壁炉旁懒洋洋地躺在舒适的安乐椅上；或在他精心梳洗之后，在教堂里毅然面向东方背诵（跪诵，假如他喜欢跪诵）信经。但这绝不意味着他相信其中的任一字句，或在他听着或哼着最低俗感伤、最浅薄的流行歌曲，虽未被感动但也并不讨厌；或在他确定谁是他最好的朋友或最喜爱的诗人；或在他选择一个群体或一个恋人；或在他打猎、射击、划船或大步走过田野；或在他挑选服装或选择职业——在他做着这一切的时候，并不是因为某一确定的理由，或目的，或外界的事物，而是他内在的情调在决定着他的取向。

　　若说这一内在的情调仅仅是对于身体状况、血液循环和消化功能的感觉，那未免过于粗浅；因为，虽然灵魂的气象全然如此，它毕竟也是深深植根于灵魂之中的某种稳定的气质和某一日臻成熟的心理倾向的见证。它给人以生活的方向感，实则是一种道德准则，宗教背后的宗教。另一方面，若它是对于一种理想的幻想或对于某一原则的忠诚，那就把它说得过于雄辩也过于抽象了。这个"内在的情调"，必须用语言来表述时，可以凝结成一句战斗口号似的简短格言或简单的理论；但那幼稚的语言并不能将它表述清楚，因为它孕育在比语言，甚至比思想还要深得多的层次上。它是一团无声的本能和忠诚的结合体，是对某种生活品质的爱，需要勇敢而坚定地予以保持。它固执地坚持很多观点，也固执地摈弃很多妄念。它在各种涌动于内心的细微见解之下进行战斗，就像一艘喷吐浓烟的战舰在各种旗帜和信号的指挥之下进行战斗一样；你所要考虑的不是它们是什么，而是它们既然已经升起就不再降落这是为什么。有时人会在绝望的时候抛弃最让他感到快活的相识——有男子汉气概、儒雅、素朴、正直、显出一副知识渊博和幽默的样子——因为他总是重弹某些老调，陷入愚蠢的琐碎教条之中而无法得到解救。改良者必须放弃他；为什么偏要改变一个比自己好得多的人呢？他就像一匹英国纯种马，行家一看就满意，轻轻一拍就能领会你的意图，和你完全融为一体，载着你在空旷的原野里驰骋。

至于他说话时如何措辞，你在乎那个干什么？你会因为云雀只唱歌而不说话就对它不耐烦吗？假使它会说话，你会对它那些奇怪的念头感到恼火吗？当然，假如有人武断地坚持与事实相反的意见，那肯定是错误的，虽然这错误未必有害；再说，人们之间大多数分歧应该引起我们的兴趣，而不是激怒我们，因为这些分歧是由于看问题的角度不同，或由于那些合乎情理的经验和兴趣的多样性而引起的。应当信任那些言语迟疑但行动迅速而坚定的人，但要警惕无休止的争论和长着长胡子的人。朱庇特只一点头就决定了最棘手的问题，而当情势所需时，英国人只需三言两语而无须比比画画，就能使人准确无误地了解他的内心世界。

就其本能而言，英国人不是传教士，不是征服者。他宁愿待在乡村，而不愿住在城市，宁愿待在家里，而不愿去陌生的地方。如果本地人还是本地人，陌生人始终是陌生人，而且和自己保持一段舒适的距离，他会很高兴，很舒心。但在外表上，他很好客，几乎任何人他都可以暂时接纳；他不是按照一成不变的计划去旅行，去征服，因为他有探索的本能。他的冒险活动都是表面的，对他自己几乎没有什么影响，所以他不怕冒险。无论他走到哪里，心里总是怀着他的"英国气象"。它已变成沙漠里一个清凉的处所，人类谵妄之中一个稳固而明智的圣堂。自从希腊的英雄时代以来，世界还没有过如此可爱、正直和孩子气的主人。若以科学上的无赖、阴谋家、吝啬鬼和狂热之徒取而代之，将是人类遭遇暗无天日之时。

| 翻译提示 |

乔治·桑塔雅那虽然多年在美国受教育并从事学术活动，但因为他的西班牙血统和他对美国社会的深刻认识，他对于古希腊传统和欧洲文明有着衷心的喜爱。他的这篇写英国人性格的散文，思想

异常深刻而比喻贴切新颖，观察洞悉入微而语言流畅自然，可谓英语文学中的名篇。这样一篇散文的翻译，自然要求一种特别的翻译方法和适当的翻译文体。这篇译文可谓细微而达旨，委曲而流畅，细心阅读，总给人以美的享受。

首先是标题和开题几句的翻译。因为作者借助英国人对于天气的偏好，用 weather（天气）和 atmosphere（气候）与 soul（灵魂）和 inner（内在自我）构成基本的比喻性搭配，即 his inner atmosphere 和 the weather in his soul。同时指出它既不是宗教上的精神（spiritual），也不是神秘莫测的（mysterious）。根据这种理解，以兼有专业性和文学意味的"气象"来译 atmosphere，而把 weather 从"情绪"推至"情调"，这样就产生了"内在的情调"和"灵魂的气象"两个基本词组，作为全篇的比喻基调。这样，标题只不过是一个扩充性的说法而已——"英国人灵魂的气象"。

比喻的贴切和精妙是桑塔雅那散文的特点之一，译文尊重原作形象，适当发挥想象，使抽象的思想明白可感，跃然纸上。下面引述的两个句子，一个是以战舰比喻英国人的性格中单一而复杂的倾向。只要想想英国曾经有过海上霸权的地位，就知道这一比喻是何等的贴切而神妙。译笔流畅达意，充分发挥了汉语的优势，译者文学想象力的运用也恰到好处：

［原文］ It fights under its trivial fluttering opinions like a smoking battleship under its flags and signals; you must consider, not what they are, but why they have been hoisted and will not be lowered.

［译文］ 它在各种涌动于内心的细微见解之下进行战斗，就像一艘喷吐浓烟的战舰在各种旗帜和信号的指挥之下进行战斗一样；你所要考虑的不是它们是什么，而是它们既然

已经升起就不再降落这是为什么。

一想起英国人喜欢赛马，就知道第二个把英国人比作纯种马的比喻，并从纯种马的角度来理解人与人的关系，这是一种多么富有暗示性的哲理阐发。而译文在不中断叙述顺序的同时，也就顺乎自然地营造了一种天人合一的崇高意境：

［原文］ He is like a thoroughbred horse, satisfying to the trained eye, docile to the light touch, and coursing in most wonderful unison with you through the open world.

［译文］ 他就像一匹英国纯种马，行家一看就满意，轻轻一拍就能领会你的意图，和你完全融为一体，载着你在空旷的原野里驰骋。

观察的仔细和运思的严密，反映在行文的流畅和思绪的激荡里，莫过于一连串现象的列举和逐渐推向一个普遍性结论的能力。这便是第一段的行文特点。在翻译上有限度地改变原文连续使用的"when…"结构，但同时保持原文分节停顿的分号"；"，可使全段文字产生统一中有变化的审美情趣。同时，长句开头处加一"设想"进行提示，列举结束时用一破折号引出下面的译文，就起到了把多归结为一的收尾作用了。

到了全篇结束的时候，同样的写作手法又出现了。不过这里是结合了比喻在内的多种归一，与现代文明的贫瘠和苍白相比，作者用荒漠之中"清凉的处所"和"人类谵妄之中的圣堂"两个比喻，把思想的境界推到了一个至高无上的地位。全篇结束时作者把英国人的性格纳入希腊以来的文明史上的一种成就，这两个比喻起到了有力的铺垫作用。

［原文］ He carries his English weather in his heart wherever he goes, and it becomes a cool spot in the desert, and a steady and sane oracle amongst all the deliriums of mankind.

［译文］ 无论他走到哪里，心里总是怀着他的"英国气象"。它已变成沙漠里一个清凉的处所，人类谵妄之中一个稳固而明智的圣堂。

　　玄思与想象的结合是造就哲人式的文学家的一个必要的条件，也是构成桑塔雅那这篇散文的个性化风格的一种成因。译者注意到这一点，是译文成功的一个重要因素。词汇平面上一个明显的标志就是，原文采用专门术语的地方，就尽量译为专门术语，而原文采用文学语言的地方，就尽量译为文学语言。而在句法平面上，则较多地改英文比较直率的语气为汉语比较委婉的语气，比如假设、虚指、让步、设问、反问、重复、提示等手段，甚至包括少量文言虚词的使用，旨在创造出中文散文波澜起伏、一唱三叹的审美趣味。

　　以下列出一些典型例句，并附以必要的提示。

［原文］ Let me come to the point boldly; what governs the Englishman is his inner atmosphere, the weather in his soul.

［译文］ 让我直接进入正题吧：左右英国人的是他内在的情调，心灵里的气象。（重复）

［原文］ To say that this atmosphere was simply a sense of physical well-being, of coursing blood and a prosperous digestion, would be far too gross…

［译文］ 若说这一内在的情调仅仅是对于身体状况、血液循环和消化功能的感觉，那未免过于粗浅……（文言虚词、假设语气、委婉讽喻）

［原文］ The reformer must give him up; but why should one wish to reform a person so much better than oneself?

［译文］ 改良者必须放弃他；为什么偏要改变一个比自己好得多的人呢？（假设语气、词类转换）

　　一篇散文的成功写作，其因素是多方面的。同样，一篇散文的成功翻译，也要求译者多方面的功底和修养。译者和作者在语言能力、文学修养、气质习性上相一致的地方越多，则译文就越成功、越自然。

（王宏印）

8

Shakespeare's Island

George Gissing（1857—1903），英国作家，早期写工人题材的小说，如 *Workers in the Dawn*，代表作有 *New Grub Street* 和 *The Private Papers of Henry Ryecroft*。"Shakespeare's Island" 选自 *The Oxford Book of English Prose*，字里行间洋溢着对莎士比亚的崇拜和对祖国的热爱之情。

Today I have read *The Tempest*... Among the many reasons which make me glad to have been born in England, one of the first is that I read Shakespeare in my mother tongue. If I try to imagine myself as one who cannot know him face to face, who hears him only speaking from afar, and that in accents which only through the labouring intelligence can touch the living soul, there comes upon me a sense of chill discouragement, of dreary deprivation. I am wont to think that I can read Homer, and, assuredly, if any man enjoys him, it is I; but can I for a moment dream that Homer yields me all his music, that his word is to me as to him who walked by the Hellenic shore when Hellas lived? I know that there reaches me across the vast of time no more than a faint and broken echo; I know that it would be fainter still, but for its blending with those memories of youth which are as a glimmer of the world's primeval glory. Let every land have joy of its poet; for the poet is the land itself, all its greatness and its sweetness, all that incommunicable heritage for which men live and die. As I close the book, love and reverence possess me. Whether does my full heart turn to the great Enchanter, or to the Island upon which he has laid his spell? I know not. I cannot think of them apart. In the love and reverence awakened by that voice of voices, Shakespeare and England are but one.

原文赏析

作者自己曾说，莎士比亚的《暴风雨》是他非常熟悉也是他最喜爱的一部剧作。这部剧他读了很多遍，越读越发现自己的知识不完善，而且，只要是关系到莎士比亚，不论他活到多大年龄，他的知识总是不完善的。

作者对莎士比亚和他的祖国充满热爱和崇敬的感情，也因能用祖国的语言阅读莎氏的作品而感到自豪。因爱诗人而爱诗人的祖国，因爱祖国而爱祖国的诗人，以至无法将这二者分开。他很感慨地说："让每个国度都为它的诗人而感到欣慰吧；因为诗人就是这国度本身，就是它的伟大和温馨所在，就是人们置生死于不顾而要继承的只可意会而不可言传的遗产。"

作者在用自己祖国的语言阅读《暴风雨》时感到无限的愉悦与自豪："Among the many reasons which make me glad to have been born in England, one of the first is that I read Shakespeare in my mother tongue."。这种愉悦与自豪使他神思驰骋，感慨万千。从莎士比亚联想到荷马，从英格兰联想到希腊，从今天联想到古代。文章的语言也因为这一想象而时空交错，错综复杂。句子里面从句套从句，理解起来有一定的难度，如下面两句话的黑体部分，当然，这样的句子翻译起来需要斟酌：

If I try to imagine myself as one who cannot know him face to face, **who hears him only speaking from afar, and that in accents which only through the labouring intelligence can touch the living soul**, there comes upon me a sense of chill discouragement, of dreary deprivation. I am wont to think that I can read Homer, and, assuredly, if any man enjoys him, it is I; **but can I for a moment dream that Homer yields me all his music, that his word is to me as to him who walked by the Hellenic shore when Hellas lived**?

| 译文 |

莎士比亚之岛

乔治·吉辛

今天我读完了《暴风雨》……我很庆幸自己出生在英格兰，在众多的理由之中首要的理由之一是，我用我的母语阅读莎士比亚。要是我想象自己不能面对面地去认识他，只能听他从遥远的地方讲话，而且是用一种费解的口音讲话，我将会感到心灰意冷，也会因为被剥夺了一种权利而感到沮丧。我常这样想，我能阅读荷马，而且可以肯定地说，要是有谁欣赏荷马的作品，那就是我；可是，我能梦想领悟他所有的音乐吗？我能像那些在古希腊海滩上漫步的古希腊人那样理解他诗篇里的每一个字吗？我知道，越过广袤的时空传到我耳际的不过是一个微弱的、断断续续的回声；我知道，若不是这回声融汇着世界远古时代荣光火花的青春记忆，这微弱的回声还会更加微弱。让每个国度都为它的诗人而感到欣慰吧；因为诗人就是这国度本身，就是它的伟大和温馨所在，就是人们置生死于不顾而要继承的只可意会而不可言传的遗产。当我合上书时，心中充满了爱和崇敬。我的心是转向这位伟大的魔法师，还是转向他施过魔法的岛屿？我不知道。我无法将他们分开。在那伟大的声音所唤起的爱和崇敬之中，莎士比亚和英格兰已经融为一体。

| 翻 译 提 示 |

一部文学名著给一个人文主义者带来的激动和感受，往往是难以用语言来形容的。而当他用母语阅读自己喜爱的作家时，他对于祖国语言的自豪感就会同他对于祖国的热爱融为一体。而当他意识到他是通过翻译阅读一篇文学名篇时，他心理上的不安全感、语言上的隔膜感以及文化上的夹生感，就会使他产生一种莫名其妙的惆怅和难以满足的向往。然而，由于对人性和人类文化的深刻洞察力，这种向往使他坚信，每一个民族都有自己的诗人——作为文化高度集中的体现，作为本民族和全人类可以引以为自豪的先进代表——在和我们交流。于是，我被感染了，我被扩大了。这就是读者面前这篇短文的作者要告诉我们的，不，准确地说，是通过译者的忠实翻译已经传达给我们的。

在这篇短短的译文中，译者以他手中运用自如的汉语，忠实地传达了原作的语义，模仿了原作的语气，有效地再现了原作的思想和意境，进而引起读者崇高的联想和对于古典文明由衷的向往。这是难能可贵的。具体而言，有几点值得强调：

其一，开头部分的抽取译法。译者将原文定语从句 which make me glad to have been born in England 抽取出来，译成"我很庆幸自己出生在英格兰"，将其单独抽出来放在句首，让它成为一个总体的感受，这样处理，不仅解决了逻辑语句上不好安排的问题，而且强化了作者对祖国的认同感。

其二，译者运用汉语重复性强的特点，造成排比句式层层推进的篇章语势（例如"就是"，"就是"；"我知道"，"我知道"；"要是……我将"等)，强化了文章的结构整体性和逻辑表现力。

其三，译者对文章里作者所表现出来的热爱诗人、热爱祖国的崇高情感有很好的理解和把握，因此，能运用与原文切合的语言将其翻译出来，效果是好的。如文章最后几句话的翻译：

当我合上书时，心中充满了爱和崇敬。我的心是转向这位伟大的魔法师，还是转向他施过魔法的岛屿？我不知道。我无法将他们分开。在那伟大的声音所唤起的爱和崇敬之中，莎士比亚和英格兰已经融为一体。

当我们阅读一篇优秀的译文并为其魅力打动时，我们享受着近乎阅读原作一样的快乐。这一在翻译理论上很难说得清的可译性问题，或者说翻译之所以存在的根据问题，会为一篇译文的阅读效果所证实。

（王宏印）

9

Salvation

Langston Hughes（1902—1967），美国黑人诗人，哈莱姆文艺复兴（Harlem Renaissance）的代表性人物。主要诗歌作品有 *The Weary Blues*、*Shakespeare in Harlem*、*One-Way Ticket*，长篇小说 *Not Without Laughter*，自传 *The Big Sea* 和 *I Wonder as I Wander*。"Salvation" 是 *The Big Sea* 中的一个小节。文章以少年口气叙事，质朴简洁。

I was saved from sin when I was going on thirteen. But not really saved. It happened like this. There was a big revival at my Auntie Reed's church. Every night for weeks there had been much preaching, singing, praying, and shouting, and some very hardened sinners had been brought to Christ, and the membership of the church had grown by leaps and bounds. Then just before the revival ended, they held a special meeting for children, "to bring the young lambs to the fold." My aunt spoke of it for days ahead. That night 1 was escorted to the front row and placed on the mourners' bench with all the other young sinners, who had not yet been brought to Jesus.

My aunt told me that when you were saved you saw a light, and something happened to you inside! And Jesus came into your life! And God was with you from then on! She said you could see and hear and feel Jesus in your soul. I believed her. I had heard a great many old people say the same thing and it seemed to me they ought to know. So I sat there calmly in the hot, crowded church, waiting for Jesus to come to me.

The preacher preached a wonderful rhythmical sermon, all moans and shouts and lonely cries and dire pictures of hell, and then he sang a song about the ninety and nine safe in the fold. But one little lamb was left out in the cold. Then he said: "Won't you come? Won't you come to Jesus? Young lambs, won't you come?" And he held out his arms to all us young sinners there on the mourners' bench. And the little girls cried. And some of them jumped up and went to Jesus right away. But most of us just sat there.

A great many old people came and knelt around us and prayed, old women with jet-black faces and braided hair, old men with work-gnarled hands. And the church sang a song about the lower lights are burning, some poor sinners to be saved. And the whole building rocked with prayer and song.

Still I kept waiting to see Jesus.

Finally all the young people had gone to the altar and were saved, but one boy and me. He was a rounder's son named Westley. Westley and I were surrounded by sisters and deacons praying. It was very hot in the church, and getting late now. Finally Westley said to me in a whisper: "God damn! I'm tired of sitting here. Let's get up and be saved." So he got up and was saved.

Then I was left all alone on the mourners' bench. My aunt came and knelt at my knees and cried, while prayers and songs swirled all around me in the little church. The whole congregation prayed for me alone, in a mighty wail of moans and voices. And I kept waiting serenely for Jesus, waiting, waiting—but he didn't come. I wanted to see him, but nothing happened to me. Nothing! I wanted something to happen to me, but nothing happened.

I heard the songs and the minister saying: "Why don't you come? My dear child, why don't you come to Jesus? Jesus is waiting for you. He wants you. Why don't you come? Sister Reed, what is this child's name?"

"Langston," my aunt sobbed. "Langston, why don't you come? Why don't you come and be saved? Oh, Lamb of God! Why don't you come?"

Now it was really getting late. I began to be ashamed of myself, holding everything up so long. I began to wonder what God thought about Westley, who certainly hadn't seen Jesus either, but who was now sitting proudly on the platform, swinging his knickerbockered legs and grinning down at me, surrounded by deacons and old women on their knees praying. God had not struck Westley dead for taking his name in vain or for lying in the temple. So I decided that maybe to save further trouble, I'd better lie, too, and say that Jesus had come, and get up and be saved.

So I got up.

Suddenly the whole room broke into a sea of shouting, as they saw me rise. Waves of rejoicing swept the place. Women leaped in the air. My aunt threw her arms around me. The minister took me by the hand and led me to the platform.

When things quieted down, in a hushed silence, punctuated by a few ecstatic "Amens," all the new young lambs were blessed in the name of God. Then joyous singing filled the room.

That night, for the last time in my life but one—for I was a big boy twelve years old—I cried. I cried, in bed alone, and couldn't stop. I buried my head under the quilts, but my aunt heard me. She woke up and told my uncle I was crying because the Holy Ghost had come into my life, and because I had seen Jesus. But I was really crying because I couldn't bear to tell her that I had lied, that I had deceived everybody in the church, that I hadn't seen Jesus, and that now I didn't believe there was a Jesus any more, since he didn't come to help me.

| 原 文 赏 析 |

本文描写作者小时候初涉教事的一段经历。文章从一个天真少年的视角看基督教，发现宗教宣传的不真实和人们信仰的盲目，由此而产生对基督教信仰的幻灭。因文章是以一个天真少年的口吻叙事，语言简单、直率，不加修饰。

拯救

兰斯敦·休斯

在我快满十三岁的时候，我从罪孽中得到拯救，但并未真正得到拯救。事情的经过是这样的：我的姑母丽德所在的教堂组织了一个声势很大的福音布道会。一连几个星期，每天晚上都有讲道、唱诗、祈祷和欢呼声。一些顽固不化的"罪人"被带到基督身边，因此，教堂信众的人数迅猛增加。在布道会结束之前，他们又专为孩子们举行了一个仪式，为了"把迷途的羔羊领回羊圈"。几天之前姑母就一直在念叨这件事。那天晚上，我被送到教堂，安顿在前排的忏悔席上，和那些还没有来到耶稣身边的"小罪人们"坐在一起。

姑母说，当你得到拯救的时候，你会看到一道光，你的心灵里也会有感觉。那是耶稣进入了你的生命，从此上帝就和你在一起！她还说，你能在心灵里听见耶稣，看见耶稣，感觉到耶稣。我相信她的话。我听很多老年人都这样说，我想，他们理应知道这些事。我就安安静静地坐在又热又挤的教堂里，等待耶稣来到我身边。

传道士用生动的、富于节奏的语言讲道，他描绘着地狱里的可怕情景：到处是呻吟、哀号和凄凉的哭声。他唱了一首歌，歌中说：九十九只羔羊安安乐乐在羊圈，只有一只流落在外受饥寒。然后他说："你们不来吗？你们不到耶稣这边来吗？年幼的羔羊们啊，你们难道不来吗？"他向我们坐在忏悔席上的小罪人伸出双臂，小女孩们都哭了，有几个女孩跳起来，立刻向耶稣奔去。可是我们大多数人仍然坐在那里。

许多老年人围拢过来——满脸乌黑发亮，头上梳着发辫的老太婆们和双手长满老茧和节瘤的老头子们，他们跪在我们周围，嗡嗡地祈祷起来。后来教堂里唱起了地狱之火在燃烧，可怜的罪人要得救的歌。祈祷声和唱歌声震撼了大厅。

我继续等着见到耶稣。

最后，除了我和另一个男孩，所有的年轻人都奔向圣坛，得到了拯救。那男孩是个无赖的儿子，名叫韦斯特利。我们两人被念念有词的女教友和教堂执事们团团围住。教堂里热极了，天色也渐渐晚了。最后韦斯特利悄声对我说："去他的上帝，我在这儿坐腻了。咱们也起来去得救吧。"于是他站起来，得到了拯救。

现在只剩下我一个人孤零零地坐在忏悔席上。这时姑母走过来，跪在我的膝下放声哭了，小教堂里的祈祷声和唱歌声像旋风一样在我周围打转。全体会众一齐哀怨地哭叫为我一个人祷告，而我呢，还是安静地在等待耶稣，我等呀，等呀，但他始终没有来。我很想看见他，可连他的影子也没有，一点也没有！我很希望发生点什么事，可什么也没有发生。

我听见唱歌声，也听见牧师在说："你为什么不来？亲爱的孩子，你为什么不到耶稣这边来？耶稣正在等你。他欢迎你。你为什么不来呢？丽德教友啊，这孩子叫什么名字？"

"叫兰斯敦。"姑母抽泣着说，"兰斯敦，你为什么不来？你为什么不来接受拯救？啊！耶稣！你为什么不来？"

现在天可真的越来越晚了。我感到很难为情，一个人把会拖延这么长。同时我也很纳闷，上帝究竟对韦斯特利怎么想呢？他根本没看见耶稣。可他却洋洋得意地坐在教坛上，晃着穿着灯笼裤的两条腿，咧着嘴直冲我笑，周围还有执事们和年老的女教友跪着祷告。上帝并没有因为韦斯特利亵渎他的圣名，因为他在教堂里撒谎而将他击毙。我决定，为了不再麻烦，我最好也撒个谎，就说耶稣已经来临，然后站起来去接受拯救。

于是我站了起来。

当人们看见我站起来，整个大厅变成了崇赞的海洋，欢乐的声浪席卷了全教堂。妇女们蹦呀，跳呀。姑母伸出双臂，把我紧紧搂住。牧师抓住我的手，把我领到教坛上。

一切安静下来，只有人们欢喜若狂地祷念"阿门"的声音断断续续打破沉寂时，所有得到新生的羔羊们都接受了上帝的祝福。这时，欢乐的歌声充满了大厅的各个角落。

那天夜里，我哭了。那是我一生中倒数第二次哭——因为我已是个十二岁的大孩子了。我一个人躺在床上哭呀，哭呀，怎么也止不住。我用被子蒙着头，可姑母还是听见了。她醒来对姑父说，我之所以哭是因为圣灵进入了我的生命，还因为我已经看见了耶稣。其实，我哭泣的真正原因是我不忍心告诉她我说了谎，我欺骗了教堂里所有的人，也不忍心对她讲我并没有看见耶稣，因此我不再相信世界上有什么耶稣，因为他没有来帮助我。

| 翻 译 提 示 |

本文叙述兰斯敦·休斯少年时代经历的一次信仰危机。儿童是相信大人的，相信大人讲的话是真理。"姑母说，当你得到拯救的时候，你会看到一道光，你的心灵里也会有感觉。那是耶稣进入了你的生命，从此上帝就和你在一起！她还说，你能在心灵里听见耶稣，看见耶稣，感觉到耶稣。"姑母所说的事情没有发生，兰斯敦很失望，从此以后，他不再相信世上有耶稣。理解和掌握好作者失望的语气对翻译好这篇文章很重要。

下面是几个译例：

［原文］ I was saved from sin when I was going on thirteen. But not really saved.

[译文] 在我快满十三岁的时候，我从罪孽中得到拯救，但并未真正得到拯救。

[原文] Then I was left all alone on the mourners' bench. My aunt came and knelt at my knees and cried, while prayers and songs swirled all around me in the little church. The whole congregation prayed for me alone, in a mighty wail of moans and voices. And I kept waiting serenely for Jesus, waiting, waiting—but he didn't come. I wanted to see him, but nothing happened to me. Nothing! I wanted something to happen to me, but nothing happened.

[译文] 现在只剩下我一个人孤零零地坐在忏悔席上。这时姑母走过来，跪在我的膝下放声哭了，小教堂里的祈祷声和唱歌声像旋风一样在我周围打转。全体会众一齐哀怨地哭叫为我一个人祷告，而我呢，还是安静地在等待耶稣，我等呀，等呀，但他始终没有来。我很想看见他，可连他的影子也没有，一点也没有！我很希望发生点什么事，可什么也没有发生。

[原文] That night, for the last time in my life but one—for I was a big boy twelve years old—I cried. I cried, in bed alone, and couldn't stop. I buried my head under the quilts, but my aunt heard me.

[译文] 那天夜里，我哭了。那是我一生中倒数第二次哭——因为我已是个十二岁的大孩子了。我一个人躺在床上哭呀，哭呀，怎么也止不住。我用被子蒙着头，可姑母还是听见了。

下面的一个段落，是以男孩的口气转述姑母的话，有一点值得注意，即句与句之间的连接方式。叙述者一连使用了六个连接词 and 和一个 so，这一方面是因为少年话语的直白，不加修饰，也正因为如此，这一段落读起来一气呵成，很有一种平和之美感。试读一下，不难体会：

My aunt told me that when you were saved you saw a light, **and** something happened to you inside! **And** Jesus came into your life! **And** God was with you from then on! She said you could see **and** hear **and** feel Jesus in your soul. I believed her. I had heard a great many old people say the same thing **and** it seemed to me they ought to know. So I sat there calmly in the hot, crowded church, waiting for Jesus to come to me.

但在汉译时，若将这几个连接词一一翻译出来，却不能产生英语原文的效果，因为汉语行文的连贯感不尽依靠形式手段，主要是依靠意思上的逻辑与递进，这也是汉语的审美特征之一。如果在相应的地方都加上"而且"之类的连接词，这种美感随即被破坏。试参照下面的译文：

姑母说，当你得到拯救的时候，你会看到一道光，你的心灵里也会有所感觉。那是耶稣进入了你的生命，从此上帝和你在一起！她还说，你能在心灵里听见耶稣，看见耶稣，感觉到耶稣。我相信她的话。我听很多老年人都这样说，我想，他们理应知道这些事。我就安安静静地坐在又热又挤的教堂里，等待耶稣来到我身边。

10

English Food

"English Food" 选自吴延迪编著的《英国风情录》（*British Scenes*），
作者不详，具有盎格鲁–撒克逊英语的特征。

English food has a bad reputation abroad. This is most probably because foreigners in England are often obliged to eat in the more "popular" type of restaurant. Here it is necessary to prepare food rapidly in large quantities, and the taste of the food inevitably suffers, though its quality, from the point of view of nourishment, is quite satisfactory. Still, it is rather dull and not always attractively presented. Moreover, the Englishman eating in a cheap or medium price restaurant is usually in a hurry—at feast at lunch—and a meal eaten in a leisurely manner in pleasant surroundings is always far more enjoyable than a meal taken hastily in a business-like atmosphere. In general, it is possible to get an adequate meal at a reasonable price; in fact, such a meal may be less expensive than similar food abroad. For those with money to spare, there are restaurants that compare favourably with the best in any country.

In many countries breakfast is a snack rather than a meal, but the traditional English breakfast is a full meal. Some people have a cereal or porridge to begin with. If porridge is prepared from coarse oatmeal (in the proper Scottish manner) it is a tasty, economical, and nourishing dish, especially when it is eaten with milk or cream, and sugar or salt. Then comes a substantial, usually cooked, course such as bacon and eggs, sausages and bacon or, sometimes, haddock or kippers. Yorkshire ham is also a breakfast speciality. Afterwards comes toast, with butter and marmalade, and perhaps some fruit. Tea or coffee is drunk with the meal. Many English people now take such a full breakfast only on Sunday morning.

The traditional English meal (lunch or dinner, lunch generally being the lighter meal) is based on plain, simply-cooked food. British beefsteak is unsurpassed (with the best steaks coming from the Scotch Angus cattle) and is accompanied by roast potatoes; a second vegetable (probably cabbage or carrots), and Yorkshire pudding (baked batter, a mixture of flour, egg, milk and salt).

English lamb chops, best when grilled, make a very tasty dish, particularly when eaten with fresh spring peas, new potatoes and mint sauce. English pork is good, but English veal is sometimes disappointing.

As regards fish, Dover soles are a delicacy. So are British trout and salmon. Unfortunately, they are not cheap!

Apple pie is a favourite sweet, and English puddings, of which there are various types, are an excellent ending to a meal, especially in winter.

English cheeses deserve to be better known than they are. The "king" of cheeses is Stilton, a blue-veined cheese both smooth and strong, and at its best when port is drunk with it. Cheddar, Cheshire, and Lancashire cheeses are all pleasing to the palate, and cream cheeses are to be had in various parts of the country. In Devon, excellent clotted cream is made, which goes well with English strawberries and raspberries.

But what, you may say, shall we drink with our meal? Many will say English beer, preferably bitter or pale ale, or cider. If it is real Devonshire country cider, be careful—it is stronger than you think when you first taste it!

In recent years the British have become more cosmopolitan in their eating habits, and many families frequently sit down to meals whose ingredients or recipes may come from India (curry is a well-liked dish), China, or anywhere in the world.

| 原 文 赏 析 |

一篇好的英文应用文，从宏观上看，有两个突出的品质：一、不论是写什么题材，总能运用与该题材相宜的语言把文章写得富有浓郁的英文韵味，读者一看，便情不自禁地说，"这是好英语"；二、文章如同口头英语一样，念起来很上口，听起来很舒服。

关于英文韵味，金岳霖说："得一语言文字所表示的意义是比较容易的事，得一语言文字所表示的味是比较困难的事……在中国学习英文的人非常之多，然而得到英文意味的人恐怕并不很多。"

他所说的符合实际情况。

当人们学英语到了一定程度时，即不满足于自己的英语只是"正确"的时候，就自然想到如何使自己的英语有"韵味"。应该说这是可能的。要达到这个目标，需要多听、多读、多领悟。王朝闻在谈到艺术的诗意时说，诗意不是可以直接看出来的，是需要领悟的。他说得很对。艺术的诗意需要领悟，文章的韵味也需要领悟。只读懂了意思，没有领悟出文章的韵味，不算真正意义上的读书。

口语化也是好文章的一个重要品质，如果文章容易上口，就像作者在面对面跟你说话一样，使人读得懂，听得懂，而且让人喜欢；作者能把读者吸引到他的作品中来，分享他的思想和情感，这说明他的写作达到了一个很高的境界。这样的文章，论其效果——不论是应用效果还是审美效果——肯定是好的。海明威说"好的文章就是好的对话"，很有道理。

下面以《英国饮食》（"English Food"）为例，把"英文韵味"和"口语化"问题综合起来，看其在文章里是如何体现的。

《英国饮食》讲的只是饮食，如果说饮食也是文化，我们在读这篇文章时就是在了解、研究英国文化，但对我们学习语言的人来说，学习承载、传播这一文化信息的语言更为重要。在任何一种文化里，饮食都只是一个很普通的话题，不过是一些吃什么喝什么的事情，谈不好可能使人感觉乏味无聊，但谈好了却很有意思。这篇小文章非同一般，写得很有韵味，很有魅力。初读时就觉得语言新鲜，再读时更觉得其语言真是神奇，怎么能把这样普通的话题谈得这样有意思，从此越读越觉得其语言巧妙，读起来有味道，爱不释手。这里除了异域文化引起我们的兴趣之外，作者用英语叙事的技巧也别具吸引力。我们不妨从修辞方面入手，对文章的语言做一些分析，看看我们在读这篇文章时所领悟到的英文韵味是以怎样的修辞方式蕴藏于文章之中的。

修辞所包含的内容很多，讲修辞的书也很多。黄任在他的《英语修辞学概论》里说，修辞可以在语言的三个层面上进行操作：字词和短语的选择；句子的多样化；段落与篇章的组织。下面就从这三个方面对这篇文章进行修辞上的分析。

1. 字词和短语的选择遵循五个原则：精确（exactness, precision），经济（economy），具体（relevant accuracy），生动（vividness, gracefulness），恰当（appropriateness）。按照这五个原则选择字词和短语，是保证文章具有英文韵味的一个重要方面。如下面黑体的词语都是很好的例子：

1) …and the taste of the food inevitably **suffers**…

2) …it is rather dull and not always attractively **presented**.

3) English lamb chops…**make** a very tasty dish…

4) …which **goes well with** English strawberries and raspberries.

5) …an excellent **ending** to a meal…all **pleasing to the palate**…

6) a breakfast **speciality**, a **delicacy**

7) in **pleasant surroundings**…in a **business-like atmosphere**…

文章里还有不少好例子。这些词语我们并不觉得难，反而觉得很简单，但我们往往不知道可以这样写。

2. 这篇文章句子多样化的程度很高，要是从其结构、功能、语态和句子的开始方式等这些不同的角度来看，每句话都有不同于其他句子的特点，几乎没有重复现象。这篇文章英文韵味很浓，可读性很强，是句子形式的多样化起了很大作用。

从句式看，文章将近一半是简单句，其余是复合句和主从句，也有少许主从复合句；从句式的功能来看，大部分是陈述句（declarative sentence），也有疑问句（interrogative sentence）和祈使句（imperative sentence）；从语态看，大部分是主动句，也有相当数量的被动句。在这篇讲饮食的文章里，被动语态用得较多是一个值得注意的现象。同时还有几个倒装句。倒装句在上下文里都有其修辞功能。

句子开头的方式也具有多样性，多数以主语开始，也有以副词（Here，Still）、连接词（But）、介词短语（In many countries，In recent years）、成语（As regards）和从句开头（If it is real Devonshire country cider）的。

句子的长短变化也是一个值得研究的现象。这篇文章分九个段落，共 31 句话，近 530 个词。最长的一句（Moreover…）45 个词；最短的一句（Unfortunately…）五个词。20 个词以上的句子九个，十个词以下的句子有十个，其余每句都在 10—20 个词之间。全篇平均每句话 17 个词。

我们在前面谈到文章的口语化问题，句子简短是使文章上口的一个重要原因。句子短了，读起来、说起来就自然顺口。

3. 这篇文章段落和篇章的组织也好。第一段是开头，说"English food has a bad reputation abroad."。第二段讲早饭。第三段讲午饭或晚饭。第四至第八段讲午饭或晚饭吃的食物以及喝的饮料。最后一段是结尾，说"In recent years the British have become more cosmopolitan in their eating habits…"。整篇文章结构是那么严密，发展是那么自然，那么顺理成章。文章内容的集中性和篇章的整体感很强，很符合写作上所要求的内容上的统一（unity）和脉络上的连贯（coherence）。

从宏观方面看，字词和短语的选择、句子的多样性、段落和篇章的组织，都对创造文章的韵味做出自己的贡献；但就句子本身而言，其形式的多样性、句子开头的不同方式和句子长短的合理间隔，这些因素综合起来，再加上插入语（parenthesis）的巧妙运用，就给文章的行文创造了一种节奏和韵律，如文中的：

1) But what,/**you may say**,/shall we drink/with our meal?

2) English lamb chops,/**best when grilled**,/make a very tasty dish,/**particularly**/when eaten with fresh spring peas,/new potatoes/and mint sauce.

第一句有四个重读音节，以一个轻读音节开始，以一个重读音节结束，其间每个重读音节后面有两个轻读音节，读起来很规律。第二句重读音节很多，很密集，重读音节之间的轻音节数和第一句比较起来不太规律。当我们朗读或口述上面的句子时，就会觉得这种音节数目基本相同又不完全相同、重读音节基本规律又不完全规律的现象是符合散文体文章的自然状态的。

文章的这种节奏和韵律可能是作者的有意安排，也可能是作者风格的自然流露。在多数情况下，后者的可能性会更大。

以上几个方面因素综合作用使文章产生了一种韵味和韵律，但这也只是一部分可视因素，肯定还有多种其他因素在起作用。但有一点需要强调，即文章绝不是从某些既定的原则出发而进行的文字的机械组合。文章的灵魂来自作者的主观世界，是作者的思想、情操、气质和审美情趣的艺术再现。客观世界为文章提供了题材，主观世界赋予文章以形式和风格。不同的作者，因为主观世界的不同，以及语言能力的差异，可能会赋予同一题材不同的形式和风格，这也就是形式与风格之所以各不相同的原因。

（与张保红合写）

| 译文 |

英国饮食

英国食品在海外的名声不佳。这很可能是因为来英国的外国人不得不常在更"大众化"的餐馆里用餐的缘故。在那里，必须迅速、大量地备餐，因此，饭菜的味道不可避免地要差一些，尽管在营养方面，其质量还是令人满意的。可是饭菜仍然显得单调，花色也常常不大讲究。此外，在价钱便宜或适中的饭店里用餐的英国人，通常是来去匆匆——至少午餐如此——而在舒适的环境中从容就餐要比在生意氛围较浓的环境里匆忙吃饭更有乐趣。一般来说，花不多的钱吃上一顿饱饭是可能的。事实上，同样的饭菜比国外或许还要便宜些。对于手头有富余的人来说，英国某些饭店和国外最好的饭店相比还要划算一些。

在许多国家，早餐只是小吃而不算正餐，但传统的英国早餐却是正餐。有的人先吃麦片或喝粥，如果粥是用粗燕麦片做的（正宗的苏格兰风味），那就既可口又经济并富有营养，特别是加了牛奶或奶油，糖或盐。然后是一道实实在在的熟菜，火腿鸡蛋、香肠火腿，有时是鳕鱼或熏鲱。约克郡火腿也是早餐的特色食品。然后是涂上黄油和果酱的吐司，也许还有些水果。吃早餐时喝茶或咖啡。许多英国人现在只在星期天才吃这样的早餐。

传统的英国正餐（午餐或晚餐；午餐一般比较简单）以清淡、烹调省事的食物为主。英国的牛排最好（用苏格兰安格斯牛的上等牛排调制），伴以烤土豆，另加第二道蔬菜（可能是卷心菜或胡萝卜），以及约克郡布丁（用面粉、蛋、牛奶和盐调制成面糊烘烤而成）。

英国的羊排美味可口，烤着吃滋味最佳，特别是和春天新鲜的豌豆、土豆和薄荷酱一起吃。英国的猪肉味道也很好，但英国的小牛肉有时却令人失望。

至于鱼类，多佛鳎鱼味道鲜美，英国的鳟鱼和鲤鱼也很好。只可惜，价格不低！

苹果饼是受欢迎的甜食，各式各样的英国布丁也是很好的饭后点心，特别是在冬天。

英国奶酪应该比现在更知名。奶酪之王是斯提耳顿干酪，带有青色纹络，细腻而味浓，喝着波尔图葡萄酒吃味道最好。切达干酪、柴郡奶酪和兰开夏郡奶酪味道都很好，而奶油干酪在全国各地都有。德文郡出产上等的浓缩奶油，用英国草莓和紫莓沾着吃味道鲜美。

可是，你也许要问，我们用餐时喝些什么呢？许多人会说：英国啤酒，最好是苦啤酒或淡啤酒，或者是苹果酒。如果是正宗的德文郡乡间产的苹果酒，那你得小心——第一次品尝时可比你所想象的要厉害。

近年来，英国人的饮食习惯越来越国际化了，许多家庭餐桌上食物的原料或烹调方法可能来自印度（咖喱食品是很受欢迎的菜肴）、中国，或世界上任何地方。

（此译文在吴延迪编著的《英国风情录》的基础上，做了一些修改，特此说明，并对东方出版中心和原译者表示感谢。）

| 翻译提示 |

这是一篇讲日常饮食的文章，语言经过锤炼，文字是朝着口语体的方向推敲的。突出表现在它的字词活泼，句式多变，节奏明快，行文流畅。在字词方面，多用盎格鲁－撒克逊语的小词，活泼而雅致。翻译时需予以注意。句式变化多，有长句，如 "Moreover, the Englishman eating in a cheap or medium price restaurant is usually in a hurry—at least at lunch—and a meal eaten in a leisurely manner in pleasant surroundings is always far more enjoyable than a meal taken hastily in a business-like atmosphere."。有短句，如 "Unfortunately, they are not cheap!"。有疑问句，如 "But what, you may say, shall we drink with our meal?"。有祈使句，如 "If it is real Devonshire country cider, **be careful**—it is stronger than you think when you first taste it!"。有被动句，如 "Tea or coffee **is drunk** with the meal."。翻译这些句子时需注意其语气上的特征。

关于句子的节奏，应注意音节的轻重读所产生的声音的起伏和速度的快慢。

行文的自然流畅取决于上下文的贯通，包括形式和意义两方面的贯通，上下文贯通了，行文就自然、流畅，就有了气势。如：

English food has a bad reputation abroad. **This** is most probably because foreigners in England are often obliged to eat in the more "popular" type of restaurant. **Here** it is necessary to prepare food rapidly in large quantities, **and** the taste of the food inevitably suffers, **though** its quality, from the point of view of nourishment, is quite satisfactory. **Still**, it is rather dull and not always attractively presented.

这是文章开始的几句话，表达了一个完整的意思。第一句是主题句（topic sentence），下面几句是对这一命题的解释。解释过程中由于使用了连接成分代词 This 和 Here，连接词 and 和 though，副词 Still，使得这段文字一气贯通，对主题句提出的命题做了十分周全的解释。译文如能注意译好这几个连接成分也可以收到同原文一样的效果：

英国食品在海外的名声不佳。这很可能是因为来英国的外国人不得不常在更"大众化"的餐馆里用餐的缘故。**在那里**，必须迅速、大量地备餐，**因此**，饭菜的味道不可避免地要差一些，**尽管在**营养方面，其质量还是令人满意的。**可是**饭菜**仍然**显得单调，花色也常常不大讲究。

下面原文中黑体的部分都是重读音节，与轻读音节的间隔虽不规律，但读的时候可以清楚地听出其轻重高低，快慢缓急的声势。翻译成汉语时虽然不可能与原文对应，因为汉语不是完全以音节计算轻重读的，有时轻重读也表现在词组上。但在汉语译文里尽量表现出原文的抑扬顿挫的效果还是可能的。

[原文]　English **lamb chops**, **best** when **gri**lled, **make** a very **tasty dish**, particularly when **eat**en with **fresh spring peas**, **new** potatoes and **mint sauce**. **Eng**lish **pork** is **good**, but **Eng**lish **veal** is **some**times disap**point**ing.

[译文]　英国的羊排美味可口，烤着吃滋味最佳，特别是和春天新鲜的豌豆、土豆和薄荷酱一起吃。英国的猪肉味道也很好，但英国的小牛肉有时却令人失望。

以下是一个包括三句话的小段落，由于里面有一个问句和一个祈使句，使得整个段落显得很活泼。把这个问句和祈使句译好，译文的效果就不会差了。

[原文]　But what, you may say, shall we drink with our meal? Many will say English beer, preferably bitter or pale ale, or cider. If it is real Devonshire country cider, be careful——it is stronger than you think when you first taste it!

[译文]　可是，你也许要问，我们用餐时喝些什么呢？许多人会说：英国啤酒，最好是苦啤酒或淡啤酒，或者是苹果酒。如果是正宗的德文郡乡间产的苹果酒，那你得小心——第一次品尝时可比你所想象的要厉害。

（与张保红合写）

下 编

散文英译
ENGLISH TRANSLATIONS
OF PROSE

1

风筝

鲁迅（1881—1936），思想家，文学家，著有短篇小说集《呐喊》
和《彷徨》，散文《朝花夕拾》，散文诗《野草》，以及大量的杂文。
《风筝》选自《野草》，笔调委婉，意蕴深邃。

北京的冬季，地上还有积雪，灰黑色的秃树枝丫杈于晴朗的天
空中，而远处有一二风筝浮动，在我是一种惊异和悲哀。

故乡的风筝时节，是春二月，倘听到沙沙的风轮声，仰头便能
看见一个淡墨色的蟹风筝或嫩蓝色的蜈蚣风筝。还有寂寞的瓦片风
筝，没有风轮，又放得很低，伶仃地显出憔悴可怜模样。但此时地
上的杨柳已经发芽，早的山桃也多吐蕾，和孩子们的天上的点缀相
照应，打成一片春日的温和。我现在在哪里呢？四面都还是严冬的
肃杀，而久经诀别的故乡的久经逝去的春天，却就在这天空中荡
漾了。

但我是向来不爱放风筝的，不但不爱，并且嫌恶他，因为我以

为这是没出息孩子所做的玩意。和我相反的是我的小兄弟，他那时大概十岁内外罢，多病，瘦得不堪，然而最喜欢风筝，自己买不起，我又不许放，他只得张着小嘴，呆看着空中出神，有时至于小半日。远处的蟹风筝突然落下来了，他惊呼；两个瓦片风筝的缠绕解开了，他高兴得跳跃。他的这些，在我看来都是笑柄，可鄙的。

有一天，我忽然想起，似乎多日不很看见他了，但记得曾见他在后园拾枯竹。我恍然大悟似的，便跑向少有人去的一间堆积杂物的小屋去，推开门，果然就在尘封的什物堆中发现了他。他向着大方凳，坐在小凳上；便很惊惶地站了起来，失了色瑟缩着。大方凳旁靠着一个蝴蝶风筝的竹骨，还没有糊上纸，凳上是一对做眼睛用的小风轮，正用红纸条装饰着，将要完工了。我在破获秘密的满足中，又很愤怒他的瞒了我的眼睛，这样苦心孤诣地来偷做没出息孩子的玩意。我即刻伸手折断了蝴蝶的一支翅骨，又将风轮掷在地下，踏扁了。论长幼，论力气，他是都敌不过我的，我当然得到完全的胜利，于是傲然走出，留他绝望地站在小屋里。后来他怎样，我不知道，也没有留心。

然而我的惩罚终于轮到了，在我们离别得很久之后，我已经是中年。我不幸偶尔看了一本外国的讲论儿童的书，才知道游戏是儿童最正当的行为，玩具是儿童的天使。于是二十年来毫不忆及的幼小时候对于精神的虐杀的这一幕，忽地在眼前展开，而我的心也仿佛同时变成铅块，很重很重地堕下去了。

但心又不竟堕下去而至于断绝，他只是很重很重地堕着，堕着。

我也知道补过的方法的：送他风筝，赞成他放，劝他放，我和他一同放。我们嚷着，跑着，笑着。——然而他其时已经和我一样，早已有了胡子了。

我也知道还有一个补过的方法的：去讨他的宽恕，等他说，"我可是毫不怪你呵。"那么，我的心一定就轻松了，这确是一个可行的方法。有一回，我们会面的时候，是脸上都已添刻了许多"生"的辛苦的条纹，而我的心很沉重。我们渐渐谈起儿时的旧事来，我便叙述到这一节，自说少年时代的糊涂。"我可是毫不怪你呵。"我想，他要说了，我即刻便受了宽恕，我的心从此也宽松了罢。

"有过这样的事吗？"他惊异地笑着说，就像旁听着别人的故事一样。他什么也不记得了。

全然忘却，毫无怨恨，又有什么宽恕之可言呢？无怨的怒，说谎罢了。

我还能希求什么呢？我的心只得沉重着。

现在，故乡的春天又在这异地的空中了，既给我久经逝去的儿时的回忆，而一并也带着无可把握的悲哀。我倒不如躲到肃杀的严冬中去吧，——但是，四面又明明是严冬，正给我非常的寒威和冷气。

| 译文 |

The Kite
Lu Xun

In the winter of Beijing, with snow still on the ground and dark-gray branches up in the brisk air, a couple of kites were fluttering up in the distance against the sunny sky—a sight that filled me with amazement and forlornness.

In my hometown, kites were flown in early spring. When you heard the whirring of wind-wheels and looked up, you saw a darkish crab-kite or a kite of limpid blue resembling a centipede. There were one or two others in the shape of old-fashioned tiles, without wind wheels. They flew at a lower level, lonely and shriveled, arousing a sense of compassion. Around this time of year, poplars and willows began to sprout, and new buds to appear on the early mountain peaches, forming a picture with the sky decorated by the kites the kids flew, a picture that gave you the feel of the warmth of spring. But, where was I now? Standing in the midst of the severe cold of the desolate winter, I felt the spring of my hometown rippling in the air, the spring that had been long gone.

I myself had never enjoyed flying kites and, further, I detested it, thinking that it was the business of the kids with little promise. My younger brother, however, about ten years of age then, weak and thin, frequently troubled with sicknesses, was crazy about kites. Unable to afford it and deprived of the access to it by this elder brother of his, he would stand there, his tiny mouth open in a gape, watching upward, sometimes for hours running. When, all of a sudden, the crab-kite in the distance plummeted, he would gasp in surprise; when two tile-kites got entangled and then fell apart, he would jump with joy. To me, all these spontaneities were contemptible and despicable.

One day, it occurred to me that I did not seem to have seen him for days, but remembered having once met him in the backyard collecting dry bamboo branches. Suddenly, as if prompted by some freakish instinct, I rushed to a small room there that was forsaken and used as a storeroom for odds and ends. I pushed the door open and, as I expected, found him nestling in the dusty junk. He was sitting on a small stool, with another one, big and square, in front. He stood up hastily, shivering all over, his face turning pale. The skeleton of a butterfly-kite was leaning against the big stool with the paper yet to be pasted and, lying on top of the stool was a pair of wind-wheels, draped with strips of red paper, to be fixed on the kite as the eyes of the butterfly—a project nearing completion. I was contented with my discovery of the secret and, at the same time, angry at his having managed to escape my notice, falling head over heels in something that was supposedly the stuff of unpromising children. I snatched up the kite and broke off one of its wings and, throwing the wheels on the ground, crushed them with my foot. He was no match for me, physically and agewise. I crowned with clean victory, of course. I walked out of the room, with my head lifted, leaving him behind where he was in despair. As for what had happened to him since then, I had no idea, nor did I ever bother to find out.

And punishment finally came down upon me. We had been apart for a long time and I was already a middle-aged man. It was not until accidentally and unfortunately, I had read a book by a foreign author about children, that I realized that children had a hundred and one reasons to play and toys were their angels. The thing I did of actually a soul-torturing nature, which had been absent from my memory for the past twenty years, suddenly began to unfold itself in my mind's eye, turning my heart into a clod of lead that kept sinking with an increasing heaviness.

The "clod of lead" kept going down, never reaching the point where it would hopefully break off.

I knew how to make up for it, then. I could give him a kite and encourage him to fly it, or I could even go and fly it with him. We would run and shout and laugh together. But by this time, just like myself, he had long been wearing a beard.

There was another way to make up, I knew. I could go and ask him to forgive me and then wait until he would say, "Why, I never put the blame on you!" With that my heart would be relieved and that was what I could fall back on. Once, we came together when both our faces were full of lines engraved with the bitterness of life, and my heart was very heavy, indeed. Soon the conversation drifted to our childhood days and I mentioned thestory about the kite, saying with regret what a barmy boy I was then. "Why, I never put the blame on you!" I thought that was what he would say and, if he had, I would have been forgiven immediately and able to get myself off the hook.

"Was there such a story, then?" He smiled with amazement, as if it were a story about someone else. Obviously he remembered nothing about it.

Since he had forgotten about that and was, therefore, not resentful of anything at all, there was no need for me to ask to be forgiven. It would be a lie to forgive without complaints.

What else did I wish to ask for then? But my heart was as heavy as ever.

Now the spring of my hometown was in the sky of a foreign place, bringing to me the memory of my long-gone childhood, along with the kind of forlornness that was hard to define. I thought 1 should retire to the depth of the severe and desolate winter, but I was right in the middle of it, exposed to the severity of the piercing cold.

| 翻 译 提 示 |

怀着对鲁迅的景仰和崇敬，试译了《野草》中的《风筝》，其时心怀迟疑，颇觉己之英语拙劣，唯恐亵渎了作者神圣的文字，曲解其委婉、深奥的本意。虽也尽力体察作者的心境，一因时隔久

远，二因思想境界差距太大，理解起来尚觉心力不足，翻译时更觉笔力不达。

刘梦溪谈《红楼梦》研究时说：思维的直观性是我们民族的思维特点，表现在艺术上则强调灵感思维，相信"文章本天成，妙手偶得之"。作品艺术形象的构成，客观物象固然离不开，但在创作主张上更突出意境和意象，这和天人合一、物我浑成的哲学思想密切相关。对艺术的理解，则崇尚妙悟，提倡心领神会。《文子·道德篇》说："上学以神听之，中学以心听之，下学以耳听之。"被列为"上学"的"以神听之"，就是通常所说的神会，也就是悟。（《传统的误读》，第194—195页）他所说的"妙悟"和"以神听之"，这对译者是真真切切地重要。

鲁迅于1934年10月9日在致萧军信中说：我的那一本《野草》，技术并不算坏，但心情太颓唐了，因为那是我碰了许多钉子之后写出来的。（《鲁迅全集》第二卷，第160页）他又说：大抵仅仅是随时的小感想。因为那时难于直说，所以有时措辞就很含糊了。（《鲁迅全集》第四卷，第356页）

鉴于《野草》是在这样的背景之下写出，后来的读者（或译者）尽可理解作者当时所处的环境以及他在那种环境里的心境，若要准确地把握住他想说而不能直说的意思以及他用"含糊"的措辞所隐约影射的内涵，再用英语以相近的语气和风格表达出来，这对母语为汉语的译者来说还是有难度的。

作者称《野草》为散文诗，即兼备散文与诗的特点。形为散文实为诗，虽无诗之格律，但有诗之韵律。作者深邃的思想波澜，微妙的感情涟漪，通过听似不规则，实为自然天成的韵律，创造了一种意境，传达了一种诗意，使人产生丰富的联想。译者反复吟诵，深入思考，体悟文章的诗意，感觉其语言的韵律，是译好文章的前提。

现举几例以做说明：

[原文] 北京的冬季，地上还有积雪，灰黑色的秃树枝丫杈于晴朗的天空中，而远处有一二风筝浮动，在我是一种惊异和悲哀。

[译文] In the winter of Beijing, with snow still on the ground and dark-gray branches up in the brisk air, a couple of kites were fluttering up in the distance against the sunny sky—a sight that filled me with amazement and forlornness.

"北京的冬季"，地上的"积雪"，"晴朗的天空"，"灰黑色的秃树枝丫"和远处浮动的"风筝"，构成一幅北京残冬的画面，使作者想起童年的往事，因而感到"惊异和悲哀"。译文用一个带时间状语的主从复合句勾勒出相应的画面和作者的感受，效果与原文接近。

[原文] 但此时地上的杨柳已经发芽，早的山桃也多吐蕾，和孩子们的天上的点缀相照应，打成一片春日的温和。

[译文] Around this time of year, poplars and willows began to sprout, and new buds to appear on the early mountain peaches, forming a picture with the sky decorated by the kites the kids flew, a picture that gave you the feel of the warmth of spring.

这里又是一幅富有诗意的画面，译文注意了行文的节奏和韵律，在第三小句的译文里用了一个分词短语 forming a picture，然后又在第四小句里重复了 a picture that gave you，这一重复使句子结构平衡饱满，意思表达充分。

[原文] 和我相反的是我的小兄弟，他那时大概十岁内外罢，多病，瘦得不堪，然而最喜欢风筝，自己买不起，我又不许放，

他只得张着小嘴，呆看着空中出神，有时至于小半日。

[译文] My younger brother, however, about ten years of age then, weak and thin, frequently troubled with sicknesses, was crazy about kites. Unable to afford it and deprived of the access to it by this elder brother of his, he would stand there, his tiny mouth open in a gape, watching upward, sometimes for hours running.

原文句子较长，短语较多，译文因此用了两个英语句子，并对短语做了适当调整和安排，因而行文比较流畅。原文里的"我又不许放"译作 deprived of the access to it by this elder brother of his，这样处理表达了作者的自责之意，效果是可以的。

[原文] 远处的蟹风筝突然落下来了，他惊呼；两个瓦片风筝的缠绕解开了，他高兴得跳跃。

[译文] When, all of a sudden, the crab-kite in the distance plummeted, he would gasp in surprise; when two tile-kites got entangled and then o fell apart, he would jump with joy.

原文属排比句，译文也做了相应的处理。文章的结尾与开头相呼应，又提到天空中早春的景象和作者悲哀的心情以及作者所处的恶劣环境。译文注意到了言辞的委婉与含蓄，效果也还是可以的吧。

2

鲁迅先生记

萧红（1911—1942），作家，著有小说《生死场》《呼兰河传》，以及短篇小说和散文。《鲁迅先生记》选自《萧红选集》，语言真挚，感情细腻。

鲁迅先生家里的花瓶，好像画上所见的西洋女子用以取水的瓶子，灰蓝色，有点从瓷釉而自然堆起的纹痕，瓶口的两边，还有两个瓶耳，瓶里种的是几棵万年青。

我第一次看到这花的时候，我就问过：

"这叫什么名字？屋中既不生火炉，也不冻死？"

第一次，走进鲁迅家里去，那是快近黄昏的时节，而且是个冬天，所以那楼下室稍微有一点暗，同时鲁迅先生的纸烟，当它离开嘴边而停在桌角的地方，那烟纹的卷痕一直升腾到他有一些白丝的发梢那么高。而且再升腾就看不见了。

"这花，叫'万年青'，永久这样！"他在花瓶旁边的烟灰盒中，抖掉了纸烟上的灰烬，那红的烟火，就越红了，好像一朵小花似的，和他的袖口相距离着。

"这花不怕冻？"以后，我又问过，记不得是在什么时候了。

许先生说："不怕的，最耐久！"而且她还拿着瓶口给我摇着。

我还看到了那花瓶的底边是一些圆石子，以后，因为熟识了的缘故，我就自己动手看过一两次，又加上这花瓶是常常摆在客厅的黑色长桌上，又加上自己是来在寒带的北方，对于这在四季里都不凋零的植物，总带着一点惊奇。而现在这"万年青"依旧活着，每次到许先生家去，看到那花，有时仍站在那黑色的长桌上，有时站在鲁迅先生照像的前面。

花瓶是换了，用一个玻璃瓶装着，看得到淡黄色的须根，站在瓶底。

有时候许先生一面和我们谈论着，一面检查着房中所有的花草。看一看叶子是不是黄了？该剪掉的剪掉，该洒水的洒水，因为不停地动作是她的习惯。有时候就检查着这"万年青"，有时候就谈着鲁迅先生，就在他的照像前面谈着，但那感觉，却像谈着古人那么悠远了。

至于那花瓶呢？站在墓地的青草上面去了，而且瓶底已经丢失，虽然丢失了也就让它空空地站在墓边。我所看到的是从春天一直站到秋天；它一直站到邻旁墓头的石榴树开了花而后结成了石榴。

从开炮以后，只有许先生绕道去过一次，别人就没有去过。当然那墓草是长得很高了，而且荒了，还说什么花瓶，恐怕鲁迅先生的瓷半身像也要被荒了的草埋没到他的胸口。

我们在这边，只能写纪念鲁迅先生的文章，而谁去努力剪齐墓上的荒草？我们是越去越远了，但无论多么远，那荒草是总要记在心上的。

A Few Memories of Mr. Lu Xun
Xiao Hong

Mr. Lu Xun had a plant pot in his sitting-room. It looked like the jar European women fetched water with, as shown in paintings. It was of a bluish-gray, with a few ripples naturally embossed with its own glaze and, on either side of it, there was a handle close to the top. Planted in it was some evergreen.

The first time I visited Mr. Lu Xun I asked:

"What is the name of this plant? There is no fire in the room, but it is not frozen."

It was toward evening one winter day. The sitting-room downstairs was dim. Mr. Lu Xun was smoking a cigarette. When he took it away from his lips, holding it between his fingers at the corner of his desk, small puffs rose as high as the top of his grayish hair and, further up, they were no longer visible.

"This plant is called evergreen. It's always like that." He flicked the cigarette ash to the ashtray next to the pot and the cigarette grew redder still like a small flower glimmering two or three inches from the cuff of his sleeve.

"It is not affected by the cold, is it?" I asked another time, not remembering exactly when.

"No, it is not," said Mrs. Lu. "It's a very tough plant." She held the pot by the top, shaking it for me to see.

I noticed there were some pebbles around the bottom. Later, as

I got to know them better, I went up to the black table once or twice for a closer look at the plant. As I came from the cold north I always wondered why this plant did not wither even in winter.

The plant was now still alive. Sometimes it was placed on the black table, other times in front of Mr. Lu Xun's photograph. But it had been transplanted into a glass pot through which their yellowish roots could be seen at the bottom.

Mrs. Lu would chat with us while moving from one plant to another, checking if any of them had turned yellow or needed clipping or watering. She would keep herself busy in her room. Sometimes she examined the evergreen, sometimes she talked of Mr. Lu Xun, in front of his photograph, as if of someone of remote past.

But where was the pot now? It was standing in the graveyard, in the grass, its bottom missing. The bottomless, empty pot had been there spring through autumn until the pomegranate at the head of the neighboring tomb had blossomed and borne fruit.

Since the Japanese bombardment of Shanghai only Mrs. Lu has made a detour to visit the tomb, but no others have ever been there. The tomb must have been overgrown with wild grass and the porcelain bust of Mr. Lu Xun buried up to the chest, not to mention what would have happened to the pot.

As for us over here, there is not much we can do but write some memorial articles. But who will go and trim the grass on his tomb? We are getting further and further away from him, but no matter how far away we are, we must remember the grass on his tomb.

　　萧红对鲁迅先生十分景仰，常以导师相称。1936 年 10 月，鲁迅逝世，萧红时在日本，心情难过，写信回来，以《海外的悲哀》为题登在当时《中流》杂志专号上。后来又连续写了几篇纪念文章，《鲁迅先生记》为其中之一，写于 1938 年。

　　萧红的小说写得好，散文写得也好。文字朴素自然，跟说话一样，不雕琢；但文章充满真情，写到苦难时，读来往往使人下泪。这是萧红散文一个特别好的地方，翻译时对这一点予以注意，可使译文有感染力；萧红具有女性作家感觉微妙、感情细腻的特点，善于描写细节，给人真实感，翻译时选词宜具体（specific）、恰当（appropriate），句子的结构与长度应宜于表达原文的思想和情感；萧红的文字常有不符合语法规范的现象，翻译时要予以调整，将其译成规范的英语，翻译严肃作家的作品应该这样，也值得这样。举例分述如下：

[原文]　鲁迅先生家里的花瓶，好像画上所见的西洋女子用以取水的瓶子，灰蓝色，有点从瓷釉而自然堆起的纹痕，瓶口的两边，还有两个瓶耳，瓶里种的是几棵万年青。

[译文]　Mr. Lu Xun had a plant pot in his sitting-room. It looked like the jar European women fetched water with, as shown in paintings. It was of a bluish-gray, with a few ripples naturally embossed with its own glaze and, on either side of it, there was a handle colse to the top. Planted in it was some evergreen.

　　这个段落是一个长句，翻译时需做一些处理。原文以"鲁迅先生家里的花瓶"开头，"花瓶"成了这个长句的主语。如果英语句子也以同样方式开始，则显陡然。略做变化，译文句子以"鲁迅先生家里有个花瓶"开始，再根据内容将长句分成几个短句，慢慢地对花瓶进行描述，这样，全段的行文速度就变得平稳、均衡，全无陡然之感。

[原文]　以后，因为熟识了的缘故，我就自己动手看过一两次，又加上这花瓶是常常摆在客厅的黑色长桌上，又加上自己是来在寒带的北方，对于这在四季里都不凋零的植物，总带着一点儿惊奇。

[译文]　Later, as I got to know them better, I went up to the black table once or twice for a closer look at the plant. As I came from the cold north I always wondered why this plant did not wither even in winter.

　　汉语里有两处用了"又加上"，这是口语里常有的现象。第一个"又加上"略有因为之意，做淡化处理之后可予忽略。第二个"又加上"等于"因为"，用现在分词短语 Coming from the cold north 或用从句 As I came from the cold north 来表示都可以。

[原文]　同时鲁迅先生的纸烟，当它离开嘴边而停在桌角的地方，那烟纹的卷痕一直升腾到他有一些白丝的发梢那么高。而且再升腾就看不见了。

[译文]　Mr. Lu Xun was smoking a cigarette. When he took it away from his lips, holding it between his fingers at the comer of his desk, small puffs rose as high as the top of his grayish hair and, further up, they were no longer visible.

这两句话描写鲁迅吸烟的细节，很细致，很逼真。用英语描写时也应选择相应的词，和符合英语规范又符合原文风格的句式，如此才能收到较好的效果。

[原文] "这花，叫'万年青'，永久这样！"他在花瓶旁边的烟灰盒中，抖掉了纸烟上的灰烬，那红的烟火，就越红了，好像一朵小花似的，和他的袖口相距离着。

[译文] "This plant is called evergreen. It's always like that." He flicked the cigarette ash to the ashtray next to the pot and the cigarette grew redder still like a small flower glimmering two or three inches from the cuff of his sleeve.

这也是一个细节，描写鲁迅先生手里点着的烟卷。翻译时选择具体、恰当的动词，如 flicked、grew、glimmering 等。

[原文] 至于那花瓶呢？站在墓地的青草上面去了，而且瓶底已经丢失，虽然丢失了也就让它空空地站在墓边。我所看到的是从春天一直站到秋天；它一直站到邻旁墓头的石榴树开了花而后结成了石榴。

[译文] But where was the pot now? It was standing in the graveyard, in the grass, its bottom missing. The bottomless, empty pot had been there spring through autumn until the pomegranate at the head of the neighboring tomb had blossomed and borne fruit.

作者在这里借花瓶抒发忧伤的心情和对已经逝世的鲁迅的牵挂，令人感到难过。从"至于"到"已经丢失"可作为一个完整的句子译。原文从"虽然"到"秋天"句，是两个主从复合句，若照原文句式将其译成两个英语的主从复合句，译文就很长，而其意只是"瓶底已经丢失，空空地站在那里，从春天到秋天，直到石榴树……"这个意思用一句话就可以说清楚，"（瓶底）丢失"用形容词 bottomless、"空空地"用 empty 来表示就行，"我所看到的"可译可不译，不译不伤害原意，而句子则更简练、更紧凑。

[原文] 我们在这边，只能写纪念鲁迅先生的文章，而谁去努力剪齐墓上的荒草？我们是越去越远了，但无论多么远，那荒草是总要记在心上的。

[译文] As for us over here, there is not much we can do but write some memorial articles. But who will go and trim the grass on his tomb? We are getting further and further away from him, but no matter how far away we are, we must remember the grass on his tomb.

从这一段文字可见萧红对鲁迅的感情之深。把"墓上的荒草""记在心上"，就是把逝者记在心上。翻译时，根据原文的叙述平铺直叙即可，不宜对文字和句子从形式上做过多雕琢。思想和感情是内在的，内涵丰富的文字多趋于平淡。

最后，说一说将译文作为独立文本来审视的问题。翻译此类文章一般都是从词句着手，努力使译文词句与原文相符，这是非常重要的一个方面。同时，还应注意译文的整体效果，包括内容的和风格的。这也就是说，始自词句的翻译最终要考虑译文作为一个独立文本的效果，当二者有了矛盾，要变通前者，以适应后者。总之，将译文作为一个独立文本加以审视，审视其整体效果——看其内容是否与原文相符，看其叙事语气与行文风格是否与原文一致，这是很重要的。

3

儿时

瞿秋白（1899—1935），中国共产党早期领导人之一，无产阶级文艺理论家，作家和翻译家，主要著作有《新俄国游记》《海上述林》。《儿时》选自《中国现代百家千字文》，思想深沉，文字含蓄。

生命没有寄托的人，青年时代和"儿时"对他格外宝贵。这种罗曼蒂克的回忆其实并不是发现了"儿时"的真正了不得，而是感觉到"中年"以后的衰退。本来，生命只有一次，对于谁都是宝贵的。但是，假使他的生命溶化在大众的里面，假使他天天在为这世界干些什么，那么，他总在生长，虽然衰老病死仍旧是逃避不了，然而他的事业——大众的事业是不死的，他会领略到"永久的青年"。而"浮生如梦"的人，从这世界里拿去的很多，而给这世界的却很少——他总有一天会觉得疲乏的死亡：他连拿都没有力量了。衰老和无能的悲哀，像铅一样的沉重，压在他的心头。青春是多么短啊！

"儿时"的可爱是无知。那时候，件件都是"知"，你每天可以做大科学家和大哲学家，每天在发现什么新的现象，新的真理。现在呢？"什么"都已经知道了，熟悉了，每一个人的脸都已经看厌了。宇宙和社会是那么陈旧，无味，虽则它们其实比"儿时"新鲜得多了。我于是想念"儿时"，祷告"儿时"。

不能够前进的时候，就愿意退后几步，替自己恢复已经走过的前途。请求"无知"回来，给我求知的快乐。可怕呵，这生命的"停止"。

过去的始终过去了，未来的还是未来。终竟感慨些什么——我问自己。

Childhood

Qu Qiubai

When you have nothing to live for in life, you tend to feel nostalgic for the days gone by—your youth and childhood. The romantic memory of the past is not at all a discovery of the sweetness of "childhood", but an awareness of life beginning to fade after "middle age". Everyone has but one life to live and, naturally, it is treasured by all. However, if his life is dedicated to the cause of the people, if he makes a point of doing something every day for the world, he is growing and, though eventually he will die, the cause he lives for—the cause of the people— will never die. In other words, he will gain a sense of "eternal youth". As for the one who lives his life drifting around as if in a dream, he takes a lot from the world but gives little in return. Sooner or later he will be feeling such deathly fatigue that he will find himself deprived of the energy to "take". Then the grief caused by age and impotence will render his heart as heavy as if loaded with lead. How fast youth goes!

What makes childhood sweet is the innocence of the heart. In childhood, whatever you see and whatever you do is "knowing". You can become a great scientist or a great philosopher, on daily basis, with the new things or the new truth you discover. But now, you seem to have learned "everything" and you are tired of the faces you see every day. The universe and the society seem to be getting old and boring, though there are more new things to discover. I miss my childhood, I bless my childhood!

When you find it hard to go forward, you tend to take a step backward to retrace the road you have come along, taking yourself back to the world of innocence and giving yourself the pleasure of "knowing" again. Oh, how terrible is the discontinuance of life.

Since what is gone is gone and what is ahead is still ahead, what is the point of getting so emotional about it—I ask myself.

| 翻 译 提 示 |

革命家、文学家瞿秋白写《儿时》讨论人生。人到"中年"有时回顾已逝的时光，但心绪不同。立志"为这世界干些什么"的人，会领略到"永久的青年"；"生命没有寄托的人"，"浮生如梦的人"，会感到"衰老"与"悲哀"。文章的情调是积极的，表达了革命者的情怀，但也流露出一丝文人的"多感"。

理解作者的思想和情绪，翻译时从整体上努力再现这种思想和情绪，是很重要的一环。

［原文］ 生命没有寄托的人，青年时代和"儿时"对他格外宝贵。

［译文］ When you have nothing to live for in life, you tend to feel nostalgic for the days gone by—your youth and childhood.

在这里，所谓"宝贵"即是常常回顾与怀念，将其译成 to feel nostalgic for 意思比较贴近原文；在翻译"青年时代"和"儿时"时，前面加了 the days gone by，是为了减缓文章开头时的行文速度，再现怀念的情绪。

［原文］ 这种罗曼蒂克的回忆其实并不是发现了"儿时"的真正了不得，而是感觉到"中年"以后的衰退。

［译文］ The romantic memory of the past is not at all a discovery of the sweetness of "childhood", but an awareness of life beginning to fade after "middle age".

"发现了"和"感觉到"在原文是动词，在英语里将它们译成动词也可以，但句子可能比较烦琐；这里译成了名词 discovery 和 awareness，一是句子简洁，二是能较好地译出"不是……而是……"的结构，语气和语速都和原文比较一致。

［原文］ 而"浮生如梦"的人，从这世界里拿去的很多，而给这世界的却很少——他总有一天会觉得疲乏的死亡：他连拿都没有力量了。

［译文］ As for the one who lives his life drifting around as if in a dream, he takes a lot from the world but gives little in return. Sooner or later he will be feeling such deathly fatigue that he will find himself deprived of the energy to "take".

句子里有几个动词要译好，"拿去的很多"，"给……的却很少"，

"连拿都没有力量了"。"拿"和"给"形成对照，和第二个"拿"又前后呼应。译文里注意到了这一点。

[原文] "儿时"的可爱是无知。那时候，件件都是"知"，你每天可以做大科学家和大哲学家，每天在发现什么新的现象，新的真理。

[译文] What makes childhood sweet is the innocence of the heart. In childhood, whatever you see and whatever you do is "knowing". You can become a great scientist or a great philosopher, on daily basis, with the new things or the new truth you discover.

这里的"可爱"译成了 sweet，和前面的 sweetness 相呼应。从"你每天……"开始到句尾本是并列的两个小句，在译文里是一个小句，用 with 短语解释前面的意思，既合乎逻辑也很紧凑。

[原文] 不能够前进的时候，就愿意退后几步，替自己恢复已经走过的前途。请求"无知"回来，给我求知的快乐。可怕呵，这生命的"停止"。

[译文] When you find it hard to go forward, you tend to take a step backward to retrace the road you have come along, taking yourself back to the world of innocence and giving yourself the pleasure of "knowing" again. Oh, how terrible is the discontinuance of life.

这一句可能是针对"生命没有寄托的人"说的，沉湎于回忆莫过于生命的"停止"，可怕啊！如果这样理解符合作者的本意，译文也许是可以接受的。

4

我的梦，我的青春！

郁达夫（1896—1945），作家，诗人，一生著有大量小说、散文、游记和诗歌。《我的梦，我的青春！》选自《郁达夫散文》，语言恣肆淋漓，乡土风情浓郁。

不晓得是在哪一本俄国作家的作品里，曾经看到过一段写一个小村落的文字，他说："譬如有许多纸折起来的房子，摆在一段高的地方，被大风一吹，这些房子就歪歪斜斜地飞落到了谷里，紧挤在一道了。"前面有一条富春江绕着，东西北的三面尽是些小山包住的富阳县城，也的确可以借了这一段文字来形容。

虽则是一个行政中心的县城，可是人家不满三千，商店不过百数；一般居民，全不晓得做什么手工业，或其他新式的生产事业，所靠以度日的，有几家自然是祖遗的一点田产，有几家则专以小房子出租，在吃两元三元一月的租金；而大多数的百姓，却还是既无恒产，又无恒业，没有目的，没有计划，只同蟑螂似的在那里出生，死亡，繁殖下去。

这些蟑螂的密集之区，总不外乎两处地方；一处是三个铜子一碗的茶店，一处是六个铜子一碗的小酒馆。他们在那里从早晨坐起，一直可以坐到晚上上排门的时候；讨论柴米油盐的价格，传播东邻西舍的新闻，为了一点不相干的细事，譬如说罢，甲以为李德泰的煤油只卖三个铜子一提，乙以为是五个铜子两提的话，双方就会得争论起来；此外的人，也马上分成甲党或乙党提出证据，互相论辩；弄到后来，也许相打起来，打得头破血流，还不能够解决。

因此，在这么小的一个县城里，茶店酒馆，竟也有五六十家之多；于是，大部分的蟑螂，就家里可以不备面盆手巾，桌椅板凳，饭锅碗筷等日常用具，而悠悠地生活过去了。离我们家里不远的大江边上，就有这样的两处蟑螂之窟。

在我们的左面，住有一家砍砍柴，卖卖菜，人家死人或娶亲，去帮帮忙跑跑腿的人家。他们的一族，男女老小的人数很多很多，而住的那一间屋，却只比牛栏马槽大了一点。他们家里的顶小的一位苗裔年纪比我大一岁，名字叫阿千，冬天穿的是同伞似的一大堆破絮，夏天，大半身是光光地裸着的；因而皮肤黝黑，臂膀粗大，脸上也像是生落地之后，只洗了一次的样子。他虽只比我大了一岁，但是跟了他们屋里的大人，茶店酒馆日日去上，婚丧的人家，也老在进出；打起架吵起嘴来，尤其勇猛。我每天见他从我们的门口走过，心里老在羡慕，以为他又上茶店酒馆去了，我要到什么时候，才可以同他一样的和大人去夹在一道呢！而他的出去和回来，不管是在清早或深夜，我总没有一次不注意到的，因为他的喉音很大，有时候一边走着，一边在绝叫着和大人谈天，若只他一个人的时候哩，总在噜苏地唱戏。

当一天的工作完了，他跟了他们家里的大人，一道上酒店去的时候，看见我羡慕地立在门口，他原也曾邀约过我；但一则怕母亲要骂，二则胆子终于太小，经不起那些大人的盘问笑说，我总是微笑摇摇头，就跑进屋里躲开了，为的是上茶酒店去的诱惑性，实在强不过。

有一天春天的早晨，母亲上父亲的坟头去扫墓去了，祖母也一清早上了一座远在三四里路外的庙里去念佛。翠花在灶下收拾早餐的碗筷，我只一个人立在门口，看有淡云浮着的青天。忽而阿千唱着戏，背着钩刀和小扁担绳索之类，从他的家里出来，看了我的那种没精打采的神气，他就立了下来和我谈天，并且说：

"鹳山后面的盘龙山上，映山红开得多着哩；并且还有乌米饭（是一种小黑果子），彤管子（也是一种刺果），刺莓等等，你跟了我来吧，我可以采一大堆给你。你们奶奶，不也在北面山脚下的真觉寺里念佛吗？等我砍了柴，我就可以送你上寺里去吃饭去。"

阿千本来是我所崇拜的英雄，而这一回又只有他一个人去砍柴，天气那么的好，今天侵早祖母出去念佛的时候，我本是嚷着要同去的，但她因为怕我走不动，就把我留下了。现在一听到了这一个提议，自然是心里急跳了起来，两只脚便也很轻松地跟他出发了，并且还只怕翠花要出来阻挠，跑路跑得比平时只有得快些。出了弄堂，向东沿着江，一口气跑出了县城之后，天地宽广起来了，我的对于这一次冒险的惊惧之心就马上被大自然的威力所压倒。这样问问，那样谈谈，阿千真像是一部小小的自然界的百科大辞典；而到盘龙山脚去的一段野路，便成了我最初学自然科学的模范小课本。

麦已经长得有好几尺高了，麦田里的桑树，也都发出了绒样的叶芽。晴天里舒叔叔的一声飞鸣过去的，是老鹰在觅食；树枝头吱吱喳喳，似在打架又像是在谈天的，大半是麻雀之类；远处的竹林丛里，既有抑扬，又带余韵，在那里唱歌的，才是深山的画眉。

上山的路旁，一拳一拳像小孩子的拳头似的小草，长得很多；

拳的左右上下，满长着了些绛黄的绒毛，仿佛是野生的虫类，我起初看了，只在害怕，走路的时候，若遇到一丛，总要绕一个弯，让开它们，但阿千却笑起来了，他说："这是薇蕨，摘了去，把下面的粗干切了，炒起来吃，味道是很好的哩！"

渐走渐高了，山上的青红杂色，迷乱了我的眼目。日光直射在山坡上，从草木泥土里蒸发出来的一种气息，使我呼吸感到了一种困难；阿千也走得热起来了，把他的一件破夹袄一脱，丢向了地下。叫我在一块大石上坐下歇着，他一个人穿着一件小衫唱着戏去砍柴采野果去了；我回身立在石上，向大江一看，又深深地深深地得到了一种新的惊异。

这世界真大呀！那宽广的水面！那澄碧的天空！那些上下的船只，究竟从哪里来，上哪里去的呢？

我一个人立在半山的大石上，近看看有一层阳炎在颤动着的绿野桑田，远看看天和水以及淡淡的青山，渐听得阿千的唱戏声音幽下去远下去了，心里就莫名其妙地起了一种渴望与愁思。我要到什么时候才能大起来呢？我要到什么时候才可以到这像在天边似的远处去呢？到了天边，那么我的家呢？我的家里的人呢？同时感到了对远处的遥念与对乡井的离愁，眼角里便自然而然地涌出了热泪。到后来，脑子也昏乱了，眼睛也模糊了，我只呆呆地立在那块大石上的太阳里做幻梦。我梦见有一只揩擦得很洁净的船，船上面张着了一面很大很饱满的白帆，我和祖母母亲翠花阿千等都在船上，吃着东西，唱着戏，顺流下去，到了一处不相识的地方。我又梦见城里的茶店酒馆，都搬上山来了，我和阿千便在这山上的酒馆里大唱大嚷，旁边的许多大人，都在那里惊奇仰视。

这一种接连不断的白日之梦，不知做了多少时候，阿千却背了一捆小小的草柴，和一包刺莓映山红乌米饭之类的野果，回到我立在那里的大石边来了；他脱下了小衫，光着了脊肋，那些野果就系包在他的小衫里面的。

他提议说，时候不早了，他还要砍一捆柴，且让我们吃着野果，先从山腰走向后山去吧，因为前山的草柴，已经被人砍完，第二捆不容易采刮拢来了。

慢慢地走到了山后，山下的那个真觉寺的钟鼓声音，早就从春空里传送到了我们的耳边，并且一条青烟，也刚从寺后的厨房里透出了屋顶。向寺里看了一眼，阿千就放下了那捆柴，对我说：

"他们在烧中饭了，大约离吃饭的时候也不很远，我还是先送你到寺里去吧！"

我们到了寺里，祖母和许多同伴者的念佛婆婆，都张大了眼睛，惊异了起来。阿千走后，她们就开始问我这一次冒险的经过，我也感到了一种得意，将如何出城，如何和阿千上山采集野果的情形，说得格外的详细。后来坐上桌去吃饭的时候，有一位老婆婆问我："你大了，打算去做什么？"我就毫不迟疑地回答她说："我愿意去砍柴。"

故乡的茶店酒馆，到现在还在风行热闹，而这一位茶店酒馆里的小英雄，初次带我上山去冒险的阿千，却在一年涨大水的时候，喝醉了酒，淹死了。他们的家族，也一个个地死的死，散的散，现在没有生存者了；他们的那一座牛栏似的房屋，已经换过了两三个主人。时间是不饶人的，盛衰起灭也绝对地无常的；阿千之死，同时也带去了我的梦，我的青春！

My Dream and My Youth
Yu Dafu

I once read a passage in a book by a Russian writer (I have forgotten the title of the book) describing how a small village looked. He says: "Supposing there are many huts made of paper standing on a high place. When a gust of wind blows, they all tumble down to the valley, tilting against each other in a cluster." This passage well fits Fuyang, the county seat with the Fuchun River winding along in the front and low hills rolling around the other three sides.

Fuyang, though the administrative center of the county, did not boast a large population; the number of households in there was less than three thousand, and of shops and stores no more than one hundred. The ordinary people in general did not know much about handicraft industry, or any of the new trades. Some of the families scraped a living on what scanty land they inherited from their forefathers, some managed to get along by renting their small huts in return for two or three yuan a month. But the majority of the people did not have their own properties, nor regular jobs. They came into the world, reproduced and then died like cockroaches, without any idea what they came for or what to do from one day to the next.

There were two places where the "cockroaches" often went to pass their time, one was the teahouse where they could spend three coppers for a cup and the other the wineshop where they could spend six coppers for a drink. They went there in the morning and stayed till closing time in the evening, talking about trifles like the prices of rice, oil and salt, circulating gossip about their neighbors. Sometimes for such trivialities as, when A said that kerosene at the Li Detai's was three coppers for a dipper, but B said no, it was five coppers for two dippers, they would burst into fierce debate, and the rest would fall into two oppositional parties, Party A and Party B, driving the debate to the point where the people involved could get a bit physical and even get someone injured. And you know what? The debate would end up nowhere.

Small as it was, the county had as many as fifty to sixty teahouses and wineshops to its credit. The cockroaches, therefore, did not have to bother about their household articles such as basins and towels, tables and chairs, bowls and chopsticks, etc. and they could fare along with plenty of leisure and pleasure nevertheless. And not far from our home on the bank of the river, there were two sheds housing such cockroaches.

Residing on our left was a family that cut firewood when there was firewood to cut and peddled vegetables when there were vegetables to peddle, or when there were funerals or weddings going on they'd offer to do legwork. It was a family of the *Miao* ethnic group with a large number of people—old and young, men and women, but the hut they lived in was scarcely larger than a stable. The youngest son of the family, named Ah Qian, was one year my senior. In winter he was wrapped in clothes patched up with rags upon rags, looking pretty much like an old umbrella and, in summer, he was bare to the waist. He had a sun-tanned complexion and a pair of muscular arms, and his face looked as if he had washed it only once since he was born. Although he was only one year older than I was, he went to teahouses and wineshops with the grown-ups of his family almost every day and, furthermore, he was often seen in and out of weddings and funerals. If he was on any account involved in a wrangle or a fight, wow, he was fearless, you bet. When he passed by our door, I'd watch him with admiration, thinking he must be on his way to the teahouse or the wineshop again. I'd wonder when I myself would be able to do the same in company with my family. Either he went early in the morning or returned late at night, I couldn't miss it, because he had a loud voice and he'd prattle away at the top of his voice and, when he was alone, he'd hum some local opera.

One day, after work, on his way to the teahouse or the wineshop with his family, he asked me to go with him when he saw me standing at the door watching him admiringly. For one thing, I was afraid that Mother would scold me and, for another, I knew I'd not be able to stand the questions put to me by adults with laughter. So, shaking my head with a smile, I retreated indoors, for I was afraid I would not be able to resist the temptation of the teahouse or the wineshop.

One morning on a spring day, Mother went to pay respects at Father's tomb and Grandma went to the temple, about three or four *li* from home, to say prayers. Cuihua was clearing the breakfast table by the stove and 1 was left standing alone at the door, looking at the light clouds gliding across the blue sky. Suddenly Ah Qian came along, humming an aria from a local opera, his shoulders slung with a sickle, a carrying pole and some ropes. Seeing that I was listles, he stopped and struck up a chat with me and then he said:

"You see, on the Dragon Hill behind the Stork Mountain there are a lot of azalea in full bloom. There are also black rice (a small black fruit), red tube (a thorny fruit) and thorny berry, and so on and so on.

Come along with me. I can pick heaps of them for you. Your grandma has gone to say prayers at the Awakening Temple at the foot of the hill, right? When I've cut enough firewood, I'll take you there for lunch."

Ah Qian had been the hero I admired, and now he was going out by himself, and in such fine weather. When Grandma left for the temple this morning, I begged her to take me with her, but she left me behind, saying I would not be able to walk that far. Now that Ah Qian offered to take me along, I readily set out with him, my heart throbbing with excitement and my feet floating with light steps. As I was afraid that Cuihua might rush out to pull me back, I began to run, and run faster than usual. At the end of the lane we turned east, running along the river. When we had run out of town at one breath we found ourselves facing a vast expanse of an open world. My apprehension about the adventure was soon overcome by the charm of nature. I was possessed by a sense of curiosity, asking about this and commenting on that, and Ah Qian was now like a pocket encyclopedia of the natural world. The wild path to the foot of the Dragon Hill became a model textbook that taught me the ABC of natural science.

Wheat was already two or three feet high and the white mulberries in the wheat field were putting forth fluffy buds. When, on a sunny day, you heard a swish overhead, it was a hawk after its prey; chirping in the branches were probably sparrows engaged in a noisy chat or a raw; the rhythmic sounds with a lingering quality were the singings of the *huamei* song birds—they were performing a concert in the bamboo groves in the distant hill.

The path uphill was lined with patches of low grass very much like babies, hands clenched; and the "hands clenched" were coated with deep yellow fluffs, resembling worms in the wilderness. I was scared to see them first and I would walk around and keep away from them when there was any in front. And that made Ah Qian laugh. He said:

"This is edible tender brake. You cut the thick stem and stir-fry it and it makes a delicious dish."

As we walked further up, my eyes were assailed and confused by the riot of mountain colors. As the sun shone direct on the hillside I had trouble in breathing from the scent rising from the plants and the earth. Ah Qian began to feel hot from walking. He took off his lined coat and threw it to the ground. He told me to rest on a big stone and then, with his small shirt on, set out for the firewood and fruits, humming some local opera aria. I stood on the stone on the hillside and, turning my eyes toward the great river, I was stunned with utter amazement.

Oh, look at the big world! Look at the blue sky! Look at the wide river and the boats sailing up and down! Where were they coming from and where were they going?

I stood there, looking at the green fields with white-mulberries shimmering with the soft sunlight in the foreground and at the horizon in the distance where the sky and the river joined and the placid mountain, and Ah Qian's singing grew fainter and fainter still. Some mysterious yearning and sadness swelled within me. When could I grow up? When could I be allowed to go to places as far-off as the edge of the sky? But if I did travel to the edge of the sky, what about my home? What about my family? I had a mixed feeling of longing for the far-off place on the one hand, and the sadness of having to leave home on the other. With those thoughts in mind I felt my eyes filled with warm tears. And then my head was befuddled and my eyes hazed. I remained on the stone flooded with sunlight, lost in a fancy dream. I dreamed of a boat scrubbed spotlessly clean sailing with a large white sail blown to the full in the air. Grandma, Mother, Cuihua, Ah Qian and I myself were all in the boat, eating some food and singing merrily along as it was drifting down the river to a foreign place. I also dreamed that all the teahouses and wineshops in town had moved into the hill. Ah Qian and I found ourselves in one of the wineshops, drinking to our hearts' content and shouting at the top of our voices and the adults sitting around all looked up with surprise.

I had no idea how long I had been dreaminging the daydreaming, but I did not wake until Ah Qian came up with a small bundle of grass and twigs and a pack of assorted fruits. He came bare-backed, having taken off his shirt and used it as a fruit wrapper.

He said, as it was getting close to midday, he had to cut some more firewood, so he suggested we go along the hillside to the mountain while eating some fruits, because the firewood in the hill had been cut by others and there was not much left for another bundle.

Soon we got around to the back of the hill. The sound of bells and drums from the temple wafted within earshot through the spring air and a wisp of smoke was rising from the roof of the kitchen behind the temple. Throwing a look toward the temple, Ah Qian laid down the bundle of grass and twigs and said to me:

"It seems they are doing the cooking and it is about lunch time, I guess. Let me take you to the temple first."

When we got there, Grandma and many other old women saying prayers with her all stared at us with surprise. After Ah Qian left they asked me about my adventure and I, beaming with pride, told them in great detail how I got out of town and how Ah Qian offered to pick the fruits for me. The moment I sat down to the table, an old woman asked, "When you grow up, what are you going to do?" I said without thinking, "I am going to cut firewood."

Teahouses and wineshops in my hometown are doing just as well as they did before, but Ah Qian, the young hero of the teahouse and wineshop who initiated me into the mountain on my first adventure was drowned in a flood one year; he had taken one cup of wine too many. Nobody survived in his family; they all died one after another, some at home, some elsewhere. Their stable-like hut has changed hands two or three times. Time, as the saying goes, is unsympathetic. Rise or fall in life has no set course to follow. Ah Qian is gone and gone with Ah Qian is my dream and my youth.

（与张保红合译）

翻 译 提 示

《我的梦，我的青春！》是郁达夫自传文章的一部分，回忆童年时代在家乡的一段生活经历。他把家乡小城的风貌和习俗，穷苦人的生活，写得很细很真，把读者带回他的家乡，带回那个时代，读来有亲临其境之感。他怀念与阿千的友谊，淳朴善良的阿千给他带来了欢乐和对生活的憧憬。读到"阿千之死，同时也带去了我的梦，我的青春！"时，我们感受到的是他对阿千的怀念之情，令人感动。

郁达夫写散文讲究"细""清""真"，"细"是"细密的描写"，"清"是"慎重的选择"，"真"是"描写的真切"。他说，这就是

"中国旧诗词里所说的以景述情，缘情叙景"。他主张，散文，特别是"抒情或写景的散文"，要有"情韵或情调"。所谓"情韵"，和"细""清""真"是一致的，也就是作者通过"细""清""真"的描写并以很含蓄的方式所抒发的情绪。作者的这种写法展现了语言的魅力，作者的这种情绪使读者受到了感染。

在这篇散文里，属于"细""清""真"的地方很多，围绕阿千的一系列描写更是如此。例如：

[原文]　冬天穿的是同伞似的一大堆破絮，夏天，大半身是光光地裸着的；因而皮肤黝黑，臂膀粗大，脸上也像是生落地之后，只洗了一次的样子。

[译文]　In winter he was wrapped in clothes patched up with rags upon rags, looking pretty much like an old umbrella and, in summer, he was bare to the waist. He had a sun-tanned complexion and a pair of muscular arms, and his face looked as if he had washed it only once since he was born.

[原文]　忽而阿千唱着戏，背着钩刀和小扁担绳索之类，从他的家里出来，看了我的那种没精打采的神气，他就立了下来和我谈天……

[译文]　Suddenly Ah Qian came along, humming an aria from a local opera, his shoulders slung with a sickle, a carrying pole and some ropes. Seeing that I was listless, he stopped and struck up a chat with me…

以上两句描写的是旧时农村穷人家孩子的真切形象，若能依照原文细细地翻译，可得原文的韵味。只是在一些很形象的地方需仔细选择符合英语用法的字词，以使其形象和原文一样鲜明，如"穿的是……一大堆破絮"，这里将其译成 he was wrapped in clothes patched up with rags upon rags，即补丁摞补丁的意思；"背着钩刀和小扁担绳索之类"，这里将其译成 his shoulders slung with a sickle, a carrying pole and some ropes，采取独立主格结构（nominative independent structure）的形式。此外，还需把句子组织好，特别要把主句和状语成分的关系处理好，在符合英语规范的前提下力求句子简洁。

文章里表现"情韵或情调"的例子也很多，比如：

［原文］ 我要到什么时候才能大起来呢？我要到什么时候才可以到这像在天边似的远处去呢？到了天边，那么我的家呢？我的家里的人呢？同时感到了对远处的遥念与对乡井的离愁，眼角里便自然而然地涌出了热泪。

［译文］ When could I grow up? When could I be allowed to go to places as far-off as the edge of the sky? But if I did travel to the edge of the sky, what about my home? What about my family? I had a mixed feeling of longing for the far-off place on the one hand, and the sadness of having to leave home on the other. With those thoughts in mind I felt my eyes filled with warm tears.

这里所写的是童年伙伴之间的真挚友谊给一个天真的孩子带来的幻想和离愁，很感人。我们将其译成 a mixed feeling of longing for the far-off place on the one hand, and the sadness of having to leave home on the other，与原文的情绪也还相符。

［原文］ 阿千，却在一年涨大水的时候，喝醉了酒，淹死了。他

们的家族，也一个个地死的死，散的散，现在没有生存
者了……

[译文] Ah Qian…was drowned in a flood one year; he had taken one
cup of wine too many. Nobody survived in his family; they all
died one after another, some at home, some elsewhere.

这段话反映了作者对死者的想念和同情。这里的英译文对原文
做了调整，将"散的散"译作死在外地，符合"没有生存者"的意
思。语序也做了相应的变通。

[原文] 阿千之死，同时也带去了我的梦，我的青春！

[译文] Ah Qian is gone and gone with Ah Qian is my dream and my
youth.

文章的"情韵或情调"集中体现在这结尾的一句话。作者与他
所崇拜的善良勇敢的少年英雄阿千相处的日子里充满对生活的憧
憬，现在阿千死了，他的死使作者对童年的回忆蒙上了一层悲哀。
这句话十分感人，且很富有诗意。译文里句子的第二部分以倒装句
形式出现，又重复了 Ah Qian，可以看作是表现作者的不舍之情，
也使句子读起来富有诗的美感。

5

落花生

许地山（1893—1941），作家，有短篇小说总集《缀网劳蛛》，散文总集《空山灵雨》，还有宗教和哲学方面的著作。《落花生》选自《空山灵雨》，语言简单朴实。

我们屋后有半亩隙地。母亲说："让它荒芜着怪可惜，既然你们那么爱吃花生，就辟来做花生园吧。"我们几姊弟和几个小丫头都很喜欢——买种的买种，动土的动土，灌园的灌园；过不了几个月，居然收获了。

妈妈说："今晚我们可以做一个收获节，也请你们爹爹来尝尝我们的新花生，如何？"我们都答应了。母亲把花生做成好几样的食品，还吩咐就在后园的茅亭里过这个节。

那晚上的天色不大好，可是爹爹也到来，实在很难得！爹爹说："你们爱吃花生吗？"

我们都争着答应："爱！"

"谁能把花生的好处说出来？"

姊姊说："花生的气味很美。"

哥哥说："花生可以制油。"

我说："无论何等人都可以用贱价买它来吃，都喜欢吃它。这就是它的好处。"

爹爹说："花生的用处固然很多；但有一样是很可贵的。这小小的豆不像那好看的苹果、桃子、石榴，把它们的果实悬在枝上，鲜红嫩绿的颜色，令人一望而发生羡慕的心。它只把果子埋在地底，等到成熟，才容人把它挖出来。你们偶然看见一棵花生瑟缩地长在地上，不能立刻辨出它有没有果实，非得等到你接触它才能知道。"

我们都说："是的。"母亲也点点头。爹爹接下去说："所以你们要像花生，因为它是有用的，不是伟大、好看的东西。"我说："那么，人要做有用的人，不要做伟大、体面的人了。"爹爹说："这是我对于你们的希望。"

我们谈到夜阑才散，所有花生食品虽然没有了，然而父亲的话现在还印在我心版上。

| 译文 |

The Peanut
Xu Dishan

At the back of our house there was half a *mu* of unused land. "It's a pity to let it lie idle like that," Mother said. "Since you all enjoy eating peanuts, let us open it up and make it a peanut garden." At that my brother, sister and 1 were all delighted and so were the young housemaids. And then some went to buy seeds, some began to dig up the ground and others watered it and, in a couple of months, we had a harvest!

"Let us have a party tonight to celebrate," Mother suggested, "and ask Dad to join us for a taste of our fresh peanuts. What do you say?" We all agreed, of course. Mother cooked the peanuts in a variety of styles and told us to go to the thatched pavilion in the garden for the celebration.

The weather was not very good that night but, to our great delight, Father came all the same. "Do you like peanuts?" Father asked.

"Yes!" We all answered eagerly.

"But who can tell me what the peanut is good for?"

"It is very delicious to eat," my sister took the lead.

"It is good for making oil," my brother followed.

"It is inexpensive," I said. "Almost everyone can afford it and everyone enjoys eating it. I think this is what it is good for."

"Peanut is good for many things," Father said, "but there is one thing that is particularly good about it. Unlike apples, peaches and pomegranates that display their fruits up in the air, attracting you with their beautiful colors, peanut buries its fruit in the earth. It does not show itself until you dig it out when it is ripe and, unless you dig it out, you can't tell whether it bears fruit or not just by its frail stem quivering above ground."

"That's true," we all said and Mother nodded her assent, too. "So you should try to be like the peanut," Father went on, "because it is useful, though not great or attractive."

"Do you mean," I asked, "we should learn to be useful but not seek to be great or attractive?"

"Yes," Father said. "This is what I expect of you."

We stayed up late that night, eating all the peanuts Mother had cooked for us. But father's words remained vivid in my memory till this day.

| 翻译提示 |

《落花生》是一篇深受读者喜爱的散文。作者回忆童年时代的一个生活片段，语言朴实、清新而自然。文中的父亲借平凡的花生，讲述人生的道理，深入浅出，富于哲理。翻译这样的文章，需注意作者的语言风格，"篇中不能有冗章，章中不可有冗句，句中不可有冗语"（林纾语）。本文译者深谙此理，精心营构，为我们提供了一篇很好的范例。下面对译者在炼词造句、布局谋篇方面的成功之处做一分析。

一个好的译者必须能够辨别文章的文体色彩，熟悉不同文体的语言风格，同时还要善于运用译入语中不同文体的语言来再现原文的语言风格，使译文与原文的文体色彩相契合。首先，译者要在遣词造句上下功夫，不可小视一词一句之工，字句之功之于翻译实为举足轻重之事体。请看下面几例：

［原文］ 我们屋后有半亩隙地。母亲说："让它荒芜着怪可惜，既然你们那么爱吃花生，就辟来做花生园罢。"我们几姊弟和几个小丫头都很喜欢——买种的买种，动土的动土，灌园的灌园；过不了几个月，居然收获了。

［译文］ At the back of our house there was half a *mu* of unused land. "It's a pity to let it lie idle like that," Mother said. " Since you all enjoy eating peanuts, let us open it up and make it a peanut garden." At that my brother, sister and I were all delighted and so were the young housemaids. And then some went to buy seeds, some began to dig up the ground and others watered it and, in a couple of months, we had a harvest!

这段译文自然，顺畅，用词妥帖，无造作之感。如，原文中"荒芜着"表示一种状态，译作 lie idle 已很好地表达出原意，但译者却在其后加了 like that，使得口语色彩更加浓厚，上下句衔接更加自然。此外，enjoy 一词较之 like，蕴涵更深。特别是"居然"一词的翻译值得一提。"居然"为副词，含有出乎意料的意思。通常情况下，会被直译成 unexpectedly 或 surprisingly 或 to our surprise，这都是可以接受的，也与原文的意思相符。本文译者没有刻意在译入语里寻找对等词，而是采用了英语的句法手段来传达这层意思，其效果堪与原文媲美。此外，在句式结构的安排上也比较讲究。如对"我们几姊弟和几个小丫头都很喜欢"的处理，译者在译文中以 At that 起句，并将"我们几姊弟"具体化，不独使译文在叙事形式上符合英语的审美要求，而且在意义上尽得原文之旨。

[原文] 那晚上的天色不大好，可是爹爹也到来，实在很难得！

[译文] The weather was not very good that night but, to our great delight, Father came all the same.

读者从"也"字和"实在很难得"的感叹中很容易体会到爹爹在家中的地位，但要把这种内涵译出来，不太容易。首先，"实在很难得"是原文的语义重点，是原文的谓语部分，其主语实质上是另一语义重点"可是爹爹也到来"这一事实，但英汉语言结构的差异决定了译文不可能从形式上与原文达到对等；其次，对"也"字的翻译，决定了能否准确地将原文的语气表达出来。本文译者并不追求源语与译语形式上的简单对等，而是将"实在很难得"译成一个插入语（to our great delight）来表达原文的语义重点，信手拈来，充分体现了译者谙熟英汉语之精理微义（就汉语而言，语义的重点一般是主语或谓语，但英语中主语或谓语却很有可能只起形式作用，语义的重点反而很可能是语法上次要的宾语或其他修饰语）的修养。

[原文]　"谁能把花生的好处说出来？"

　　　　……

　　　　我说："……这就是它的好处。"

　　　　爹爹说："花生的用处固然很多；但有一样是很可贵的……"

[译文]　"But who can tell me what the peanut is **good for**?"

　　　　…

　　　　…I said, "…I think this is what it is **good for**."

　　　　"Peanut is **good for** many things," Father said…

　　"花生的好处"，在汉语只是一个词组，一般情况下，译者可能会把它译成对应的英语词组。这里译者采取了一个语义对应的英语句式，准确地译出了原文的意思，译文连贯，效果很好。

[原文]　爹爹说："花生的用处固然很多；但有一样是很可贵的。这小小的豆不像那好看的苹果、桃子、石榴，把它们的果实悬在枝上，鲜红嫩绿的颜色，令人一望而发生美慕的心。它只把果子埋在地底，等到成熟，才容人把它挖出来。你们偶然看见一棵花生瑟缩地长在地上，不能立

刻辨出它有没有果实，非得等到你接触它才能知道。"

[译文] "Peanut is good for many things," Father said, "but there is one thing that is particularly good about it. Unlike apples, peaches and pomegranates that display their fruits up in the air, attracting you with their beautiful colors, peanut buries its fruit in the earth. It does not show itself until you dig it out when it is ripe and, unless you dig it out, you can't tell whether it bears fruit or not just by its frail stem quivering above ground."

这段赞扬花生的议论哲理性很强，翻译起来难度也较大。整段议论跳跃性强，视角变化多，爹爹分别从"这小小的豆""苹果、桃子、石榴""它""你们"等不同的视角谈花生的好处。如果按照原文句子结构套译，可能会造成译文逻辑混乱。这里，译者打破了原文句子的限制，从整个段落出发，重组原文的概念，调整视角，改变语序。虽然译文与原文在字面上有一定的距离，但译文终不失原文本旨。

总之，翻译是一种再创造。它要求译者像作家一样善于炼词、炼句。刘大櫆在《论文偶记》中曾说："神气者，文之最精处也；音节者，文之稍粗处也；字句者，文之最粗处也；然论文而至于字句，则文之能事尽矣。"可见，字句对于文章是何等重要。

（温秀颖）

6

荼蘼

许地山（1893—1941），作家，有短篇小说总集《缀网劳蛛》，散文总集《空山灵雨》，还有宗教和哲学方面的著作。《荼蘼》选自《空山灵雨》，语言淳厚朴实，却又耐人寻味，引人思索。

我常得着男子送给我的东西，总没有当它们做宝贝看。我的朋友师松却不如此，因为她从不曾受过男子的赠予。

自鸣钟敲过四下以后，山上礼拜寺的聚会就完了。男男女女像出圈的羊，争要下到山坡觅食一般。那边有一个男学生跟着我们走，他的正名字我忘记了，我只记得人家都叫他做"宗之"。他手里拿着一枝荼蘼，且行且嗅。荼蘼本不是香花，他嗅着，不过是一种无聊举动便了。

"松姑娘，这枝荼蘼送给你。"他在我们后面嚷着。松姑娘回头看见他满脸堆着笑容递着那花，就速速伸手去接。她接着说："很多谢，很多谢。"宗之只笑着点点头，随即从西边的山径转回家去。

"他给我这个，是什么意思？"

"你想他有什么意思，他就有什么意思。"我这样回答她。走不多远，我们也分途各自家去了。

她自下午到晚上不歇把弄那枝荼蘼。那花像有极大的魔力，不让她撒手一样。她要放下时，每觉得花儿对她说："为什么离夺我？我不是从宗之手里递给你，交你照管的吗？"

呀，宗之的眼、鼻、口、齿、手、足、动作，没有一件不在花心跳跃着，没有一件不在她眼前的花枝显现出来！她心里说："你这美男子，为甚缘故送给我这花儿？"她又想起那天经坛上的讲章，就自己回答说："因为他顾念他使女的卑微，从今而后，万代要称我为有福。"

这是她爱荼蘼花，还是宗之爱她呢？我也说不清。只记得有一天我和宗之正坐在榕树根谈话的时候，他家的人跑来对他说："松姑娘吃了一朵什么花，说是你给她的，现在病了。她家的人要找你去问话咧。"

他吓了一跳，也摸不着头脑，只说："我哪时节给她东西吃？这真是……！"

我说："你细想一想。"他怎么也想不起来。我才提醒他说："你前个月在斜道上不是给了她一朵荼蘼吗？"

"对呀，可不是给了她一朵荼蘼！可是我那里教她吃了呢？"

"为什么你单给她，不给别人？"我这样问。

他很直接地说："我并没有什么意思，不过随手摘下，随手送给别人就是了。我平素送了许多东西给人，也没有什么事；怎么一朵小小的荼蘼就可使她着了魔？"

他还坐在那里沉吟，我便促他说："你还能在这里坐着吗？不管她是误会，你是有意，你既然给了她，现在就得去看她一看才是。"

"我哪有什么意思？"

我说："你且去看看罢。蚌蛤何尝立志要生珠子呢？也不过是外间的沙粒偶然渗入它的壳里，它就不得不用尽工夫分泌些黏液把那小沙裹起来罢了。你虽无心，可是你的花一到她手里，管保她不因花而爱起你来吗？你敢保她不把那花当作你所赐给爱的标识，就纳入她的怀中，用心里无限的情思把它围绕得非常严密吗？也许她本无心，但因你那美意的沙无意中掉在她爱的贝壳里，使她不得不如此。不用踌躇了，且去看看罢。"

宗之这才站起来，皱一皱他那副冷静的脸庞，跟着来人从林菁的深处走出去了。

| 译文 |

A *Tumi* Flower
Xu Dishan

From time to time I would receive something from my fellow boy students but I did not attach much sentimental value to them. But it was not the case with my friend Shi Song who had never been approached by boys with any present at all.

When the chime clock struck four, the congregation held in the Christian church on the hill was over. Boys and girls were swarming out, like sheep released from their pen scrambling for the first bite of grass on the hillside. A boy student was walking behind us. His full name slipped my mind and I only remembered that people called him Zongzhi. He had a *tumi* flower in his hand, sniffing at it as he walked along. As *tumi* flowers have no scent, he did it just out of habit, I guessed.

"Miss Song, let me give you this flower," he said aloud, coming up from behind. Miss Song turned and Zongzhi, all smiles, was reaching out the flower to her. She hastened to take it and said, "many thanks, many thanks." Zongzhi nodded with a smile and then, veering to the path on the west hillside, was off on his way home.

"What does he mean, giving me this flower?"

"He means what you think he means," I replied. And soon we parted; she went her way home and I went mine.

For the rest of the afternoon and the whole of that evening she kept fiddling with the flower as if it had some magic power to cling to her hands. Each time she was about to put it down she seemed to hear the flower murmuring: "Why are you letting go of me? Don't you know when Zongzhi left me in your hands he meant for you to take care of me?"

She was excited with the illusion that its stamens began to vibrate with Zongzhi's eyes, lips, teeth, hands, feet and every gesture he made, dancing on each and every petal of the flower. And then she said in her heart, "you the Adonis, what did you give me this flower for?" Reflecting on the sermon delivered in the church that afternoon she answered for herself: "For he has looked with favor on the lowliness of his servant. Surely, from now on all generations will call me blessed."

Did she love the flower, or did Zongzhi love her? I could not figure out, but I remembered that one day Zongzhi and I were chatting under a banyan tree when someone of his family came running up and said to him: "Miss Song has eaten some flower and she says she had it from you and she is now feeling unwell. Her family wants to have a word with you."

Zongzhi was bewildered with a spasm of shock. He did not know what to say except "When did I ever give her anything to eat? How incredible!"

I said, "Think carefully." When I saw that he failed to recall anything, I brought it up to remind him: "About two months ago, along the path on the hillside you gave her a *tumi* flower. Remember?"

"Oh, yes! I did. But I did not tell her to eat it, did I?"

"But why did you give it to her in particular, not anyone else?" I asked.

He said frankly: "But I did not mean anything. I just picked it from the tree as I passed by and then gave it to her, that's all. I have given many things to others and nothing has happened. Why should she have become infatuated with such a tiny flower?"

He was still sitting there, upset. I urged him to get up and go and I said: "How can you still hang around here like this? Since you gave the flower to her, you should go and see her right away, whether she misunderstood you, or you intended it."

"I did not intend anything at all."

"Just go and see how things are with her. The oyster has no intention to cultivate pearls, has it? But when a sand grain happens to end up in its shells, it has to secrete mucus to wrap it up. True, you did not mean it, but don't you think it's probable that she fell in love with you the moment you put the flower into her hands? Who can doubt that she accepted the flower as a symbol of love from you and then began to cherish it with all her feelings from the bottom of her heart? She might not be expecting it, but when your well-intentioned 'sand' dropped in her 'shells of love', she had to act this way. Don't hesitate any more. Get going."

Zongzhi got up and, with a fleeting frown on his well-composed face, went with the one from his family out of the exuberance of the trees.

| 翻 译 提 示 |

做汉英翻译，写好英语句子是一个基本的要求，也是一个很高的追求。英语句子一方面结构严密，一方面又变化无穷。严谨规范的句法形式，相对稳定的动词搭配和灵活多样的表达方式，使英语句子呈现万千气象。好的英语作家写起句子来，真是如鱼游水，如鹤浮云，"从心所欲，不逾矩"。他们用简单的词语构筑多变的句子，表达复杂的概念。在这"简单""多变"和"复杂"之中，渗透着英语的丰韵和风姿。

学习翻译英语句子大概要经过三个阶段：句法阶段，语义结构阶段，审美阶段。在句法阶段，学好语法规则和句法关系。在语义结构阶段，培养对英语的"语感"，学习翻译符合英语表达习惯的句子，这个阶段需要较长的时间。在审美阶段，除了句法和语义结构方面的训练以外，主观上的审美修养起着很大作用，影响到译者对具有艺术感染力的句子的判断和感悟。

本文译者仍在第一、二阶段里摸索，仍在努力使翻译出来的句子正确无误，符合英语表达习惯。这不仅是现在也是今后很长时间里的奋斗目标。

下面所举的各个译例，也是想说明译者对于译句准确性的追求。

关于"荼蘼"的翻译

"荼蘼"是一种花，其名称写法不一。《现代汉语词典》（修订本）里没有"荼蘼"这一词条，而有"荼蘪"，其解释是，"落叶小灌木，攀缘茎，茎上有钩状的刺，羽状复叶，小叶椭圆形，花白色，有香气。供观赏。也作酴醾。"《辞源》里有"荼蘼"条，其解释是，"荼蘼"即酴醾。由此看来，"荼蘼""酴醾"和"荼蘪"是指同一种花。为方便，这里以"荼蘼"作为通用之名。

"荼蘼"偶尔出现在古诗里。《辞源》在解释"荼蘼"时引了苏轼的诗句："酴醾不争春，寂寞开最晚。"《红楼梦》第六十三回《寿怡红群芳开夜宴 死金丹独艳理亲丧》，宝玉和众姑娘玩"占花名儿"游戏，麝月掣得一签，上有一枝荼蘼花，题着"韶华胜极"四字，并有一句诗："开到荼蘼花事了。"蔡义江在《红楼韵语》（中华书局，2004 年版）里说，此诗句出自宋代王淇《春暮游小园》："一从梅粉褪残汝，涂抹新红上海棠。开到荼蘼花事了，丝丝天棘出莓墙。"

"开到荼蘼花事了"一句，霍克斯译作"After sweet Rose there is no more blooming."；杨宪益和戴乃迭译作"When the rose blooms, spring flowers fade."。一是将"荼蘼"译作 sweet Rose，一是将其译作 rose。两个译文都用了 rose，各有自己的考虑，这里不做讨论。

如何翻译作为标题的《荼蘼》，很费一些踌躇。

吴光华主编的《汉英大辞典》（上海交通大学出版社，1993 年版）给"荼蘼"和"酴醾"词条下的英译文都是 roseleaf raspberry，并附有拉丁文，这可能是植物学的分类名称，用作一篇散文的标题似乎缺少诗意。再从文章的上下文看，文章《荼蘼》里的荼蘼花与《辞源》里的"荼蘼"（酴醾）和《现代汉语词典》（修订本）里所描述的"荼蘪"（酴醾）是同一种花无疑，但文章里却说，"他手里拿着一枝荼蘼，且行且嗅。荼蘼本不是香花，他嗅着，不过是一种无聊举动便了。"这又与《现代汉语词典》（修订本）所描述的"有香气"的特征不一致。

考虑到以上种种因素，在没有找到更合适的译法之前，暂且用音译方式处理。"A *Tumi* Flower"，听起来不错，在行文里使用起来也方便。

［原文］ 我常得着男子送给我的东西，总没有当它们做宝贝看。

［译文］ From time to time I would receive something from my fellow boy students but I did not attach much sentimental value to them.

这里的"总没有当它们做宝贝看"，意思是，"我"对此并不很敏感，没有因此而动感情。这反衬了下面的"我的朋友师松却不如此"，意思是，师松对这类事情很敏感，动了感情。考虑到后面发生的事情，考虑到文章"情调"的一致，开头的这句话没有直译。

［原文］ 荼蘼本不是香花，他嗅着，不过是一种无聊举动便了。

［译文］ As *tumi* flowers have no scent, he did it just out of habit, I guessed.

这里"无聊举动"里的"无聊"和一般意义上的无聊不同，是说那是很自然的习惯动作，手里有了花，不论香不香，会习惯性地嗅一嗅。因此，就做了这样的处理。

［原文］ ……就速速伸手去接。

［译文］ …hastened to take it…

"速速"在这里是一个重要的副词，需要将其含义译出来，所以用了动词 hastened。

［原文］ "我不是从宗之手里递给你，交你照管的吗？"

［译文］ "Don't you know when Zongzhi left me in your hands he meant for you to take care of me?"

这样译只是为了更自然，比"Didn't Zongzhi leave me…"更顺口些。

［原文］ 呀，宗之的眼、鼻、口、齿、手、足、动作，没有一件不在花心跳跃着，没有一件不在她眼前的花枝显现出来！

［译文］ She was excited with the illusion that its stamens began to vibrate with Zongzhi's eyes, lips, teeth, hands, feet and every gesture he made, dancing on each and every petal of the flower.

这里的"呀"表示女主人公激动的心情，译文没有用感叹词，而用了 excited；眼、鼻等在花心的跳跃是女主人公的幻觉，因此用了 illusion，并用动词 vibrate 和分词 dancing 表示"跳跃"和"显现"。这样译句子形式简洁，符合英语的表达习惯。

［原文］ 这真是……！

［译文］ How incredible!

"这真是……"后面是什么，作者没有说出来。根据上下文，可能是"令人难以置信"或"不可思议"之类，所以译成"How incredible!"。

［原文］ 怎么一朵小小的荼蘼就可使她着了魔？

［译文］ Why should she have become infatuated with such a tiny flower?

"着了魔"的意思可用不同的词来表示，infatuated 可能是其中最合适的，《牛津高级英语词典》（第六版）对 infatuated 的解释是：having a very strong feeling of love or attraction for sb/sth so that you cannot think clearly and in a sensible way，这个意思符合女主人公所处的情境。

［原文］ 你敢保她不把那花当作你所赐给爱的标识，就纳入她的怀中，用心里无限的情思把它围绕得非常严密吗？

［译文］ Who can doubt that she accepted the flower as a symbol of love from you and then began to cherish it with all her feelings from the bottom of her heart?

这里的译文对原文做了一些梳理，意思却没有走样。有时需要做类似的处理。

［原文］ ……皱一皱他那副冷静的脸庞……

［译文］ ...with a fleeting frown on his well-composed face...

with a fleeting frown 和 with a frown 意思有出入，区别在于是"皱一皱"，还是一直皱着眉头。

总之，散文往往是作者抒发感情和宣称信仰的媒介，不同的作者有不同的表达方式，在句子组织层面上，有时差异更明显。翻译时虽然主要是以原文的句子为单位进行处理，但不能太受制于原文的句子形式，要做变通。这种变通需要考虑两个方面的要求，一是所译句子符合英语表达习惯，二是适于传达原文的感情和氛围。为了这个目的，翻译时变通句子是十分重要的，有时是十分必要的。

7

野草

夏衍（1900—1995），剧作家，著有话剧《赛金花》《上海屋檐下》，杂文集《劫余随笔》等。《野草》选自《中国现代百家千字文》，语言通俗幽默。

有这样一个故事。

有人问：世界上什么东西的气力最大？回答纷纭的很，有的说"象"，有的说"狮"，有人开玩笑似的说，是"金刚"。金刚有多少气力，当然大家全不知道。

结果，这一切答案完全不对，世界上气力最大的，是植物的种子。一粒种子所可以显现出来的力，简直是超越一切，这儿又是一个故事。

人的头盖骨，结合得非常致密与坚固，生理学家和解剖学者用尽了一切的方法，要把它完整地分出来，都没有这种力气，后来忽然有人发明了一个方法，就是把一些植物的种子放在要剖析的头盖骨里，给它以温度与湿度，使它发芽，一发芽，这些种子便以可怕的力量，将一切机械力所不能分开的骨骼，完整地分开了，植物种子力量之大，如此如此。

这，也许特殊了一点，常人不容易理解。那么，你看见笋的成长吗？你看见过被压在瓦砾和石块下面的一棵小草的生成吗？他为着向往阳光，为着达成它的生之意志，不管上面的石块如何重，石块与石块之间如何狭，它必定要曲曲折折地，但是顽强不屈地透到地面上来，它的根往土壤钻，它的芽往地面挺，这是一种不可抗的力，阻止它的石块，结果也被它掀翻，一粒种子的力量的大，如此如此。

没有一个人将小草叫作"大力士"，但是它的力量之大，的确是世界无比。这种力，是一般人看不见的生命力，只要生命存在，这种力就要显现，上面的石块，丝毫不足以阻挡，因为它是一种"长期抗战"的力，有弹性，能屈能伸的力，有韧性，不达目的不止的力。

种子不落在肥土而落在瓦砾中，有生命力的种子决不会悲观和叹气，因为有了阻力才有磨炼。生命开始的一瞬间就带了斗争来的草，才是坚韧的草，也只有这种草，才可以傲然地对那些玻璃棚中养育着的盆花哄笑。

| 译文 |

Wild Grass
Xia Yan

There is a story that goes like this:

Someone asks, "What is the most powerful thing in the world?"

The question is answered in a variety of ways. Someone says, "Elephant." Someone else says, "Lion." Another one says half-jokingly, "The Buddha's guardian warrior." As to how powerful the Buddha's guardian warrior is, no one can tell, of course.

In fact, none of the answers is correct. The most powerful thing in the world is the seeds of plants. The force generated by a seed is incredible. Here goes another story:

The bones of a human skull are tightly and firmly joined so much so that no physiologist or anatomist has ever succeeded in taking them apart whatever means they try. Then someone has a brilliant idea. He puts some seeds of a plant in the skull to be dissected and provides the necessary temperature and moisture to make them germinate. Once the seeds germinate, they generate a terrible force that opens up the human skull that has defied even mechanical means. You see how powerful the seeds of a plant can be.

You may think this is too unusual a case for the common mind to come to terms with. Well, have you ever seen how bamboo shoots grow? Have you ever seen how the tender young grass comes out from under debris and rubble? In order to get to the sunshine and satisfy its will to grow, it persistently winds its way up, no matter how heavy the rocks above and how narrow the space between the rocks. Its roots drill downward and its sprouts shoot upward. This is an irresistible force. Any rock lying in its way is overturned. This shows how powerful a seed can be.

Though the little grass has never been compared to a Hercules, the power it produces is matchless in the world. It is an invisible life-force. So long as there is life, the force will show itself. The rock on top of it is not heavy enough to stop it, because it is a force that remains active over a long period of time, because it is an elastic force that shrinks and expands, because it is a tenacious force that will not stop until it achieves its end.

The seed does not fall on fertile land but in debris, instead. The seed with life is never pessimistic nor crestfallen, for, having overcome resistance and pressure, it is tempered. Only the grass that has been fighting its way out since its birth is strong and tenacious and, therefore, it can smile with pride at the potted plants in glassed green houses.

| 翻 译 提 示 |

《野草》是夏衍抗战时期写的一篇寓理散文，借生命力顽强的小草，喻相信抗战必胜的国人。文章语言质朴简练，蕴藉深厚，耐人寻味。如何译好这篇文章，值得仔细探讨。

翻译是语言的转换过程，也是文化的移植过程；语言的相互转换需遵循语言的规律，文化的移植则需适应读者的需求。做好这项工作在于译者驾驭语言的能力、文化知识的广博，以及译者的审美经验等。王国维在《人间词话》中论及境界的创造时说："诗人对宇宙人生须入乎其内，又须出乎其外。入乎其内，故能写之。出乎其外，故能观之。入乎其内，故有生气。出乎其外，故有高致。"由此兼及译者，也须"入乎其内"，以了解原文的意图，体会文章的神韵，与原作所表现的情态融为一体；译者又须"出乎其外"，既能不受原文表层语言形式的羁绊，又能用流畅自然的译语传达原作情志，唯此能保证译文生动，与原文气韵相符。兹对《野草》英译文试做分析：

一、得原文精髓，译真实形象

夏衍笔下的野草既是自然的野草，也是被赋予灵性的野草。把握野草的双重属性，对整篇文章的翻译很重要。译者熟悉野草的天然特点，也深谙野草的灵性，且看以下译例：

1) Once the seeds **germinate**, they generate a terrible force…

2) Its roots **drill downward** and its sprouts **shoot upward**.

3) The seed does not **fall** on fertile land but in debris, instead.

4) Only the grass **that has been fighting its way** out since its birth is strong and tenacious and, therefore, it can **smile** with pride at the potted plants in glassed green houses.

例 1 和例 2 的黑体部分译的是野草的天然属性；例 3 和例 4 的黑体部分译的是野草顽强不屈的品质。

二、字句的斟酌

字句是构成语篇的基本要素，也是文本情感、信息、文化等的基本载体。翻译过程中，结合语篇、语境斟酌字句，是成功移译的一个重要环节。且看以下译例：

1) In order to get to the sunshine and satisfy its will to grow, it persistently **winds its way up**, no matter how heavy the rocks above and how narrow the space between the rocks. Its roots **drill downward** and its sprouts **shoot upward**. This is an irresistible force. Any rock lying in its way is **upset**.

2) The rock on top of it is not heavy enough to stop it, because it is a force that **remains active over a long period of time**, because it is an elastic force that shrinks and expands, because it is a tenacious force that **will not stop until it achieves its end**.

以上两个译例不受词法、句法束缚，译得简洁凝练，文从字顺，原文韵味字里行间得之，娓娓而谈的叙事风格再现得体。

3) Have you ever seen how the tender young grass comes out from under debris and rubble?

4) Only the grass that has been fighting its way out since its birth is strong and tenacious and, therefore, it can smile with pride at the potted plants in glassed green houses.

以上两例更是炼字精到，意蕴豁然的典范。tender 一字写小草的孱弱，而联系语境实则通过情景对比表达了"草虽弱小，而生命顽强"的语义内涵。smile with pride at 的择用，突出了小草高尚的形象与品质。

三、依实出华，译形传神

翻译中的形式因素往往为人们所忽视，大概是人们通常认为源语的形式在诸多时候与其意义的表现关联不大所致，然而，"如果表达的形式是所表达的意思的一个基本的组成部分，情况就不同了"（奈达语）。为此，转存源语的形式有时是尤显重要的，甚至可以这么说，形之不存，神将焉附？《野草》的英译者正是充分考虑到原文"形与神"的关系，所以便译出了形神两全的文字。且看下例：

There is a story that goes like this:

Someone asks, "What is the most powerful thing in the world?" The question is answered in a variety of ways. Someone says, "Elephant." Someone else says, "Lion." Another one says half-jokingly, "The Buddha's guardian warrior." As to how powerful the Buddha's guardian warrior is, no one can tell, of course.

In fact, none of the answers is correct. The most powerful thing in the world is the seeds of plants. The force generated by a seed is incredible. Here goes another story…

这段文字译得传神，如"As to how powerful the Buddha's guardian warrior is, no one can tell, of course. In fact, none of the answers is correct."。译句不仅词语选择、句法结构很似原文，也将原句略带调侃的味道再现了。

总之，《野草》英译文译笔质朴、自然、流畅。无论是从形式到内容，还是从遣词造句到谋篇布局，均与原文谋得了对应和统一，是我们从事翻译研究、探索翻译艺术的一篇较好的译文。

8

小麻雀

老舍（1899—1966），作家，主要作品有《骆驼祥子》《茶馆》等。《小麻雀》选自《老舍散文选集》，语言通俗活泼。

　　雨后，院里来了个麻雀，刚长全了羽毛。它在院里跳，有时飞一下，不过是由地上飞到花盆沿上，或由花盆上飞下来。看它这么飞了两三次，我看出来：它并不会飞得再高一些，它的左翅的几根长翎拧在一处，有一根特别的长，似乎要脱落下来。我试着往前凑，它跳一跳，可是又停住，看着我，小黑豆眼带出点要亲近我又不完全信任的神气。我想到了：这是个熟鸟，也许是自幼便养在笼中的。所以它不十分怕人。可是它的左翅也许是被养着它的或别个孩子给扯坏，所以它爱人，又不完全信任，想到这个，我忽然的很难过。一个飞禽失去翅膀是多么可怜。这个小鸟离了人恐怕不会活，可是人又那么狠心，伤了它的翎羽。它被人毁坏了，而还想依靠人。多么可怜！它的眼带出进退为难的神情，虽然只是那么个小而不美的小鸟，它的举动与表情可露出极大的委屈与为难。它是要保全它那点生命，而不晓得如何是好。对它自己与人都没有信心，而又愿找到些倚靠。它跳一跳，停一停，看着我，又不敢过来。我想拿几个饭粒诱它前来，又不敢离开，我怕小猫来扑它。可是小猫并没在院里，我很快地跑进厨房，抓来了几个饭粒。及至我回来，小鸟已不见了。我向外院跑去，小猫在影壁前的花盆旁蹲着呢。我忙去驱逐它，它只一扑，把小鸟擒住！被人养惯的小麻雀，连挣扎都不会，尾与爪在猫嘴旁拢拉着，和死去差不多。

瞧着小鸟，猫一头跑进厨房，又一头跑到西屋。我不敢紧追，怕它更咬紧了，可又不能不追。虽然看不见小鸟的头部，我还没忘了那个眼神。那个预知生命危险的眼神。那个眼神与我的好心中间隔着一只小白猫。来回跑了几次，我不追了。追上也没用了，我想，小鸟至少已半死了。猫又进了厨房，我愣了一会儿，赶紧地又追了去；那两个黑豆眼仿佛在我心内睁着呢。

进了厨房，猫在一条铁筒——冬天生火通烟用的，春天拆下来便放在厨房的墙角——旁蹲着呢。小鸟已不见了。铁筒的下端未完全扣在地上，开着一个不小的缝儿，小猫用脚往里探。我的希望回来了，小鸟没死。小猫本来才四个来月大，还没捉住过老鼠，或者还不会杀生，只是叼着小鸟玩一玩。正在这么想，小鸟，忽然出来了，猫倒像吓了一跳，往后躲了躲。小鸟的样子，我一眼便看清了，登时使我要闭上了眼。小鸟几乎是蹲着，胸离地很近，像人害肚痛蹲在地上那样。它身上并没血。身子可似乎是蜷在一块，非常的短。头低着，小嘴指着地。那两个黑眼珠！非常的黑，非常的大，不看什么，就那么顶黑顶大的愣着。它只有那么一点活气，都在眼里，像是等着猫再扑它，它没力量反抗或逃避；又像是等着猫赦免了它，或是来个救星。生与死都在这俩眼里，而并不是清醒的。它是糊涂了，昏迷了；不然为什么由铁筒中出来呢？可是，虽然昏迷，到底有那么一点说不清的，生命根源的，希望。这个希望使它注视着地上，等着，等着生或死。它怕得非常的忠诚，完全把自己交给了一线的希望，一点也不动。像把生命要从两眼中流出，它不叫也不动。

小猫没再扑它，只试着用小脚碰它。它随着击碰倾侧，头不动，眼不动，还呆呆地注视着地上。但求它能活着，它就决不反抗。可是并非全无勇气，它是在猫的面前不动！我轻轻地过去，把猫抓住。将猫放在门外，小鸟还没动。我双手把它捧起来。它确是没受了多大的伤，虽然胸上落了点毛。它看了我一眼！

我没主意：把它放了吧，它准是死？养着它吧，家中没有笼子。我捧着它好像世上一切生命都在我的掌中似的，我不知怎样好。小鸟不动，蜷着身，两眼还那么黑，等着！愣了好久，我把它捧到卧室里，放在桌子上，看着它，它又愣了半天，忽然头向左右歪了歪，用它的黑眼睁了一下；又不动了，可是身子长出来一些，还低头看着，似乎明白了点什么。

| 译 文 |

A Young Sparrow
Lao She

As soon as the rain stops, a young sparrow, almost full-fledged, comes to the courtyard. It hops and flutters, up to the edge of a plant pot or back to the ground again. After it has done this a couple of times, I realize that it cannot fly any higher as the plumes on its left wing have got entangled, and one is sticking out as if about to come off any moment. When I make an attempt to move toward it, it hops off a bit and stops again, staring back at me with its small, black-bean-like eyes that have a mixed look of wanting to be friends with me but not sure that I am a friend to be trusted. At that moment it occurs to me that it must be a tame bird, having been caged perhaps since it was hatched. No wonder it does not bother much about my presence. As its left wing has been injured either by its owner or some other kid, there is distrust in its look though it loves to stay close with man. Suddenly I am filled with sadness. How miserable it is for a bird to lose its wings. I am sure, without someone taking care of this young sparrow, it will not be able to survive. How cruel is man who has injured its wing! Nevertheless, it still looks for help from man. Poor thing! The look in its eyes shows that the little creature is of two minds. Though it is small and ugly, its gestures and expressions seem to tell me that it has been terribly wronged and it has now ended up helpless. It wants to save its diminishing life, but it does not know what to do. It has little confidence in itself and less in man, but it needs someone to fall back on. It begins to hop again and then stops, its eyes looking at me, but too shy to come over. I think of fetching some cooked rice to lure it over, but I cannot afford to leave it alone; I am afraid it might fall prey to the kitte. As at the moment the kitten is not around, I hurry off to the kitchen for some grains of rice but on my return the bird is not there anymore. I run to the outer yard and find the kitten crouching by a plant pot in front of the screen wall. I quicken my steps to scare her off but she pounced on the bird and gets hold of it. The tamed sparrow, with its tail and claws dangling from the kitten's mouth, does not even know how to struggle. It looks more dead than alive.

I watch the kitten run first to the kitchen and then to the west room, my eyes fixed on the bird. I know I must not keep too close after her, but I must not give up either. I cannot see the bird's head, but its look—the look with anticipated danger in its eyes—is still vivid in my mind.

Between the pitiable look and my sympathy stands that small white kitten. Having run a few rounds after her, I quit, thinking it is pointless to chase her like that because, by the time I get hold of her, the bird will have been half dead. The kitten slips back to the kitchen again and I, hesitating for a second, hurry over there too. I seem to see in my mind's eye that the little bird is still keeping its two black-bean-like eyes open.

Coming into the kitchen I notice that the kitten is crouching by a tin pipe which is installed as smoke duct in winter and dismantled in spring, but the bird is not with her. The pipe leans against the corner and, between its lower end and the floor, there is an opening through which the kitten is probing with her paws. My hope revives: the bird is not dead. As the kitten is less than four months old, it has not learned how to catch mice, or how to kill for that matter. She wants to hold the bird in her mouth just for fun. While I am thinking along these lines the little bird is out and the kitten, taken aback, bolts backward. The way the little bird looks has such an effect on me that I feel like shutting my eyes immediately. It is virtually crouching, with its chest close to the floor, like a man does when suffering from a stomachache. There is no stain of blood on its body, but it seems to have become very short, shrinking up into itself. Its head drops low, its small beak pointing to the floor. The two black eyes, unseeing, are very black and large, looking lost. It has its little life left all in the eyes, as if waiting to be charged again for lack of the strength to resist or run, or for the kitten to pardon it or some savior to come to its rescue. There is death as well life in its eyes. It must be confused or stunned, or else why has it come out from under the pipe? Stunned as it is, it still cherishes some hope that, though hard to define, keeps it going for life. With that hope it looks at the floor, expecting either to die or survive. It is so scared that it is completely motionless, entrusting itself entirely to the precarious hope. It keeps quiet and still as if waiting for its life to flow out of its eyes.

The kitten makes no more attempts to attack the bird, merely touching it with her little paws, with the bird tilting from side to side, its head undisturbed and its eyes looking blank at the floor. It will not fight back so long as there is a chance of survival. But the bird has not lost all of its courage; it keeps still in front of the kitten only. I go over light-footed, grab the kitten and put her outside the door, and the sparrow stands where it is. When I pick it up with my hands. I find it is not seriously injured, though some fluff has come off its chest. It throws a look at me.

I have no idea what to do. If I let it go, it is sure to die; if I keep it with me, I do not have a cage for it. I hold it in both hands as if holding all the lives in the world, not knowing what to do about it. The sparrow huddles up, motionless, its eyes as black as ever, still expectant. It remains that way for quite a while. I take it to my bedroom, put it on the desk and watch it for a few moments. Suddenly it tilts its head left and then right, winking its black eyes once or twice, and becomes still again. By now its body seems to have stretched a bit, but it still keeps its head low as if it has cottoned on to something.

这篇散文通过对小麻雀、小猫细腻生动的描绘，对自己内心活动的揭示，表现了作者热爱生命、热爱生活的情趣。"译者应成为所译作品的原作者的再现"（美国翻译家 Gregory Rabassa 语），这也就是说，应再现作者对人情物态的生动描绘和作者对生活的情趣。本文拟从这两方面对《小麻雀》英译文做一分析。

一、作者情真、译者意切

翻译是译者与作者的对话，是译者与作者情感的交流与融通。译者透过文字体察作者的内心活动，用另一种文字再现作者内心情感的起伏。《小麻雀》中的"我"既怜爱受伤的小鸟，也喜爱活泼可爱的小猫；"我"、小麻雀、小猫在作者的笔下既互相有别，也和谐相处，共同生活在"我"的院落之中。在译者的笔下，"我"、小麻雀、小猫依然和谐相处。"我"对小麻雀、小猫的怜爱或喜爱之情依然如故；猫雀相遇看似一场生死劫杀，实则游戏游戏而已等等。诸如此类从以下几个方面可以看出。

1. 对"小麻雀"与"小猫"的理解与翻译

在译者的笔下，"小麻雀"分别译为 a young sparrow、a tame bird、poor thing、the little creature、the bird、the little bird 等；"小猫"则译为 the kitten，在文中出现十几次，可见译者对作者心情体会的贴切。

2. 对"小猫"的动作神态的理解与翻译

作者笔下的小猫其实不是杀生的猫，它的一举一动其实也不带明显的攻击性。译者把握了这点，才有意味深长的译文。兹举数例，加以说明。

［原文］ 我想拿几个饭粒诱它前来，又不敢离开，我怕小猫来**扑它**。

［译文］ I think of fetching some cooked rice to lure it over, but I cannot afford to leave it alone; I am afraid it might fall prey to the kitten.

［原文］ 我忙去驱逐它，它只一**扑**，把小鸟擒住！

［译文］ I quicken my steps to scare her off but she pounced on the bird and gets hold of it.

［原文］ ……（小麻雀）像是等着猫再**扑**它，它没有力量反抗或逃避……

［译文］ …as if waiting to be charged again for lack of the strength to resist or run…

［原文］ 小猫没再**扑**它，只试着用小脚碰它。

［译文］ The kitten makes no more attempts to attack the bird, merely touching it with her little paws…

以上几例中有四个"扑"字，在译者的笔下，每一次"扑"各有侧重，且表达妥帖，既从多角度勾勒出这只活泼可爱的小猫，又再现了作者对小猫的喜爱之情。

3. 对"小麻雀"怜爱之情的理解与翻译

作者对小麻雀的同情，对其处境的关切，以及对它的喜爱，充溢于文章的字里行间。译者将这种情感在译文里表现得饱满充分。

［原文］ ……有一根特别的长，似乎要脱落下来。

［译文］ …and one is sticking out as if about to come off **any moment**.

［原文］ 这个小鸟离了人恐怕不会活……

［译文］ I am sure, without someone taking care of this young sparrow, it will not be able to **survive**.

［原文］ （它被人毁坏了，……）多么可怜！
［译文］ **Poor thing!**

［原文］ 它是要保全它那点生命……
［译文］ It wants to save **its diminishing life**, but it does not know what to do.

［原文］ 我不敢紧追……
［译文］ I know I must not **keep too close** after her…

［原文］ 我捧着它好像世上一切生命都在我的掌中似的……
［译文］ **I hold it in both hands as if holding all the lives in the world**…

［原文］ 我把它捧到卧室里，放在桌子上，看着它……
［译文］ I take it to my bedroom, put it on the desk and **watch it for a few moments**.

以上诸例的黑体部分将作者对小麻雀的关爱之情可谓昭示得呼之欲出！

二、原文生动形象，译文妥帖传神

翻译是信息的传递，也是风格的移植。只注重信息的传递而忽略了风格的移植，译文往往会显得干瘪，失却原有的魅力与感人的力量。原文简洁凝练，译文也应简洁凝练；原文形象生动，译文也应形象生动。这种风格的移植离不开译者对原文的感悟，更离不开译者精湛的译笔。

［原文］ 它在院里跳，有时飞一下，不过是由地上飞到花盆沿上，或由花盆上飞下来。

［译文］ It hops and flutters, up to the edge of a plant pot or back to the ground again.

译文既传递了原文的意义，也移植了原文的情景，且显得简洁凝练。

［原文］ 所以它不十分怕人。

［译文］ No wonder it does not bother much about my presence.

［原文］ 来回跑了几次，我不追了。追上也没用了……

［译文］ Having run a few rounds after her, I quit, thinking it is pointless to chase her like that…

译文形象生动，予人亲临其境、亲历其事之感。

［原文］ 猫又进了厨房，我愣了一会儿，赶紧地又追了去……

［译文］ The kitten slips back to the kitchen again and I, hesitating for a second, hurry over there too.

［原文］ 正在这么想，小鸟，忽然出来了，猫倒像吓了一跳，往后躲了躲。

［译文］ While I am thinking along these lines the little bird is out and the kitten, taken aback, bolts backward.

［原文］ ……开着一个不小的缝儿，小猫用脚往里探。

［译文］ …there is an opening through which the kitten is probing with her paws.

［原文］ 可是并非全无勇气，它是在猫的面前不动！

［译文］ But the bird has not lost all of its courage; it keeps still in front of the kitten only.

以上诸例，译笔用字精巧，准确简练，生动传神，将字里行间体现出的情、景、意提炼得准确精练！

（张保红）

9

书籍

孙犁（1913—2002），作家，著有《风云初集》《荷花淀》，散文集《晚华集》等。《书籍》选自《中华散文珍藏本·孙犁卷》，语言简洁凝练。

　　我同书籍，即将分离。我虽非英雄，颇有垓下之感，即无可奈何。

　　这些书，都是在全国解放以后，来到我家的。最初零零碎碎，中间成套成批。有的来自京沪，有的来自苏杭。最初，囊中羞涩，也曾交臂相失。中间也曾一掷百金，稍有豪气。总之，时历三十余年，我同它们，可称故旧。

　　十年浩劫，我自顾不暇，无心也无力顾及它们。但它们辗转多处，经受折磨、潮湿、践踏、撞破，终于还是回来了。失去了一些，我有些惋惜，但也不愿去寻觅它们，因为我失去的东西，比起它们，更多也更重要。

它们回到寒舍以后，我对它们的情感如故。书无分大小、贵贱、古今、新旧，只要是我想保存的，因之也同我共过患难的，一视同仁。洗尘，安置，抚慰，唏嘘，它们大概是已经体味到了。

近几年，又为它们添加了一些新伙伴。当这些新书，进入我的书架，我不再打印章，写名字，只是给它们包裹一层新装，记下到此的岁月。

这是因为，我意识到，我不久就会同它们告别了。我的命运是注定了的。但它们各自的命运，我是不能预知，也不能担保的。

| 译 文 |

My Books
Sun Li

Soon I'll part with my books; I'll have to, the way the ancient hero Xiang Yu parted with his favorite lady Yu at Gaixia.

The books had arrived at my home since 1949, the year the country was liberated (from KMT rule). At first they came piecemeal and, later, in set or in bulk, some from Beijing and Shanghai, some from Suzhou and Hangzhou. During the first few years, as I was financially embarrassed, sometimes I had to turn from the books that I would have liked to give everything in exchange for. However, there were occasions on which I threw my money on books with quite a sense of lavish generosity. In short, having kept them company for over 30 years, I felt lifelong intimacy with them all.

During the ten years of the disastrous Cultural Revolution I was not in the mood to, nor was I fit enough to bother about my books, as

I was not even sure where I myself would end up. But, having been taken from place to place, getting moistened and damaged, tortured and trampled underfoot, they eventually had come back to me. Some of them had got lost, for which I was really sorry, but I thought I would not go and retrieve them, for I had had more to lose in those years and what I had lost was far more important than the books.

After their return home I felt about them with the same affection as I did earlier. I treated them alike, whether they were big or small, old or new, expensive or inexpensive, classical or contemporary, since they had been in my collection and, therefore, gone through thick and thin with me. I would sigh with significance, when I dusted and caressed them and then found a place for them to go to. I guessed they must have sensed how I felt about their return.

During the past couple of years I had found them some new companions. I no longer stamped my seal or wrote my name on them. When I put them onto the bookshelves, I only clothed them with a new cover and marked the date of their arrival.

This was because I was well aware that it would not be long before I bid farewell to my books; my fate had been predestined. As for what would happen to theirs, I could not foretell, much less could I guarantee.

(与高巍合译)

| 翻 译 提 示 |

作家孙犁，秉性刚正；对国家、对民族充满忧患。他与书同生活，共命运。"文革"期间，书籍遭劫，孙犁的心灵遭受创伤。后来一些书籍退回来了，也还购买新书，但他不再在上面"打印章，

写名字"，"这是因为……它们各自的命运，我是不能预知，也不能担保的"。

孙犁有很深的文字功夫，他的文字虽平淡，但有丰富的内涵。赵改燕在谈孙犁散文的美学追求时说："孙犁在晚年审视历史与现实，反思人生与自身，有许多人生体验的积淀，在写作时，以理性注入，含有哲学意味。作家把对历史人生的观照诉诸平淡的文字中，作品就具备了很强的生命意识。"

了解、研究作家的为人及其作品对译者很重要，对把握作家的情感分寸、传译作家的思想气度、传达作品的内蕴内涵都很重要。对作家的为人了解越多越细越好，对其作品研读越深越透越好，要使译文达意传神需要这样。

以下是文字处理方面的几点想法。

［原文］ 我同书籍，即将分离。我虽非英雄，颇有垓下之感，即无可奈何。

［译文］ Soon I'll part with my books; I'll have to, the way the ancient hero Xiang Yu parted with his favorite lady Yu at Gaixia.

孙犁晚年想到即将与书分离，自言"颇有垓下之感"。《史记·项羽本纪》有这样的记载："项王军壁垓下，兵少食尽。汉军及诸侯兵围数重。夜闻汉军四面皆楚歌，项王乃大惊曰：'汉皆得楚乎？是何楚人之多也！'项王则夜起，饮帐中。有美人名虞，常幸从；骏马名骓，常骑之。于是项王乃悲歌慷慨，自为诗曰：'力拔山兮气盖世！时不利兮骓不逝！骓不逝兮可奈何！虞兮虞兮奈若何！'歌数阕，美人和之。项王泣数行下，左右皆泣，莫能仰视。"作者顺手拈来的一个典故道出他对书的眷恋之情和即将与之别离的悲壮。

翻译这段文字，即使给"垓下之感"加注释，仍不好照字面直译。其中心意思是"我同书籍，即将分离……无可奈何"。将这个中心意思准确译出，句子其余部分可略做变通。

[原文] 最初，囊中羞涩，也曾交臂相失。

[译文] During the first few years, as I was financially embarrassed, sometimes I had to turn from the books that I would have liked to give everything in exchange for.

"交臂相失"也即"失之交臂"，是汉语成语，其含义是"十分喜爱，想买而又无力购买，因而感到遗憾"。翻译时如有相应的英语成语，可以直接拿来用，但译文无论如何要与原文的意思相符。

[原文] 中间也曾一掷百金，稍有豪气。

[译文] However, there were occasions on which I threw my money on books with quite a sense of lavish generosity.

这里的"豪气"就是"为了购买心爱的书籍，不惜花钱"所表现的气派。翻译时想到了 generosity，是可取的。

[原文] ……因为我失去的东西，比起它们，更多也更重要。

[译文] …for I had had more to lose in those years and what I had lost was far more important than the books.

这样处理，译文没有歧义，也把"更多"和"也更重要"的两层意思都说清楚了。

[原文] ……只要是我想保存的，因之也同我共过患难的，一视同仁。

［译文］ I treated them alike...since they had been in my collection and, therefore, gone through thick and thin with me.

　　这里把"只要"的意思改成"既然"，似乎更合逻辑，而且无损原意。

　　关于文章的衔接与连贯，也顺便提一下。全文分六个段落，每一段都有其所侧重的与主题相关的中心内容，先说什么后说什么作者是思考过了的，翻译时遵照作者的意图逐段处理即可，自然形成一个经纬严密的篇章。重要的是把每个段落内部各个句子衔接好，段落的组织就会好，每个段落组织好了，篇章大体不会差。所谓"篇之彪炳，章无疵也"，就是这个道理。举第三段为例，对句子的衔接做简略分析。英译文中的黑体字可看作是将各个句子组成一个有机整体的衔接成分，靠了这些成分的帮助便有了组织较完好的段落。

　　During the ten years of the disastrous Cultural Revolution **I was not** in the mood to, nor was I fit enough to bother about my books, **as** I was not even sure where I myself would end up. (1) **But**, having been taken from place to place, getting moistened, damaged, tortured and trampled underfoot, **they** eventually had come back to me. (2) **Some** of them had got lost, for which I was really sorry, **but** I thought I would not go and retrieve them, **for** I had had more to lose in those years and what I had lost was far more important than the books. (3)

　　此段有三句话，第一句，"文革"期间顾不上书，因为（as）连自己都顾不上；第二句，可是（But）书又回来了，出乎意料；第三句，（书没有全回来）丢了一些，但也（but）不想去找，因为（for）失去的东西比书"更多也更重要"。这样处理，句子的逻辑发展合理，因而段落的整体性和叙事效果也可以。

语篇的衔接与连贯是翻译过程中要注意的重要问题，在不伤害原意的前提下，为了取得好的衔接与连贯效果，有时可对语句做适当调整和变通，以使译文具有"欲停不止"的语势。

（与高巍合写）

10

哀互生

朱自清（1898—1948），作家，著有散文集《背影》《欧游杂记》等。《哀互生》选自《中国现代百家千字文》，语言深沉，有时代感。

三月里刘熏宇君来信，说互生病了，而且是没有希望的病，医生说只好等日子了。四月底在《时事新报》上见到立达学会的通告，想不到这么快互生就殁了！后来听说他病中的光景，那实在太惨；为他想，早点去，少吃些苦头，也未尝不好的。但丢下立达这个学校，这班朋友，这班学生，他一定不甘心，不瞑目！

互生最叫我们纪念的是他做人的态度。他本来是一副铜筋铁骨，黑皮肤衬着那一套大布之衣，看去像个乡下人。他什么苦都吃得，从不晓得享用，也像乡下人。他心里那一团火，也像乡下人。那一团火是热，是力，是光。他不爱多说话，但常常微笑；那微笑是自然的，温暖的。在他看，人是可以互相爱着的，除了一些成见已深，不愿打开窗户说亮话的。他对这些人却有些憎恶，不肯假借一点颜色。世界上只有能憎的人才能爱；爱憎没有定见，只是毫无作为的角色。互生觉得青年成见还少，希望最多；所以愿意将自己的生命一滴不剩而献给他们，让爱的宗教在他们中间发荣滋长，让他们都走向新世界去。互生不好发议论，只埋着头干干干，是儒家的真正精神。我和他并没有深谈过，但从他的行事看来，相信我是认识他的。

互生办事的专心，少有人及得他。他办立达便饮食坐卧只惦着立达，再不想别的。立达好像他的情人，他的独子。他性情本有些狷介，但为了立达，也常去看一班大人先生，更常去看那些有钱可借的老板之类。他东补西凑地为立达筹款子，还要跑北京，跑南京。有一回他本可以留学去，但丢不下立达，到底没有去。他将生命献给立达，立达也便是他的生命。他办立达这么多年，并没有让多少人知道他个人的名字，他早忘记了自己。现在他那样壮健的身子到底为立达牺牲了。他殉了自己的理想，是有意义的。只是这理想刚在萌芽；我们都该想想，立达怎样才可不死呢？立达不死，互生其实也便不死了。

Mourning for Husheng
Zhu Ziqing

In March I heard from Mr. Liu Xunyu that Husheng was sick and hopelessly at that. The doctor said there was not much he could do but wait for the day to arrive. Toward the end of April, I came across an obituary issued by Lida Association in *The New Current Affairs*. How quickly the day had arrived! Later, when I learned how he had suffered while lying in bed, I thought it was too miserable. From his point of view, however, his passing away was not a bad thing after all because, going earlier, he had less to suffer. But it must have been very hard for him to close his eyes and resign himself to the fact that he had to leave his Lida School, his friends and his students behind.

What was most memorable about Husheng was his attitude toward life. He was as strong as a man of steel and, with his dark complexion set off by clothes of coarse cloth, looked like a countryman. He could withstand any hardship, never seeking ease and comfort. In this sense he was like a countryman, too. Also like a countryman, he had a heart as warm as fire radiating warmth, light and power. He was a man of few words, but of all smiles. His smile was natural and friendly. In his view, people should love each other, except those with deep prejudices and those who could not bring themselves out in the open. He disliked those people, and wouldn't show anything like gentleness to them. In this world, only those who could hate could love. Those who did not know what to love and what to hate were useless people. Husheng believed that young people had little prejudice but lots of promise, so he was willing to dedicate his life to them without reservation, letting the religion of love grow and flourish among them so that they could all go to a new world. Husheng was not fond of talking but he set his mind on work and work and nothing but work—an embodiment of the Confucian spirit. Though I never had a chance to talk with him deeply, I was convinced that I understood him from the way he conducted himself in relation with others.

Few people I knew of had the same sense of dedication as

Husheng. When he was running Lida School, he had all his thoughts on the school whatever he did. Lida was like his sweetheart, his only son. He was by nature an honest man but, for the sake of Lida, he had to go and see nobs, bosses and the like from whom he hoped to raise money. To raise money, he had to run to places as far as Beijing and Nanjing. Once he could have been arranged to go and study abroad, but he did not go because he could not leave the school behind. He had sacrificed his life for Lida and Lida had become his life too. Though he was head of the school for many years, he never tried to make his name known to the public. He had forgotten himself altogether. Now he had consumed himself for Lida despite his robust constitution. He had died for his ideal and that was a meaningful death. As his ideal was just beginning to bud, we should all think about one question: what should we do to keep Lida alive? If Lida was alive, Husheng was alive with it.

| 翻译提示 |

从文章所叙的内容看，作者与互生之间并没有很深的交往。但互生身上很多好的品质使他感动，令他敬佩。互生做人的态度，狷介的性格，只知吃苦，不知享用，爱憎分明，埋头苦干，办事专心，忘我牺牲，以及他为理想而殉职的高贵品质，使作者在互生身上看到了民族的精神，国家的希望。出于文学家的责任感，朱自清写了这篇短文章，这是一篇很好的文章。有实在的内容，有真挚的感情，用不加雕琢的文字表达出来，就是好文章。

不加雕琢的文字表现在用词、语域和句式的结构上，形成一种有个性的叙事风格，这种风格其实就是与所写内容以及作者性情相关联的叙事方式。翻译之前从用词、语域和句式结构上研究文章的

语气，体会作者的心情，翻译时选择恰当的词汇和句式，译文可得
与原文接近的风格。

朱自清的这篇文章语言简单朴素，不着意修饰，通篇如此，下
面仅以第一段的几个句子为例说明一下。

［原文］ 三月里刘薰宇君来信，说互生病了，而且是没有希望的病，
医生说只好等日子了。

［译文］ In March I heard from Mr. Liu Xunyu that Husheng was sick
and hopelessly at that. The doctor said there was not much he
could do but wait for the day to arrive.

汉语的"等日子"是一个委婉的说法，英语 wait for the day to
arrive 可以表达相同的意思，容易理解。

［原文］ 四月底在《时事新报》上见到立达学会的通告，想不到
这么快互生就殁了！

［译文］ Toward the end of April, I came across an obituary issued by
Lida Association in *The New Current Affairs*. How quickly
the day had arrived!

翻译"想不到这么快互生就殁了！"这句话时与上句联系起来，
有前后呼应的效果。

［原文］ 为他想，早点去，少吃些苦头，也未尝不好的。

［译文］ From his point of view, however, his passing away was not a
bad thing after all because, going earlier, he had less to suffer.

汉语的"早点去"和英语的 going earlier 都是常听到的口语
形式。

［原文］ 但丢下立达这个学校，这班朋友，这班学生，他一定不甘心，不瞑目！

［译文］ But it must have been very hard for him to close his eyes and resign himself to the fact that he had to leave his Lida School, his friends and his students behind.

"不甘心"和"不瞑目"的译文与原文是相符的。

11

老人和他的三个儿子

冯雪峰（1903—1976），作家，诗人，参加过二万五千里长征，经历坎坷。著有散文集《乡风与市风》《有进无退》等。《老人和他的三个儿子》选自《中国现代百家千字文》，语言练达，思想深沉。

　　一位老人有三个儿子。大儿子是一个非凡的水手：坚强、勇敢、尽职，而且富于冒险精神。老人真的爱他，认为这是一个做父亲的值得骄傲的光荣。可是，在一次暴风雨中，这个儿子以他的大胆和勇猛，葬身于大海的狂涛骇浪里了。

　　二儿子是一个不知道辛苦和疲劳的、力气比一般伙伴都更大的壮健的矿工，又很诚实和守信义，乐意帮助伙伴和朋友，所以矿工们，尤其是青年们，都和他做朋友，以得到他的友谊为快乐。那父亲也真爱他，尤其是在大儿子死了以后，更认为这是上天给他的最大的弥补。可是，不久，二儿子也殉身于自己的勇敢和自我牺牲的行为了，因为这一天他在煤矿中工作，矿坑因为支柱损坏而崩坍，他英勇撑住一根支柱，救出了许多伙伴，而他自己是被压死了。

老人的伤痛是不用说的，他马上变成一个非常衰败的软弱的人了。不过，还剩下一个小儿子，是做父亲的唯一的安慰。老人改变了主意，决心不让小儿子成为一个出众的英雄好汉的人物，因为他实在不能再忍受那种折损儿子的痛苦。他叹着气说："唉，与其因为他有才能而被夺，我宁愿他是一个一无所长的没出息的人呵。"这样，老人就亲自教育这个小儿子，采取了一种连那些老婆婆们教育女娃娃都很少采用的教育方法。而这个小儿子，也真孝顺。果然没有叫父亲失望。就是说，他让自己成为一个又懦弱又自私而真的一无用处的人了。可是，真没有想到，到了这时候，这个老人感到从来没有过的悲哀和不幸了。他一边痛悔自己的错误，一边憎恨而又可怜自己的小儿子说：

"这就叫作废物，这就叫作脓包，是我一向所痛恨的。现在因为我自私，亲手把他制造出来了！嗳，嗳，这样的一个海淹不死、山压不死的人，他活着到底做什么的？"

这个老人实在无法爱他的小儿子，因为他只能爱波浪壮阔的海和巍峨坚实的山以及像他大儿子二儿子那样的人。因此，他现在做父亲的心，不得不无限地痛苦，这是他一度错误的想法和他亲手毁坏了小儿子这件事情的一个惩罚。

| 译文 |

An Old Man and His Three Sons
Feng Xuefeng

An old man had three sons. The eldest was an extraordinary sailor—brave, dutiful, tough and adventurous. The old man loved him indeed, thinking he was the kind of son to do credit to a father. But one day he was caught in a tempest and this brave and tough son of his was engulfed in the stormy waves.

His second son was a strong coal miner, stronger than the other miners, not knowing what was hardship and fatigue. And he was honest and trustworthy, always ready to help. Therefore, his fellow miners, especially the younger ones, sought his friendship and took pleasure in being friends with him. His father cherished him as a godsend—a great compensation for the loss of his eldest son. But unfortunately he also lost his life in a brave act of self-sacrifice. One day when he was working down the pit, the decaying props gave way and the pit caved in. He grasped one prop that was falling and held fast to it. Many of the miners were saved but he was buried in it.

His grief was beyond words. Soon he became a weak and flabby old man. Fortunately, he had his youngest son left and he was the only comfort to him. But the old man changed his mind. He did not encourage him to become a hero, because he could no longer stand the grief of losing his last child. He said with a sigh, "I'd like him to be a mediocrity rather than a talented person who may lose his life." He set about educating him in such a fashion that even old women would not follow in educating their granddaughters. And this son of his, very obedient indeed, did not let him down. In other words, he became a weak, selfish and worthless person. It was not until then that the old man found himself a sad and most unfortunate man he had never been. He was full of remorse for the mistake he had made. He said in a mixed tone of anger and pity about his son.

"This is what is called good-for-nothing—the kind of person I dislike. I am to blame though, for I've made him like this as a result of my selfishness. Ai, I wonder if life has any meaning to such a callous creature that cannot even be drowned in the sea or crushed by the mountain?"

The old man could not bring himself to love this son of his any more, for he only had love for stormy seas, lofty mountains and heroic people like his first two sons. Being a father, he was now suffering from a broken heart—a punishment imposed on himself for ruining his youngest son with his own idea and by his own doing.

| 翻 译 提 示 |

　　这是冯雪峰的一个寓言故事，情节简单，寓意深刻。翻译时需遵循原文的行文方式和风格，但有时为了取得好的译文，要对原文做一些调整。例如：

［原文］　大儿子是一个非凡的水手：坚强、勇敢、尽职，而且富
　　　　　于冒险精神。

［译文］　The eldest was an extraordinary sailor—brave, dutiful, tough
　　　　　and adventurous.

　　关于形容词的顺序，可根据对译文的感觉和需要做调整，这里以 brave 开始，接着说 dutiful，也算自然，再把 tough and adventurous 放在一起，搁在后面，因为这二者的意思联系更紧密。这样处理也许比按照原文顺序翻译，效果要好些。

［原文］　可是，在一次暴风雨中，这个儿子以他的大胆和勇猛，
　　　　　葬身于大海的狂涛骇浪里了。

［译文］But one day he was caught in a tempest and this brave and tough son of his was engulfed in the stormy waves.

"在一次暴风雨中"，译成"But one day he was caught in a tempest..."比简单地译成 in a tempest 要生动，使全句有平衡感；"（以他的）大胆和勇猛"在原文属名词，在 this brave and tough son 里属形容词，结合下文的"葬身于……"考虑，这样处理是可以的，更符合英语语言习惯。

［原文］……都和他做朋友，以得到他的友谊为快乐。
［译文］...sought his friendship and took pleasure in being friends with him.

这样译略与原文有出入，但意思与原文相符，行文既不违反原文风格，也符合英语叙事习惯，读起来比较顺。

［原文］那父亲也真爱他，尤其是在大儿子死了以后，更认为这是上天给他的最大的弥补。
［译文］His father cherished him as a godsend—a great compensation for the loss of his eldest son.

这样翻译行文简洁，用一个简单的句子和很少的词传达了原文的意思。

［原文］……二儿子也殉身于自己的勇敢和自我牺牲的行为了……
［译文］...he also lost his life in a brave act of self-sacrifice.

原文里两个形容词在译文里只保留了一个——勇敢，另一个形容词"自我牺牲的"，译成了名词形式。

［原文］ ……这样的一个海淹不死、山压不死的人，他活着到底做什么的？

［译文］ …I wonder if life has any meaning to such a callous creature that cannot even be drowned in the sea or crushed by the mountain?

这里译文加了一个 callous 来形容 creature，使后面的 that cannot even be drowned in the sea or crushed by the mountain 对前面的行文有了交代。在汉语里，读者不会对这样的句子产生误解，因为汉语里有这样的修辞；在英语里加上一个词，以建立前后的联系。

12

我若为王

聂绀弩（1903—1986），作家，诗人，经历坎坷。著有《绀弩杂文选》，散文集《沉吟》，诗集《聂绀弩诗全编》等。《我若为王》选自《中国现代百家千字文》，文笔恣肆，冷嘲热讽。

在电影刊物上看见一个影片的名字：《我若为王》。从这影片的名字，我想到和影片毫无关系的另外的事。我想，自己如果做了王，这世界会成为一种怎样的光景呢？这自然是一种完全可笑的幻想，我根本不想做王，也根本看不起王，王是什么东西呢？难道我脑中还有如此封建的残物么？而且真想做王的人，他将用他的手去打天下，决不会放在口里说的。但是假定又假定，我若为王，这世界会成为一种怎样的光景？

我若为王，自然我的妻就是王后了。我的妻的德性，我不怀疑，为王后只会有余的。但纵然没有任何德性，纵然不过是个娼妓，那时候，她也仍旧是王后。一个王后是如何的尊贵呀，会如何地被人们像捧着天上的星星一样捧来捧去呀。假如我能够想象，那一定是一件有趣的事情。

我若为王，我的儿子，假如我有儿子，就是太子或王子了。我并不以为我的儿子会是一无所知，一无所能的白痴；但纵然是一无所知一无所能的白痴，也仍旧是太子或王子。一个太子或王子是如何的尊贵呀，会如何地被人们像捧天上的星星一样地捧来捧去呀。假如我能够想象，倒是件不是没有趣味的事。

我若为王，我的女儿就是公主；我的亲眷都是皇亲国戚。无论他们怎样丑陋，怎样顽劣，怎样……也会被人们像捧天上的星星一样地捧来捧去，因为他们是贵人。

我若为王，我的姓名就会改作："万岁"，我的每一句话都成为："圣旨"。我的意欲，我的贪念，乃至每一个幻想，都可竭尽全体臣民的力量去实现，即使是无法实现的。我将没有任何过失，因为没有人敢说它是过失；我将没有任何罪行，因为没有人敢说它是罪行。没有人敢呵斥我，指摘我，除非把我从王位上赶下来。但是赶下来，就是我不为王了。我将看见所有的人们在我面前低头，鞠躬，匍匐，连同我的尊长，我的师友，和从前曾在我面前昂头阔步耀武扬威的人们。我将看不见一个人的脸，所看见的只是他们的头顶和帽盔。或者所能够看见的脸都是谄媚的，乞求的，快乐的时候不敢笑，不快乐的时候不敢不笑，悲戚的时候不敢哭，不悲戚的时候不敢不哭的脸。我将听不见人们的真正的声音，所能听见的都是低微的，柔婉的，畏葸和娇痴的，唱小旦的声音："万岁，万岁，万万岁！"这是他们的全部语言："有道明君！伟大的主上啊！"这就是那语言的全部内容。没有在我之上的人了，没有和我同等的人了，我甚至会感到单调，寂寞和孤独。

为什么人们要这样呢？为什么要捧我的妻，捧我的儿女和亲眷呢？因为我是王，是他们的主子，我将恍然大悟，我生活在这些奴才们中间，连我所敬畏的尊长和师友也无一不是奴才，而我自己也不过是一个奴才的首领。

我是民国国民，民国国民的思想和生活习惯使我深深地憎恶一切奴才或奴才相，连同敬畏的尊长和师友们。请科学家们不要见笑，我以为世界之所以还大有待于改进者，全因为有这些奴才的缘故。生活在奴才们中间，作奴才们的首领，我将引为生平的最大的耻辱，最大的悲哀。我将变成一个暴君，或者反而正是明君：我将把我的臣民一齐杀死，连同尊长和师友，不准一个奴种留在人间。我将没有一个臣民，我将不再是奴才们的君主。

我若为王，将终于不能为王，却也真的为古今中外最大的王了。"万岁，万岁，万万岁！"我将和全世界的真的人们一同三呼。

| 译文 |

If I Were King
Nie Gannu

In a movie magazine I have come across the title of a film: *If I Were King*. It reminds me of something totally irrelevant to the film. I wonder what the world would be like if I were mounted on the throne. This, of course, is absurd fantasy. I don't want to be King, nor do I have the slightest respect for him. What kind of stuff is King made of? Are there any such feudal remnants still left in my head? He who really wants to be King will fight for it with his hands instead of mouthing it in words. But let me suppose and suppose in the strict sense of the word that I were King, what would the world look like?

If I were King, naturally my wife would be Queen. I am not

skeptical of my wife's virtue. She has more virtue than we expect in a queen. Even if she were a virtueless woman, or a shameless whore, she would be Queen nevertheless. How respectable and honorable a queen would be and how she would be praised to the skies and worshiped like stars! If I could stretch my imagination a bit, it would be very interesting.

If I were King, my son (if I ever had a son) would be Prince or Crown Prince. I would not believe my son was an ignorant and worthless idiot but, even if he were, he would still be Prince or Crown Prince. How respectable and honorable Prince or Crown Prince would be and how he would be praised to the skies and worshiped like stars! If I could stretch my imagination a bit, it would not be anything uninteresting.

If I were King, my daughter would be Princess and my relatives imperial kinsfolk. No matter how ugly or mean they might be, or whatever you name it, they would be praised to the skies and worshiped like stars because of their noble origin.

If I were King, I would be renamed "Your Majesty" and every word I said would be an "imperial edict". My will, my avaricious desires, or my wild fantasies would be carried out by my subjects with the greatest efforts they could ever make, even if they were impossible to be carried out. I would be immune to mistakes; no one had the guts to call them mistakes. I would be immune to crimes; no one had the guts to call them crimes. No one would dare to reproach me or find fault with me, unless they pulled me off the throne (in which case I would be no King at all). I would see all the people bowing with their heads dropped, and prostrating themselves at my feet, including my respected elders, teachers, friends and those who had once swaggered around in front of me. I would not be able to see their faces; all I could see was the top of their heads or hats or helmets. Or, if I ever got a glimpse of their faces, they were ingratiating and begging faces, faces that dared not smile when they were happy and dared not refuse to smile when they were unhappy, and faces that dared not weep when they were grieved and dared not refuse to weep when they were not so grieved. I would not be able to hear their real voices; all I could hear was their low, soft, timid and silly shouts of "A long life, a long life and a long long life", like the faint singing of young maids in Beijing opera. All they could say was: "Our enlightened King, our Great Lord." This was all they could utter. There was no one else above me and no one else claimed to be my equal. I was isolated, bored and lonely.

Why did they behave this way? Why did they praise my wife, my son and daughter and my relatives? Because I was King, their Lord. I would soon find that I was living among the despicable flunkeys, including my revered elders, teachers and friends, and that I was nothing but their chieftain.

I was a citizen of the Republic and my thinking and life habits as a citizen of the Republic had developed a strong disgust for flunkeys and servility, my revered elders, teachers and friends and all. I hoped that scientists would be kind enough not to laugh at me. The reason I believed there was still room for improvement on the world was that there were despicable flunkeys in it. I considered it my greatest shame and tragedy to live amid them and be their leader. I would rather be a tyrant, or therefore, in my case, a wise king to be exact, and slaughter all my subjects, including my respected elders, teachers and friends, leaving none of them to propagate in the world. I would have not a single subject under me and, therefore, I would be no King of the despicable flunkeys.

If I were King (as a matter of fact I could never be the king) I would be the greatest king ever. I would shout along with the people—people in the true sense—of the world, "A long life, a long life, and a long, long life."

| 翻 译 提 示 |

好的文学作品，对于源语读者来说，是作者心灵的外显。经过翻译家之手，该作品的生命力得以伸张。这是文学作品的价值所在，也是翻译家劳动的价值所在。合格的译者可以做到双语转换上的精巧，而好的翻译家，能做到与原作者心灵上的沟通。因为文学翻译从本质上讲，是一次译者与作者之间的对话。

译者的工作首先从选择原文开始。译者的翻译动机，或他的首要动机，总是想把自己认为有价值的东西呈现给新的读者。从译者的翻译实践来看，他所翻译的散文都透发着一种人本的、内心的力量：做真正的人，做有利于社会的人。读罢此篇译作"If I Were King"，一个真切的感受就是，他之所以选择翻译《我若为王》，是因为受到作者心灵力量的触动，并且是在与作者达到心灵上的契合之后才动笔的。

原文从一个有趣的电影名字展开联想，从小我想到大我，再回到小我。侃侃而谈，肆意泼辣之中不乏对"大王"头上虚伪光环的蔑视，对奴才相的憎恶。表面之下潜流着作者对民族劣根性的切齿痛恨。原文行文流畅，逻辑清晰。译者的用笔犹如一列磁悬浮列车，既没有亦步亦趋地贴在原作的文字上，却又飘然自得地运行在作者的心灵轨道上。如：

[原文] 从这影片的名字，我想到和影片毫无关系的另外的事。

[译文] It reminds me of something totally irrelevant to the film.

"从……我想到"在英语里能找到对应的现成句式 remind sb of sth。合格的译者可以做到双语转换上的精巧，好的翻译家，还能做到与作者心灵上的沟通。如：

[原文] 我根本不想做王，也根本看不起王，王是什么东西呢？

[译文] I don't want to be King, nor do I have the slightest respect for him. What kind of stuff is King made of?

原文中两个"根本（不）"（not, nor）承载的憎恶之极的情绪通过一个最高级 the slightest 足额传达出来。（王是）"什么东西"，本来是一个名词，但用动词句式 what kind of stuff is (King) made of 来表达，进一步强化了蔑视的语气。这是作者对所谓的"王"的概念的鲜明态度。作者以一指十，向封建的帝王制度发起猛烈攻击。"王"虽然是天生的，但更是一种腐朽制度"制造"出来的，更是奴性十足的臣民人为"创造"出来的。译者使用 is made of 有力地服务了原作在下文对王和"创造"王的奴才相进行层层剥离的意图。译文句式的变动看似简单，却体现出译者与作者心灵上的契合。做到这一点，才能最佳地用另一种语言再现作者心灵的写照。

下面一个例子更能说明这一点：

[原文] 没有在我之上的人了，没有和我同等的人了，我甚至会感到单调，寂寞和孤独。

[译文] There was no one else above me and no one else claimed to be my equal. I was isolated, bored and lonely.

与原文粗略对照，译者的"创造"似乎太过了些。本来是相同结构的两个句子，其中一个却在译文中做了明显的变动。claim 的使用，衬托了奴才臣民都想为王的梦想，不能为王，在自己的王面前便不敢"宣称"任何属于自己的东西。作者意图在此，译者把握于心。可以说，译者的一个 claim 比原文更传神地总结了作为王的对立面的封建臣子的真实心态，可谓是闪亮的一笔。

再看原文三个形容词的翻译。"单调""寂寞""孤独"并列开来，似有递进关联。若照直翻译，再容易不过。但是译者追随作者的思绪，揣摩出作者在简单的表达上要传达的真实感受：简简单单三个词，乃是上文四个长长排比句（"我将……"）的高度浓缩。三个词要传达的意思是一个正常的人，更确切地说是一个正直的人，在如此悲哀的"王"的环境中必然的、真切的感受。其中有主有次，有原因和结果之分。只有深入到作者的内心，设身处地，才能理顺三个词的内在逻辑关系。isolated 重在外部环境的压抑，而 bored 和 lonely 偏于内心世界的感受。

译者需要知识面宽些。原文有两处涉及中国京剧的知识：

所能听见的都是低微的，柔婉的，畏葸和妓痌的，唱小旦的声音："万岁，万岁，万万岁！"

"万岁，万岁，万万岁！"我将和全世界的真的人们一同三呼。

"唱小旦的声音""三呼"是中国京剧文化独具的术语，虽为"声音"，传达的却是神态；虽是"三"呼，却是感叹。如果对此不了解，翻译时很容易出错。作者应该是听过京剧小旦唱腔的，使用前四个形容词来刻画奴才臣子的声音。这种声音并不是在本质上像"唱小旦的声音"，而只是"声"似。而且，小旦的声音是"唱"出来的。译者采用 like the faint singing of young maids in Beijing opera，将一个"唱小旦的"的神态动感地描绘出来。这样一副有气无力、没有自我的模样，恰好是作者要传达给读者的奴相的写照。译者把握了作者的意图，充分传译出原作中富有动感的声音效果。

至于"三呼"，既是确数，又是情感的发泄。看过京剧的人都知道，臣子面见主子便三呼"万岁"。一句三顿，其中饱含多少敬拜、依附和感恩。作者的高明之处在于在文章结尾使用了双关修辞法。同为顿呼，我和"真正的人"岂能像（上文）奴才臣民的一般?！这确实给译者制造了困难，译者译作"A long life, a long life, and a long, long life."。在符号处理上采用三个逗号，突出"三呼"发自内心的欢乐，突出欢快的鲜明节奏，以示截然区别于作者深恶痛绝的奴才臣子那奴颜婢膝、急不可耐，却又缺乏真情的"唱小旦"般的三呼："A long life, a long life and a long long life."。这样的技术处理，不仅再现了原作的"双关"修辞效果，而且与作者真正达到了心灵上的契合。看似技术处理，其实是艺术的匠心。

（任东升）

13

冬夜

艾芜（1904—1992），作家，著有短篇小说集《南行记》，散文集《漂泊杂记》等。《冬夜》选自《中国现代百家千字文》，语言有乡土风味。

冬天，一个冰寒的晚上。在寂寞的马路旁边，疏枝交横的树下，候着最后一辆搭客汽车的，只我一人。虽然不远的墙边，也蹲有一团黑影，但他却是伸手讨钱的。马路两旁，远远近近都立着灯窗明灿的别墅，向暗蓝的天空静静地微笑着。在马路上是冷冰冰的，还刮着一阵阵猛厉的风。留在枝头的一两片枯叶，也不时发出破碎的哭声。

那蹲着的黑影，接了我的一枚铜板，就高兴地站起来向我搭话，一面抱怨着天气："真冷呀，再没有比这里更冷了！……先生，你说是不是？"

看见他并不是个讨厌的老头子，便也高兴地说道："乡下怕更要冷些吧？"

"不，不，"他接着咳嗽起来，要吐出的话，塞在喉管里了。

我说："为什么？你看见一下霜，乡下的房屋和田野，便在早上白了起来，街上却一点也看不见。"

他捶了几下胸口之后，兴奋地接着说道："是的，是的……乡下冷，你往人家门前的稻草堆上一钻就暖了哪……这街上，哼，鬼地方！……还有那些山里呵，比乡下更冷哩，咳，那才好哪！火烧一大堆，大大小小一家人，闹热呀！……"

接着他便说到壮年之日，在南方那些山中冬夜走路的事情。一个人的漂泊生活，我是喜欢打听的，同时车又没有驰来，便怂恿他说了下去。他说晚上在那些山里，只要你是一个正派的人，就可以朝灯火人家一直走去，迎着犬声，敲开树荫下的柴门，大胆地闯进。对着火堆周围的人们，不管他男的女的，用两手向他们两肩头一分，就把你带着风寒露湿的身子，轻轻地放了进去。烧山芋和热茶的香味，便一下子扑入你的鼻子。抬头看，四周闪着微笑的眼睛，欢迎着，毫没有怪你唐突的神情。你刚开口说由哪儿来的时候，一杯很热的浓茶，就递在你的下巴边上。老太婆吩咐她的孙女，快把火拨大些，多添点子柴，说是客人要烘暖他的身子；你暖和了，还不觉得疲倦的话，你可以摸摸小孩子的下巴，拧拧他们的脸蛋，做一点奇怪的样子，给他们嬉笑。年轻的妈妈，一高兴了，便会怂恿他的孩子把拿着要吃的烧山芋，分开一半，放在你这位客人的手上。如果你要在他们家过夜，他们的招待，就更来得殷勤些。倘若歇一会，暖暖身子，还要朝前赶路，一出柴门，还可听见一片欢送的声音："转来时，请来玩呀！"老头子讲着讲着，给冷风一吹，便又咳嗽起来。我听得冷都忘记了，突然老头子忘形地拉着我问道：

"先生，这到底是什么原因哪？……这里的人家，火堆一定烧得多的，看窗子多么亮哪……他们为什么不准一个异乡人进去烤烤手哩？"

搭客汽车从远处轰轰地驰来了，我赶忙摆他的手，高声说道："因为他们是文明的人，不像那些山里的……"

再跳进通明的汽车里，蓦地离开他了。但远的南国山中，小小的灯火人家里面，那些丰美的醉人的温暖，却留在我的冬夜的胸中了。

| 译 文 |

A Winter Night
Ai Wu

It was a cold winter night. The street was deserted. I stood alone under a tree with an entanglement of bare branches overhead, waiting for the last bus to arrive. A few paces off in the darkness there was a shadowy figure squatting against the wall, but he turned out to be a tramp. The street was lined with fine houses, their illuminated windows beaming quietly towards the dark blue sky. It was icy cold with a gust of strong wind howling around. A couple of withered leaves, still clinging to the branches, rustled mournfully from time to time.

The shadowy figure, taking a copper coin from me with thanks, straightened up to attempt a conversation with me.

"It's really cold here," he complained. "It couldn't be colder anywhere else…What do you think, sir?"

Seeing that he was not too nasty an old man, I readily responded, "It must be colder in the country, I'm afraid."

"No, no," he disagreed and began to cough, his words stuck up in his throat.

"Why?" I asked. "In the country when it frosts, you always find the roofs and the fields turning white in the morning, but you don't see that here on the streets."

He patted his chest to ease off his coughing and went on excitedly:

"True, true…it's cold in the country, but when you get into somebody's straw stack, you get warmed up at once…But this street, humm, what a terrible place! In the mountains, it's even colder, but when they have a fire in the house with the whole family sitting around it, wow, it's heaven!"

Then he began to relate to me the adventures of his younger days— travelling alone in winter nights through the mountains in the south. As I was interested in stories about wanderers and since the bus had not arrived yet, I encouraged him to go on.

"When you end up in the mountains at night," he said, "and if you are a decent person, you can always turn where there is a light flickering and a dog barking. You push open the bramble gate under the shade and walk in without hesitation. Part the people, men or women, around the fire with your hands and you bring yourself—a cold and wet man with dew—among them. Immediately your nose is filled with the aroma of hot tea and roast sweet potatoes. When you look round you see friendly faces smiling at you; there is no hint of anything like blame for what elsewhere might be considered as brusqueness. Scarcely have you begun to tell them where you come from when a cup of hot and strong tea is handed over to you. Grandma will tell her granddaughter to feed the fire with more wood, saying that the guest needs more heat to warm up. When you are recovered from cold and fatigue, you tend to tease the kid, stroking his chin, giving a gentle pinch to his cheek or making a face to provoke him to gurgle. The delighted young mother will encourage her kid to share his sweet potato with you. The kid will then break it in two and thrust one half into your hand. If you intend to stay overnight, you will be entertained with all possible hospitality. If you just drop in to warm up and then go on your way, they will see you off at the gate, saying, "please do drop in on us again on your way back."

In the middle of his babbling another gust of wind brushed by and the old man began to cough again. I was so intrigued by his story that I did not feel the cold any more. Suddenly he grabbed my hand, forgetting that we were strangers, and asked:

"Sir, could you tell me why the people here even do not allow a countryman in to warm his hands? They must've got bigger fires in their houses. Look at their bright windows…"

The bus came rumbling up. Withdrawing my hand from his, I answered at the top of my voice:

"Because they are more civilized than the mountain people…"

With that I jumped onto the brightly-lit bus which started moving on, leaving the old man behind. But the little houses with flickering oil lamps in the remote mountains and the intoxicating warmth and friendliness of their inhabitants left a deep impress on my memory.

| 翻 译 提 示 |

唐代王维的诗中有画，画中有诗。诗何以蕴画，画何以蕴诗？这要靠艺术家对生活的观察、对艺术的感悟以及对审美的体验。一

句话，功夫在诗外。文学翻译也一样，要达到神形兼备的境界，也是功夫在诗外。

《冬夜》借一个街头乞讨的老人之口，描述了山民的淳朴和市民的冷漠。文字质朴平淡，洗练流畅，寓意深隽。英译文也成功地再现了原文意蕴。

意蕴无论多空灵、多虚幻，总是有形可依。奈达认为，翻译是"在译入语中复制出与译出语信息意义和风格最近似的自然对等物"。这个对等是形式与内容双重的。内容对等又分现实对等和心理感受对等。形与意构成一虚一实。汉英翻译的神似，虚实变换是关键。

虚与实之别由结构衔接体现。汉语常以简练之形蕴深刻内涵，故意合多于形合，多隐性衔接。各小句如竹节一般，主次模糊，这是"虚"。英语的结构较"实"，等级分明，轻重有序，多显性衔接。《冬夜》的译者深谙两者之差异，虚实变换，常有令人赞叹之笔。例如下一句原文乍看很模糊，译出来条理清晰明了：

[原文]　还有那些山里呵，比乡下更冷哩，咳，那才好哪！火烧一大堆，大大小小一家人，闹热呀！

[译文]　In the mountains, it's even colder, but when they have a fire in the house with the whole family sitting around it, wow, it's heaven!

"咳"一句是指前面的"……更冷哩"，还是指后面的"火烧一大堆……"似乎都行，译者准确把握了原文的"意"，用 but 和 when 衔接，使各成分之间的关系豁然明显。然后再用介词 with 将 a fire in the house 和 the whole family sitting around it 衔接。这种条理的清晰是英语结构所要求的。

汉语结构不怕头重脚轻，英语则讲究头轻脚重。这一句很典型：

[原文] 在寂寞的马路旁边，疏枝交横的树下，候着最后一辆搭客汽车的，只我一人。

[译文] The street was deserted. I stood alone under a tree with an entanglement of bare branches overhead, waiting for the last bus to arrive.

主语前有三个修饰成分。汉语里各种短语组成的复杂词组或分句都可以名正言顺地置到句首之位；而英语应利用多种句法手段来减轻句首可能出现的重叠。本句这样译，将原文理出了主次，"树下"，"候着……汽车"等信息便被置于次要地位，这也是一种虚实转换，句子内容没有受到影响。

汉语句中信息中心多置句末，英语经常把主语放在句首，不一定照顾信息中心的位置，譬如：

[原文] 一个人的漂泊生活，我是喜欢打听的……

[译文] As I was interested in stories about wanderers...

本例前面有句"接着他便说到壮年之日，在南方那些山中冬夜走路的事情"。本例的"漂泊生活"即指前文"走路的事情"，属已知信息，置于句首作"主位"，符合汉语习惯。英译文则用 As I was interested 句式以突出主语。As 在此起衔接下句 I encouraged him to go on 的作用，其本意在原文也有，只是没有显现，英译文化虚为实。于是，汉语句式在译文中了无痕迹。

内容对等的一个重要方面是现实对等。这不但需要译者有驾驭语言的能力，还要求译者有敏锐的观察和悟性，透过形式，把握文中意蕴。

［原文］ ……只要你是一个正派的人，就可以朝灯火人家一直走去，迎着犬声…

［译文］ …and if you are a decent person, you can always turn where there is a light flickering and a dog barking.

原文没提"灯火"点燃的方式，译文添了 flickering，可又不是凭空而添。原文用"晚上""山里""灯火人家""犬""柴门"等字眼勾勒出一幅画面，译者体味到了，通过 flickering 将"灯火人家"动态化，保留了原作的美感，同时与后面的 dog barking 形成对称，凸现了原文的意境之美，可谓异曲同工。为了再现意蕴可以添，也可以减。譬如：

［原文］ 你刚开口说由哪儿来的时候，一杯很热的浓茶，就递在你的下巴边上。

［译文］ Scarcely have you begun to tell them where you come from when a cup of hot and strong tea is handed over to you.

"下巴边上"未译，现实中，客人不会等主人把茶递到嘴边。原文显然意在强调主人殷勤好客。译文若以同样方式夸张未必好。将其省略，反而自然，因为这符合读者头脑中的现实。

［原文］ 他说晚上在那些山里，只要你……

［译文］ "When you end up in the mountains at night," he said, "and if you…"

形式上，原文没有 end up 之意，原文描述的现实却有：旅途中，行人匆匆赶路，夜幕降临时，蓦然发现自己来到了一个小山村。英译文既没漏掉这一意境，也没完全将其点实，可说是虚实结合，浑然含蓄。

衔接是多层次的网络。句际、词语间等无不成衔接，进而形成语言、意义以及文体的连贯，并影响内容的现实对等和心理对等。只有把握了全文意境，并使每一细节融会于整体之中，才能使译文有神韵。译者很善于把词语具体化，以取得这种效果。例如：

[原文] 年轻的妈妈，一高兴了，便会怂恿她的孩子把拿着要吃的烧山芋，分开一半，放在你这位客人的手上。

[译文] The delighted young mother will encourage her kid to share his sweet potato with you. The kid will then break it in two and thrust one half into your hand.

原文的动词"分"与"放"单独理解是很笼统的。用 break 与 thrust 来译"分"与"放"很恰当，将孩子掰开山芋，把其中一半往客人前面一伸的情景描写得栩栩如生。

"随心所欲，不逾矩"，译者在选择词语时，在不违背生活真实的前提下，不囿于原文的形式意义，依情度势，随机应变，笔法灵巧。文中"高兴"一词的翻译就是一例：

[原文] 那蹲着的黑影，接了我的一枚铜板，就高兴地站起来向我搭话……

[译文] The shadowy figure, taking a copper coin from me with thanks, straightened up to attempt a conversation with me.

前例中的"高兴"译成 delighted，是形式意义对等，这里将"高兴"译成 with thanks，这是领会原文之后调整的结果。落魄之人受人恩惠表示感谢是合乎情理的，因而 with thanks 在这里成了表达高兴的方式。

　　再，译者洞幽烛微，很注意词汇对读者的心理感受产生的效果。

[原文]　马路两旁，远远近近都立着灯窗明灿的别墅，向暗蓝的天空静静地微笑着。

[译文]　The street was lined with fine houses, their illuminated windows beaming quietly towards the dark blue sky.

　　原文用了拟人手法。字面上，"向暗蓝的天空静静地微笑"的是别墅，不是窗户。实际上，读者心里只会将"微笑"与"明灿的窗户"联系起来，所以以 window 为逻辑主语的独立主格结构来译拟人化辞格，足见译者对生活体察的细微。更妙的是，译文没用 smiling 而用 beaming；后者不仅有"微笑"之意，也有"发光"之意，可谓一语双关。

[原文]　抬头看，四周闪着微笑的眼睛，欢迎着，毫没有怪你唐突的神情。

[译文]　When you look round you see friendly faces smiling at you; there is no hint of anything like blame for what elsewhere might be considered as brusqueness.

　　原文"眼睛"与译文中的 faces 都不可能说出欢迎的话，只能是带着"友好的"表情，译成 friendly 既符合生活真实，也忠实地传达了人物感受。相比"眼睛微笑"，"唐突"似乎不难译。但推敲一下原文的现实：山区民风淳厚，主人并不怪罪陌生人来家避寒，尽管"别的地方"会视之为唐突。若直译为 there is no hint of anything like blame for your brusqueness，读者会想：原来在主人内心，这毕竟还是唐突呵，只是不计较罢了。将 elsewhere 一用，清清楚楚消除了这一误会。一个小词，信手拈来，效果很好。

[原文] 看见他并不是个讨厌的老头子，便也高兴地说道："乡下怕更要冷些吧？"

[译文] Seeing that he was not too nasty an old man, I readily responded: "It must be colder in the country, I'm afraid."

此句的第一个小句不妨译成 Seeing that he was not too nasty an old man，但译者洞察了"我"的心理。老者来自乡下，且是要饭的，"我"呢，是城里人，对他倒不一定十分厌恶，却也未必多么喜欢，用 not too nasty 来译很恰当。

在翻译寓情于景的拟人化修辞格时，用词也很灵活。如：

[原文] 留在枝头的一两片枯叶，也不时发出破碎的哭声。

[译文] A couple of withered leaves, still clinging to the branches, rustled mournfully from time to time.

"发出破碎的哭声"烘托寂冷街头上孤独的老人，凄凉情景尽寓其中；译文是 rustled mournfully from time to time。rustle 是照顾与 leaves 的搭配，更偏重"悲"而无"哭"，这似乎削弱了原文的意境。然而，译者以 clinging 译"留"，不用 staying 或 (being) left，较之 clinging，后者不带感情，而 clinging 则使枯叶仿佛害怕随风飘落的悲凄跃然纸上。这算是对 rustled 之不足的一个补偿吧。译文从总体上仍传达了原文的气氛。

将原作与译作对照读，可见译文之天成。总之，再现原作神韵，译者需有对语言的敏感，需有想象力和审美体验。

（余东）

14

花床

缪崇群（1907—1945），作家，著有散文集《晞露集》《石屏随笔》等。《花床》选自《中华散文百年精华》，语言富有感染力。

冬天，在四周围都是山地的这里，看见太阳的日子真是太少了。今天，难得雾是这么稀薄，空中融融地混合着金黄的阳光，把地上的一切，好像也照上一层欢笑的颜色。

我走出了这黝暗的小阁，这个作为我们办公的地方，（它整年关住我！）我扬着脖子，张开了我的双臂，恨不得要把谁紧紧地拥抱起来。

由一条小径，我慢慢地走进了一个新村。这里很幽静，很精致，像一个美丽的园子。可是那些别墅里的窗帘和纱门都垂锁着，我想，富人们大概过不惯冷清的郊野的冬天，都集向热闹的城市里去了。

我停在一架小木桥上，眺望着对面山上的一片绿色，草已经枯萎了，唯有新生的麦，占有着冬天的土地。

说不出的一股香气，幽然地吹进了我的鼻孔，我一回头，才发现了在背后的一段矮坡上，铺满着一片金钱似的小花，也许是一些耐寒的雏菊，仿佛交头接耳地在私议着我这个陌生的来人：为探寻着什么而来的呢？

我低着头，看见我的影子正好像在地面上蜷伏着。我也真的愿意把自己的身子卧倒下来了，这么一片孤寂宁馥的花朵，她们自然地成就了一张可爱的床铺。虽然在冬天，土下也还是温暖的罢？

在远方，埋葬着我的亡失了的伴侣的那块土地上，在冬天，是不是只披着衰草，也还生长着不知名的花朵，为她铺着一张花床呢？

我相信，埋葬着爱的地方，在那里也蕴藏着温暖。

让悼亡的泪水，悄悄地洒在这张花床上罢。有一天，终归有一天，我也将寂寞地长眠在它的下面，这下面一定是温暖的。

仿佛为探寻什么而来，然而，我永远不能寻见什么了，除非我也睡在花床的下面，土地连接着土地，在那里面或许还有一种温暖的，爱的交流？

| 译 文 |

Flower Bed
Miao Chongqun

In winter, sunny days were scarce here, as it was surrounded by hills all around. Today, however, the fog was wonderfully thin and the air was filtered through with golden sunlight that tinted everything on the ground with a joyful hue.

I stepped out of the small dim garret—our office—where I was shut in all year round. I lifted my head and opened my arms wide as if to embrace someone in front.

I went ambling along a narrow path and came to a new village. It was a quiet and well-knit cluster of villas, like a beautiful garden. As I noticed the curtains of the windows were drawn and the screen doors locked, I guessed the wealthy residents, unaccustomed to the cold and lonesome winter there, must have swarmed into the bustling city.

Coming to a small wooden bridge, I looked toward the hill opposite and saw a patch of green spread out on the slope. The grass there had withered and new wheat was sprouting up across the wintry hillside.

As a faint aromatic scent seemed to be wafting into my nostrils, I turned, only to find a stretch of a gentle incline thickly strewn with golden-coin-like flowers. They were probably the tough daisies, whispering in private to each other about this intruder: what on earth is he looking for here?

Looking down I saw my own shadow nestling on the ground. To be sure, I would like to nestle on the ground, for these lonely and fragrant flowers would naturally make a lovely bed. Though it was winter, it had to be warm underground, I guessed.

I thought of the place in the distance where my departed life companion was buried. I hoped that it was not covered with withered grass only, but also flowers, known or unknown, growing thick enough to make a flower bed for her.

I believe where love is buried, there is warmth there.

Let my memorial tears drop quietly on the flower bed and, one day, I believe the day will eventually come, I'll be lying underneath it in my long sleep and it must be warm there.

I seem to have come here in search of something, but I'll never be able to find anything, except hoping that some day I'll go and sleep underneath the flower bed where the land is one where warmth and love interflow.

（与高巍合译）

翻 译 提 示

在这篇文章里，作者借大自然之景，抒发对亡妻的怀念之情，是一篇非同一般意义的悼文。

作者走出"黝暗的小阁"，离开"整年关住"他的地方，仰起头，张开双臂，去拥抱"金黄的阳光"。走进大自然，他看见"新生的麦"，闻见雏菊的花香，低头看见地上"孤寂宁馥的花朵……自然地成就了一张可爱的花床"，想到"虽然在冬天，土下也还是温暖的罢"？进而想起埋葬在远方的亡妻，地上是否"也还生长着不知名的花朵，为她铺着一张花床呢"？作者相信，"埋葬着爱的地方，在那里也蕴藏着温暖"。写到这里，作者的泪水洒在花床之上，期待着终有一天他将长眠地下，与亡妻共享温暖，继叙爱恋。

在这篇悼文里，我们从作者的情绪中所感受到的除了淡淡的凄婉和感伤，更多的是对冰冷无情的现实生活的远疏，以及对"温暖"和"爱"的憧憬。人间难以寻觅的东西，只有到地下去与亡妻共享。

这篇散文的感人之处是选取朴素自然的字词和句型，运用婉转含蓄的象征和联想，抒发作者对妻子真诚的怀念和向往。这虽是一篇散文，却有神话的味道。

翻译这篇文章似有两点值得考虑：

一、写景是为了抒情

下面的例句能说明这一点。

[原文] 今天，**难得**雾是这么稀薄，空中**融融地**混合着金黄的阳光，把地上的一切，好像也照上一层**欢笑的颜色**。

[译文] Today, however, the fog was **wonderfully** thin and the air was **filtered** through with golden sunlight that **tinted** everything on the ground with **a joyful hue**.

这句话里黑体的地方需做些推敲。"难得"一词在汉语里是常用词，在英语里也能设法把它的意思表达出来，如"Today, however, the fog was very thin which was rare…"，若从作者的角度体验一下他的感受，他说"难得雾是这么稀薄"时一定是怀着十分喜悦的心情，鉴于此，可将这句话译成 the fog was wonderfully thin，虽然 wonderfully 和"难得"在词义上并不对应，但从再现作者当时的心情来看，似也能产生较好的效果；"融融地"用英语怎样表达好呢？如有与其对应的词固然好，但翻译时也不必非要一字一词地对着译，若想象一下阳光透过薄雾照射到地面时的情景，将这一情景做一简单的描述，"融融地"的景象也就很自然地呈现出来，由此想到了 filter 这个字；"照上一层欢笑的颜色"，其实颜色本身并不欢笑，是作者心里高兴。综合以上几点考虑，故将这句话译成了这样。

二、抒情不是直抒其情，而是通过叙事和描写婉转含蓄地抒情

为了取得这样的效果，常需调整和变通句子结构，使其通顺、自然，符合原文的语气，下面的例句都能说明这一点。

[原文] 冬天，在四周围都是山地的这里，看见太阳的日子真是太少了。

[译文] In winter, sunny days were scarce here, as it was surrounded by hills all around.

"在四周围都是山地的这里"，在原文是一个指明地点的状语，将其译成英语的状语也可以，但实际翻译起来不太好处理，因为在汉语里，"这里"是一个状语副词，可以直译成英语的 here；可是，"这里"的前面有"在四周围都是山地的"作它的定语，这在汉语里并不少见，但在英语里却不好在 here 前面再加一个定语。从这句话的意义逻辑看，它是为"看见太阳的日子真是太少了"说明原因，因此，将其译成一个表示原因的从句也未尝不可。

[原文] 这里很幽静，**很精致**，像一个美丽的园子。

[译文] It was a quiet and **well-knit** cluster of villas, like a beautiful garden.

这句话里的"精致"需要确定它的含义，"很精致"指什么？否则译文的概念就会模糊。为了说清它的含义，特将其在汉语里作表语（形容词性谓语）的成分变成英语里形容词性的定语成分，并将后面一句话里的"别墅"提到前面来，加上一个 cluster，这样，用 well-knit 来修饰 cluster of villas，它在句中的概念就清楚了，行文也自然。

[原文] 说不出的一股香气，**幽然地**吹进了我的鼻孔……

[译文] As a **faint** aromatic scent seemed to be **wafting** into my nostrils...

这里"说不出的"和"幽然地"两个词语都没有按字面意义翻译。"说不出的"其实就是 faint，根据 *New World Dictionary* 的解释，faint 的意思是 dim，或 indistinct，这就和汉语的"说不出的"意思十分吻合；"幽然地"也无须特别翻译出来，其意已包含在动词 waft 之中，*The New Oxford Dictionary of English* 解释 waft 的意思时说，pass or cause to pass easily or gently through or as if through the air，这里的 easily or gently 很恰当地表达了"幽然地"的意思。

[原文] 在远方，埋葬着我的亡失了的伴侣的那块土地上，在冬天，是不是不只披着衰草，也还生长着不知名的花朵，为她铺着一张花床呢？

[译文] I thought of the place in the distance where my departed life companion was buried. I hoped that it was not covered with withered grass only, but also flowers, known or unknown, growing thick enough to make a flower bed for her.

此句的译文做了几处调整：第一部分的"在远方……"变成"我想到了埋葬在远方的伴侣"，这样做，句子本身的行文和与上下文的衔接都自然；"在冬天"不必译了，因为文章所说的都是冬天的事；最后一部分的问句实际上是作者的希望。

[原文] 仿佛为探寻什么而来，然而，我永远不能寻见什么了，除非我也睡在花床的下面，土地连接着土地，在那里面或许还有一种温暖的，爱的交流？

［译文］ I seem to have come here in search of something, but I'll never be able to find anything, except hoping that some day I'll go and sleep underneath the flower bed where the land is one where warmth and love interflow.

此句后一部分"除非……"的问句形式也作为"希望"处理了，因而将问句变成叙述句，顺便也把句中"或许"的意思解决了。

以上几个句子的译文都对原文做了调整，这样做是为了在忠实于原意的前提下，再现其婉转含蓄的抒情语气；若严格地按照原文的词义或句法翻译，难免出现行文不自然的现象，有悖原文叙事和描写的风格。

（与高巍合写）

15

我可能是天津人

侯宝林（1917—1993），杰出相声演员，人民艺术家。《我可能是天津人》选自《我的青少年时代》，语言雅俗共赏，幽默风趣。

　　还是从火车上说起吧！大约在我四岁多的时候，我坐过火车。当时带我坐车的人，是我的舅舅，叫张全斌。我记得那时我的打扮挺滑稽的，穿着蓝布大褂、小坎肩，戴瓜皮小帽。那时候，小孩儿打扮成那个样子，够不错了。在我的童年中，也就只有过这么一次。在火车上，因为小，没坐过火车，也很少见过家里以外的人，觉得挺新鲜。也许人在幼年时代终归想要些温暖吧！那时舅舅抱着我，哄着我，我觉得很温暖。一路上吃了半斤炒栗子，睡了一会儿觉，就到了北京。根据这个情况，现在估计起来，我可能是从天津来的。我现在对我原来的父母还有个模糊不清的印象，父亲、母亲的形象还能回忆起一点儿，但很模糊。究竟家里姓什么？哪里人？

不知道。我只知道自己的生日和乳名。生日是自己长大以后听家里大人说的，是农历十月十五酉时生人，所以我的乳名叫"酉"，北京人的习惯爱用儿化韵，前面加个"小"，后面加"儿"，就叫"小酉儿"。关于我个人的历史情况，我就知道这一些，再多一点都记不起来了。

| 译文 |

I May Have Come from Tianjin
Hou Baolin

Let me begin with my trip on the train. When I was about four years old I had traveled by train. The man I traveled with was my uncle Zhang Quanbin. I still remember how funny I looked the way I was dressed—in a blue cloth gown with a short sleeveless jacket over it, and with a skullcap on the head. In those days it was good enough for small kids to be dressed like that. However, it was my only experience to boast about in my childhood. As I had never traveled by train before, nor had I met anyone outside my family, I found that everything I saw on the train was new to me. Probably, in childhood, one always needs some comfort. Sitting in my uncle's lap, being humored all the way, I was feeling very good. We ate half a *jin* of roast chestnuts, had a nap and soon arrived in Beijing. I assume, from what I mentioned above, I may have come from Tianjin. Even today I can recollect what my parents looked like but, of course, my impression is blurry. As for what my family name was and where my parents came from, I really don't know. I only remember my birthday and my infant name. I was told about my birthday by my foster parents when I grew up. I was born in the "you" period (between 5—7 p.m.), 15th of the 10th month of the Chinese lunar year. So I was named *You*. Prefixed with *Xiao*—young, and suffixed with a diminutive *er*—an intimate way of addressing young and small things by Beijingers, my name, therefore, became *Xiao You'r*. This is all I know about my childhood and beyond that I do not remember much else.

| 翻 译 提 示 |

1982 年，侯宝林为年轻人写了《我的青少年时代》，这里选了该书的开头一段。侯宝林是伟大的相声演员，天才艺术家，他说相声的造诣，无人能与之相提并论。他经历过艰苦的磨难，对生活有自己的体验；他有敏锐的艺术感受力，能从历史和现实中察觉美与丑；他有艺术家的天赋和气质，他懂得什么是幽默；他的语言好，有魅力。他没上过学，可他的语言，各个文化层次的人都喜欢。

这段文字是一个意思和形式都完整的段落，作者讲述自己幼年时代的经历，文字通俗、活泼、含蓄，使人感觉亲切。译文从整体上应表现这个风格。

下面举几个例子来说明：

［原文］ 还是从火车上说起吧！
［译文］ Let me begin with my trip on the train。

这是一个常用的汉语祈使句，翻译时也用英语祈使句式，但不能照字面直说 "Let me begin from the train."。作者要说的是从他在火车上的经历开始。"Let me begin with my trip on the train."，这样符合作者的意思，口气也与原文吻合。

[原文] 大约在我四岁多的时候，我坐过火车。
[译文] When I was about four years old I had traveled by train.

"坐过火车"或"坐过飞机"，都是指旅行，而不是指曾经在什么上"坐过"。所以此句译成 I had traveled by train 为好。

[原文] 当时带我坐车的人，是我的舅舅，叫张全斌。
[译文] The man I traveled with was my uncle Zhang Quanbin.

这句话里的"带"不是狭义的带，是"跟我一起"或"照看我"的意思，若译成 The man I traveled with 或 The man who was with me was 或 The man who took care of me was 等，较接近原文。

[原文] 我记得那时我的打扮挺滑稽的，穿着蓝布大褂、小坎肩，戴瓜皮小帽。
[译文] I still remember how funny I looked **the way** I was dressed——in a blue cloth gown with a short sleeveless jacket over it, and with a skullcap on the head.

这个句子前半句说"滑稽"，后半句说为什么"滑稽"，虽没有连接词，但前后连贯，意思完整、紧凑。英译文也应努力做到这样。用 the way 连接前后两个半句，关联着前面的 funny，也照应了后面的"打扮"，然后在 dressed 的后面加一个破折号，说明是如何 dressed。这个英语句子可算完整、紧凑，也是一个符合英语习惯的句型。

[原文] 那时舅舅抱着我，哄着我，我觉得很温暖。

［译文］ Sitting in my uncle's lap, being humored all the way, I was feeling very good.

这是一个很短的句子，却有主语转移现象，在汉语这种现象很自然，用英语将其直译出来也未尝不可，但若把句子做适当调整，由一个主语领衔似乎更好。

［原文］ 生日是自己长大以后听家里大人说的，是农历十月十五酉时生人，所以我的乳名叫"酉"，北京人的习惯爱用儿化韵，前面加个"小"，后面加"儿"，就叫"小酉儿"。

［译文］ I was told about my birthday by my foster parents when I grew up. I was born in the "you" period (between 5—7 p.m.), 15th of the 10th month of the Chinese lunar year. So I was named *You*. Prefixed with *Xiao*—young, and suffixed with a diminutive *er*—an intimate way of addressing young and small things by Beijingers, my name, therefore, became *Xiao You'r*.

这句话涉及了汉语里特有的文化现象，"酉时生人"及"儿化韵"，"酉"做音译，但需附解释，"I was born in the 'you' period (between 5—7 p.m.), 15th of the 10th month of the Chinese lunar year."。"儿化韵"也做同样处理。此句的核心部分是"前面加个'小'，后面加'儿'，（我的名字）就叫'小酉儿'"。"北京人的习惯爱用儿化韵"，因为"儿化韵"的意思已经由 diminutive *er* 表示了，后面用破折号的形式解释一下就可以了。

16

生命的三分之一

邓拓（1912—1966），新闻工作者，历史学家，政论家，诗人。《生命的三分之一》选自《中国现代百家千字文》，语言有说服力。

一个人的生命究竟有多大意义，这有什么标准可以衡量吗？提出一个绝对的标准当然很困难；但是，大体上看一个人对待生命的态度是否严肃认真，看他对待劳动、工作等等的态度如何，也就不难对这个人的存在意义做出适当的估计了。

古来一切有成就的人，都很严肃地对待自己的生命，当他活着一天，总要尽量多劳动、多工作、多学习，不肯虚度年华，不让时间白白地浪费掉。我国历代的劳动人民以及大政治家、大思想家等等都莫不如此。

班固写的《汉书·食货志》上有下面的记载："冬，民既入；妇人同巷，相从夜绩，女工一月得四十五日。"

这几句读起来很奇怪，怎么一月能有四十五天呢？再看原文底下颜师古做了注解，他说："一月之中，又得夜半为十五日，共四十五日。"

这就很清楚了。原来我国的古人不但比西方各国的人更早地懂得科学地、合理地计算劳动日，而且我们的古人老早就知道对于日班和夜班的计算方法。

一个月本来只有三十天，古人把每个夜晚的时间算作半日，就多了十五天，从这个意义上说来，夜晚的时间实际上不就等于生命的三分之一吗？

对于这三分之一的生命，不但历代的劳动人民如此重视，而且有许多大政治家也十分重视。班固在《汉书·刑法志》里还写道："秦始皇躬操文墨，昼断狱，夜理书。"

有的人一听说秦始皇就不喜欢他，其实秦始皇毕竟是中国历史上的一个伟大人物，班固对他也还有一些公平的评价。这里写的是秦始皇在夜间看书学习的情形。

据刘向的《说苑》所载，春秋战国时有许多国君都很注意学习。如："晋平公问于师旷曰：吾年七十，欲学恐已暮矣。师旷曰：何不炳烛乎？"

在这里，师旷劝七十岁的晋平公点灯夜读，拼命抢时间，争取这三分之一的生命不至于继续浪费，这种精神多么可贵啊！

《北史·吕思礼传》记述这个北周大政治家生平勤学的情形是："虽务兼军国，而手不释卷。昼理政事，夜即读书，令苍头执烛，烛烬夜有数升。"

光是烛灰一夜就有几升之多，可见他夜读何等勤奋了。像这样的例子还有很多。

为什么古人对于夜晚的时间都这样重视，不肯轻轻放过呢？我认为这就是他们对待自己生命的三分之一的严肃认真态度，这正是我们所应该学习的。

我之所以想利用夜晚的时间，向读者同志们做这样的谈话，目的也不过是要引起大家注意珍惜这三分之一的生命，使大家在整天的劳动、工作以后，以轻松的心情，领略一些古今有用的知识而已。

| 译文 |

One Third of Our Lifetime
Deng Tuo

What is the significance of life? Is there a standard by which we can measure it? It is difficult, of course, to advance a well-defined standard. However, the significance of one's existence can more or less be evaluated by examining his attitude toward life and work.

Since ancient times all people of accomplishment are serious about their lives. So long as they are alive, they try to work as hard as they can and learn as much as possible, never letting a day slip by doing nothing. This is true of the working people, and the great statesmen and thinkers in our history.

The great historian Ban Gu, in his "Foods and Goods" of *The Chronicles of the Han Dynasty*, says:

"In winter people stay indoors. Women get together to spin hemp threads at night. They work forty-five days a month."

It sounds strange. How come there are forty-five days in a month? Let us see how it is annotated by Yan Shigu:

"Every night they work an extra of half a day's time and, therefore, they have forty-five days in a month."

Now it's clear. Our ancestors had learned, earlier than the westerners, how to calculate workdays accurately and sensibly. They had also learned how to distinguish between day shift and night shift.

Our forefathers, counting the time of one night for half a day, managed to extend the thirty-day-month by fifteen days. In this sense the night time gained makes up one third of our lives, doesn't it?

This one third of our lifetime is not only treasured by the working people but also by the great statesmen in our history. Ban Gu also says in "Criminal Law" of *The Chronicles of the Han Dynasty*:

"The First Emperor of the Qin Dynasty set a good example of industry, disposing of lawsuits during the day and reading at night." This is about how he tried to find time to read at night.

To some people the First Emperor of Qin isn't a pleasant name to hear but there is no denying that he was a great figure in the history of China. Even Ban Gu has an impartial comment to make on him.

Liu Xiang, the great scholar of the Han Dynasty, cites in his *Historical Anecdotes* many princes of the Spring and Autumn and the Warring States period who set great store by learning. For example:

"Duke Ping of the State of Jin asked Shikuang: 'I am already seventy years old. Isn't it too late for me to learn?' Shikuang suggested: 'Why not make use of your night time?'"

Here Shikuang encouraged the seventy-year-old Duke Ping to read at night, making up for the one third of the lifetime. What a great spirit!

"The biography of Lu Sili" in *The History of the Four Northern Dynasties*, in stating what a diligent learner this great statesman was, says:

"Though he took responsibilities for both administrative and military affairs, he was never seen without a book in his hands. He tended state affairs during the day and read at night with a servant holding a wood torch for him. At the end of each reading you would find so much ash in his study as to fill several *sheng*."

We can imagine how avidly he read at night. There are more examples of this kind in the book.

Why did the people in the past make such effective use of night time? I think this is positive proof of their attitude toward the one third of their lives. This is exactly where we should learn from them.

My idea of writing this little essay tonight is to call the reader's attention to the one third of his lifetime so that, after the day's work, he can sit relaxed at home, browsing through and appreciating the useful knowledge of the past and of the present.

（与段钧金合译）

| 翻 译 提 示 |

邓拓的杂文多是有感而发，有较强的思想性和知识性。《生命的三分之一》就是这样。他旁征博引，评古论今，劝说人们珍惜光阴努力学习，文章很有意义。

作者广博的历史知识和驾驭汉语的能力也给文章翻译带来了困难。但是，这篇译文读来却是译笔流畅，衔接自然，意义连贯。即使对中国历史知之不多的读者，读后也能一目了然，并能感受到说理文（essay）的魅力。我们分别来看。

一、篇章的衔接和连贯

有学者指出衔接是篇章的一种特征，连贯则是对篇章评价的一个方面；前者是客观的，后者是主观的。英汉两种语言中衔接的手段差不太多，但在具体篇章中的运用却有差别。如果把汉语中自然衔接的语句都直接翻译成英语，不一定是好的译文。本文译者在译文的衔接和意义的连贯上处理得当。来看几个译例：

1) **Now** it's clear. **Our ancestors** had learned, earlier than the westerners, how to calculate workdays accurately and sensibly. **They** had also learned how to distinguish between day shift and night shift.

2) **The great historian Ban Gu**, in his "Foods and Goods" of *The Chronicles of the Han Dynasty*, says…

3) In this sense the night time gained makes up **one third of our lives**, doesn't it?

4) To some people, the First Emperor of Qin isn't a pleasant name to hear but there is no denying that he was…

篇章衔接的手段不外乎指称（reference）、省略（ellipsis）、替代（substitution）、连接（conjunction）和词汇衔接（lexical cohesion），它们是篇章客观上表现出来的特征，但在中英两种语言中体现出的效果却是不同。在例1里，译者在原文中的指示指称词"这"之前巧妙地增加了时间副词 Now，贴切自然。而后面原文中的"我国的古人"和"我们的古人"是利用了词汇衔接中重述的衔接手段；译者翻译时使用了指示 They，这样在英文中既指代明确，又符合英语表达习惯。例2、3、4的英译较之原文不是增添了一些衔接的词句就是在语序上做了重大调整，译文衔接流畅，逻辑清晰，而且还补译出了英文读者不具备的言外知识，意义连贯，处理恰当。

二、译文的文体与措辞

这篇文章属于论说文体，前半部分多以稍微正式的非个人性口吻（impersonal tone）来论证观点，后半部分又以较为随便的个人性口吻（personal tone）作结，规劝读者珍惜光阴。文字简洁准确，说理充分且无赘言。译文也同样做到了句子节奏明快，措辞轻重有别，使得全文形神俱现。例如：

5) What is the significance of life? Is there a standard by which we can **measure** it? It is difficult, of course, to **advance a well-defined standard**. However, the significance of one's existence can **more or less** be evaluated by examining his attitude toward life and work.

6) Since ancient times all **people of accomplishment** are serious about their lives…**This is true of** the working people, and the great statesmen and thinkers in our history.

7) "Duke Ping of the State of Jin asked Shikuang: 'I am already seventy years old. **Isn't it too late for me to learn?**' Shikuang suggested: '**Why not make use of your night time?**'"

例 5 是文章的开头，原文以两个分句构成一个问句，译文很自然地把它转成两个问句，有很强的节奏感。而 advance a well-defined standards 和 more or less 以及例 6 中 people of accomplishment 和 This is true of 都是相对于论说文体使用的较为正式的词语或句子结构，这样不但符合叙述者说话的语气，也增强了文章的文学色彩。例 7 中黑体部分是两个反问句，加之上述例 3，总起来是本篇所使用的三个不同形式的修辞性疑问句。这样处理不仅保留了原文的形式，而且准确传达了原文的精神，以较为口语化的句式拉近了读者与文章的距离，使得论述深入浅出。读者亦能从这篇措辞严谨、文体把握准确的译文中感受到英文说理文的力与美。

总体看来，这篇英译文衔接自然，节奏紧凑，语义连贯完整，逻辑性强，在文体的把握上是很好的。

（丁连普）

17

枯叶蝴蝶

徐迟（1914—1996），作家，主要著作有报告文学集《我们这时代的人》《哥德巴赫猜想》等。《枯叶蝴蝶》选自《中国现代百家千字文》，语言犀利。

峨眉山下，伏虎寺旁，有一种蝴蝶，比最美丽的蝴蝶可能还要美丽些，是峨眉山最珍贵的特产之一。

当它阖起两张翅膀的时候，像生长在树枝上的一张干枯了的树叶。谁也不去注意它，谁也不会瞧它一眼。

它收敛了它的花纹、图案，隐藏了它的粉墨、彩色，逸出了繁华的花丛，停止了它翱翔的姿态，变成了一张憔悴的，干枯了的，甚至不是枯黄的，而是枯槁的，如同死灰颜色的枯叶。

它这样伪装，是为了保护自己。但是它还是逃不脱被捕捉的命运。不仅因为它的美丽，更因为它那用来隐蔽它的美丽的枯槁与憔悴。

它以为它这样做可以保护自己，殊不知它这样做更教人去搜捕它。有一种生物比它还聪明，这种生物的特技之一是装假作伪，因此装假作伪这种行径是瞒不过这种生物——人的。

人把它捕捉，将它制成标本，作为一种商品去出售，价钱越来越高。最后几乎把它捕捉得再也没有了。这一生物品种快要绝种了。

到这时候，国家才下令禁止捕捉枯叶蝶。但是，已经来不及了。国家的禁止更增加了它的身价。枯叶蝶真是因此而要绝对的绝灭了。

我们既然有一对美丽的和真理的翅膀，我们永远也不愿意阖上它们。做什么要装模作样，化为一只枯叶蝶，最后也还是被售，反而不如那翅膀两面都光彩夺目的蝴蝶到处飞翔，被捕捉而又生生不息。

我要我的翅膀两面都光彩夺目。

我愿这自然界的一切都显出它们的真相。

Lappet Butterflies
Xu Chi

At the foot of Mount Emei, around Fuhu Temple, there lives a species of butterfly—one of the rarest rarities of the mountain that is probably even more beautiful than the most beautiful butterflies in the world.

When it closes its wings it resembles a withered tree leaf hanging from a branch—scarcely noticeable to the human eye. When it gathers its wings full of exquisite patterns, it conceals its beautiful colors.

When it flutters out from a cluster of blooming flowers and alights somewhere in the middle of its graceful flight, it turns into a dried leaf, not even of a withering yellow, but of a deathly grey.

It disguises its shape and colors in order to protect itself, but it can't help ending up in being captured, nevertheless, not just because of its beauty, but more because of the withered quality of its appearance that covers up its beauty.

It is misled to believe that by so doing it can keep itself out of danger. Unfortunately, it doesn't understand that by so doing it makes itself more vulnerable, because there is another creature—man—that is cleverer than this butterfly. This creature is extremely skilled in the trade of masquerading; no other masquerading can slide by under his nose.

Man captures it, makes a specimen of it and sells it in the market at increasingly high prices. What happens as a result is that there is hardly any of the butterflies to be found—the species is on the brink of dying out.

The government has now decided to put a ban on its capture, but it's too late. The ban, instead, has helped to escalate its price. The butterfly is virtuely on the verge of extinction.

Since we have got a pair of wings of beauty and truth, we will never close them up. Why do you have to put on the appearance of a withered-leaf-like butterfly, as you are sure to be netted and sold at the market anyway? Isn't it better to fly around freely on your colorful, flashing wings and, despite of the danger of falling prey to man, keep up the line of your species?

I want both sides of my wings to shine.

I like everything in the world to show their true colors.

| 翻 译 提 示 |

作者借自然现象说明生活哲理，既描绘了自然生态之美，又阐释了作者的生活哲学，很有情趣，富有寓意。第一段是对枯叶蝴蝶的概括描写，谈了它的生活环境和它的审美价值——它的美丽和它的稀有。文字简明准确。然后是对枯叶蝴蝶的外观和特性的描写，作者借以抒发了自己的处世准则。这两点是文章的主要内容。下面看几个句子的翻译：

[原文] 峨眉山下，伏虎寺旁，有一种蝴蝶，比最美丽的蝴蝶可能还要美丽些，是峨眉山最珍贵的特产之一。

[译文] At the foot of Mount Emei, around Fuhu Temple, there lives a species of butterfly—one of the rarest rarities of the mountain that is probably even more beautiful than the most beautiful butterflies in the world.

这是一个比较自然的句子，而且读起来有一种向前的语势。翻译时应把这句话的自然和向前的语势反映出来。后面两个小句的次序做了颠倒，这是因为英译文 that is probably even more beautiful than the most beautiful butterflies in the world 中的意思更重要，句子也长些，更适合放在句尾。

[原文] 当它阖起两张翅膀的时候，像生长在树枝上的一张干枯了的树叶。谁也不去注意它，谁也不会瞧它一眼。

[译文] When it closes its wings it resembles a withered tree leaf hanging from a branch—scarcely noticeable to the human eye.

"谁也不去注意它，谁也不会瞧它一眼"，意即不易引起人的注意，将这句话译成上面的样子，符合原文的意思。

[原文] 不仅因为它的美丽，更因为它那用来隐蔽它的美丽的枯槁与憔悴。

[译文] …not just because of its beauty, but more because of the withered quality of its appearance that covers up its beauty.

译文用 the withered quality of its appearance 概括了汉语的"枯槁与憔悴"，也应该是可以的。

[原文] 人把它捕捉，将它制成标本，作为一种商品去出售，价钱越来越高。最后几乎把它捕捉得再也没有了。这一生物品种快要绝种了。

[译文] Man captures it, makes a specimen of it and sells it in the market at increasingly high prices. What happens as a result is that there is hardly any of the butterflies to be found—the species is on the brink of dying out.

这个句子节奏短促，翻译时也尽量用短句，保持原文的节奏。"最后"二字，没有译成 Finally，而是译成了 What happens as a result，也是考虑到节奏应与前面一致。快节奏表达的是一种焦急忧虑的心情。

[原文] 我们既然有一对美丽的和真理的翅膀，我们永远也不愿意阖上它们。做什么要装模作样，化为一只枯叶蝶，最后也还是被售，反而不如那翅膀两面都光彩夺目的蝴蝶到处飞翔，被捕捉而又生生不息。

[译文] Since we have got a pair of wings of beauty and truth, we will never close them up. Why do you have to put on the appearance of a withered-leaf-like butterfly, as you are sure to be netted and sold at the market anyway? Isn't it better to fly around freely on your colorful, flashing wings and, despite of the danger of falling prey to man, keep up the line of your species?

这一段（以及结尾两句话）是作者在这篇文章里要点明的意图。原文第二句的前半句是反问句（rhetorical question），译文用了反问句；后半句是陈述句（declarative sentence），译文也用了反问句，而且两个反问句连起来，更突出地表达了作者的意思。

（与马会娟合写）

18

向日葵

冯亦代（1913—2005），出版家，作家，翻译家。著有散文集《书人书事》《漫步纽约》等。《向日葵》选自《中华散文百年精华》，文章情真感人。

看到外国报刊登载了久已不见的梵高名画《向日葵》，以三千九百万美元的高价，在伦敦拍卖成交，特别是又一次看到原画的照片，心中怏怏若有所失者久之；因为这是一幅我所钟爱的画。当然我永远不会有可以收藏这幅画的家财，但这也禁不住我对它的喜欢。如今归为私人所有，总有种今后不复再能为人们欣赏的遗憾。我虽无缘亲见此画，但我觉得名画有若美人，美人而有所属，不免是件憾事。

记得自己也曾经有过这幅同名而布局略异的复制品。是抗战胜利后在上海买的。有天在陕西南路街头散步，在一家白俄经营小书店的橱窗里看到陈列着一幅梵高名画集的复制品。梵高是 19 世纪以来对现代绘画形成颇有影响的大师，我不懂画，但我喜欢他的强烈色调，明亮的画幅上带着些淡淡的哀愁和寂寞感。《向日葵》是他的系列名画，一共画了七幅，四幅收藏在博物馆里，一幅毁于第二次世界大战时的日本横滨，这次拍卖的则是留在私人手中的最后两幅之一；当下我花了四分之一的月薪，买下了这幅梵高的精致复制品。

我特别喜欢他的那幅《向日葵》，朵朵黄花有如明亮的珍珠，耀人眼目，但孤零零插在花瓶里，配着黄色的背景，给人的是种凄凉的感觉，似乎是盛宴散后，灯烛未灭的那种空荡荡的光景，令人为之心沉。我原是爱看向日葵的，每天清晨看它们缓缓转向阳光，洒着露珠，是那样的楚楚可怜亦复可爱。如今得了这幅画便把它装上镜框，挂在寓所餐室里。向日葵衬在一片明亮亮的黄色阳光里，挂在漆成墨绿色的墙壁上。宛如亭亭伫立在一望无际的原野中。特别怡目，但又显得孤清。每天我就这样坐在这幅画的对面，看到了欢欣，也尝到了寂寞。以后我读了欧文·斯通的《生活的渴望》，是关于梵高短暂一生的传记。他只活了三十七岁；半生在探索色彩的癫狂中生活，最后自杀了。他不善谋生，但在艺术上却走出了自己的道路，虽然到死后很久，才为人们所承认。我读了这本书，为他执著的生涯所感动，因此更宝贵他那得含蓄多姿的向日葵。我似乎懂得了他的画为什么一半欢欣，一半寂寞的道理。

解放了，我到北京工作，这幅画却没有带来；总觉得这幅画面与当时四周的气氛不相合拍似的。因为解放了，周围已没有落寞之感，一切都沉浸在节日的欢乐之中。但是曾几何时，我又怀恋起这幅画来了。似乎人就像是这束向日葵，即使在落日的余晖里，都拼命要抓住这逐渐远去的夕阳。我想起了深绿色的那面墙，它一时掩没了这一片耀眼的金黄；我曾努力驱散那随着我身影的孤寂，在作无望的挣扎。以后星移斗转，慢慢这一片金黄，在我的记忆里也不自觉地淡漠起来，逐渐疏远得几乎被遗忘了。

十年动乱中，我被谪放到南荒的劳改农场，每天做着我力所不及的劳役，心情惨淡得自己也害怕。有天我推着粪车，走过一家农民的茅屋，从篱笆里探出头来的是几朵嫩黄的向日葵，衬托在一抹碧蓝的天色里。我突然想起了上海寓所那面墨绿色墙上挂着的梵高《向日葵》。我忆起那时家庭的欢欣，三岁女儿在学着大人腔说话，接着她也发觉自己学得不像，便嘻嘻笑了起来，爬上桌子指着我在念的书，说"等我大了，我也要念这个"。而现在眼前只有几朵向日葵招呼着我，我的心不住沉落又飘浮，没个去处。以后每天拾粪，即使要多走不少路，也宁愿到这处来兜个圈。我只是想看一眼那几朵慢慢变成灰黄色的向日葵，重温一些旧时的欢乐：一直到有一天农民把熟透了的果实收藏了进去。我记得那一天我走过这家农家时，篱笆里孩子们正在争夺丰收的果实，一片笑声里夹着尖叫；我也想到了我远在北国的女儿，她现在如果就夹杂在这群孩子的喧哗中，该多幸福！但如果她看见自己的父亲，衣衫褴褛，推着沉重的粪车，她又作何感想？我噙着眼里的泪水往回走。我又想起了梵高那幅《向日葵》，他在画这画时，心头也许远比我尝到人世更大的孤凄，要不他为什么画出行将衰败的花朵呢？但他也梦想欢欣，要不他又为什么要用这耀眼的黄色作底呢？

梵高的《向日葵》已经卖入富人家，可那幅复制品，却永远陪伴着我的记忆；难免想起作画者对生活的疯狂渴望。人的一生尽管有多少波涛起伏，对生活的热爱却难能泯灭。阳光的金色不断出现在我的眼前，这原是梵高的《向日葵》说出了我未能一表的心思。

Sunflowers

Feng Yidai

When I learned from a foreign newspaper that Vincent van Gogh's *Sunflowers* was auctioned off in London for 39 million U.S. dollars, especially when again I saw its photo that I had long missed seeing, I was kind of depressed, as if something were getting away from me, because it was the painting I loved with all my heart. I knew I could never be wealthy enough to afford it, but I cherished a great love for it. Now, having fallen into some private collection, it would not be available for the public to appreciate any more. What a pity! I had never had the good luck to see the original but, to me, a masterpiece is like a beauty and when the beauty is claimed by someone else you feel deprived of your access to her.

I remember once having a reproduction of the painting under the same title with a slightly different composition. I bought it in Shanghai after the War of Resistance against Japanese Aggression. One day, I was strolling along southern-Shaanxi Street when I caught sight of the painting in the window of a small bookstore run by some Russian. It was a copy from the collection of van Gogh's masterpieces. Vincent van Gogh was a master having a great influence on modern painting since the 19th century. I do not know much about art, but I like the intense hues with a tinge of forlornness against the brilliance in his paintings. *Sunflowers* is one of the seven masterpieces of a series, four of which were in museums, one damaged in Yokohama, Japan, during World War

II and the one auctioned in London was one of the last two in private collections. I took the exquisite reproduction there and then, for a quarter of my salary of that month.

I like his *Sunflowers* in particular, with its glorious blossoms glittering like pearls, but the blossoms, placed in a vase against a yellow background, look lonesome and make you feel miserable, the way you feel when the feast is over and the guests are gone but the lights and candles are still glimmering in the deserted hall. I enjoyed seeing the sunflowers when in the morning they slowly turned to the sun, dripping with dew—pitiful but gorgeous. I mounted the painting in a frame and hung it on the wall of our dining room. The wall was painted dark green and the sunflowers in the painting, as if standing in an endless field bathed in bright sunshine, looked pleasing but solitary. Every day I sat in front of it, filled with joy and shrouded in loneliness. Later I came to know from Irving Stone's *Lust for Life*, a biography of van Gogh's short life, that he lived for 37 years only but spent half of his lifetime trying crazily to find out about the mystery of colors until he ended up in death by suicide. Vincent van Gogh was not good at making a living, but he had carved a new path for himself in art, though the artist was not recognized until many years after his death. Having read this book, I was moved by his devotedness to art and loved his *Sunflowers* all the more for its gracefulness and suggestiveness. I seemed to understand why joyfulness and loneliness are inherently mixed in his works.

After 1949 I was transferred to Beijing. I did not take the painting with me, as I felt that it was quite out of tune with the milieu of the time. In the liberated society we were immersed in a festival atmosphere and there was not the slightest suggestion of loneliness. But soon I began to miss the painting again. It seemed as if man, like this bunch of sunflowers, would try to hang on to the setting sun in its afterglow. I thought of that dark green wall that seemed to have engulfed the brilliant yellow. I tried desperately to disperse the loneliness that followed me like a shadow but in vain. With the passage of time the golden yellow in my memory had grown dim, so dim that I had gradually forgotten about it.

During the chaotic ten years (1966—1976) I was banished to a farm in Nanhuang to reform through labor. I was forced to work beyond my endurance and I was in such a gloomy state of mind that I often found myself scared. One day as I was pushing a dung-cart past a farmer's thatched hut, I saw some fresh yellowish sunflowers craning out of its fence sky. They reminded me of van Gogh's *Sunflowers* on the dark green wall in my house in Shanghai, calling back to mind the joys of the family: our three-year-old daughter was trying to speak the way adults do and, when she realized that her mimicking was funny, she giggled and then, climbing up to the desk and pointing to the book I was reading, said, "when I am grown, I will read this too." But now in front of me, there were only a few sunflowers nodding at me and that sent my heart sinking and floating around, not knowing where to stop. Since then each time I went dung-collecting, I would go and pass that hut even if I had to walk a longer distance in the round of my daily journey. I wanted to see the sunflowers that were turning grayish yellow, reminiscing the cheerfulness of the days gone by, until one day the farmer got the crops in. When I passed the farmers hut that day, I heard some kids laughing and screaming inside the fence, each trying to get a fair share of the seeds from the crops. I then thought of my daughter in the far north.

How excited she would be if she were among the kids, making such noises with them. However, if she had seen her own dad pushing the heavy dung-cart in his shabby clothes as they were, how would that have made her feel? As I was on my way back with tears in my eyes my thoughts turned to van Gogh and his *Sunflowers* again. When he was working on the painting, he might have felt more loneliness and misery of life, otherwise why did he paint the pedals going to wither? He must have dreamed of joy, otherwise why should he have placed the petals against an intense yellow background?

Now van Gogh's *Sunflowers* has become a rich man's private property but that reproduction of the painting lives on in my memory, reminding me of the artist's crazy lust for life. Though one has ups and downs to face down the road, his love for life is hard to fade away. That the golden color of the sunshine keeps popping up before my eyes is an indication that van Gogh's *Sunflowers* voices the feelings I have been unable to express myself.

（与温秀颖合译）

| 翻 译 提 示 |

"阅历知书味，艰难识世情。"读罢这篇文章，感到作者对人生对艺术的感受是那样的真挚，那样的深入事理。世事艰难，人生多舛，他仍能看见"阳光的金色不断出现在……眼前"。作者对梵高《向日葵》的阐释得益于一个饱经世事的老人对人生的体验和一个作家与画家心灵的相通。

《向日葵》是一篇好文章，所写的事情不论是从生活的还是从艺术的角度看都是那样的真实。作者在篇幅不长的文字里，组织了纵横交错的多层内容。从《向日葵》的原作联想到自己当年购买的复制品；从艺术的《向日葵》写到长在农家庭院里植物的向日葵；从"解放"前对《向日葵》的挚爱到"解放"后感到它的与"四周的气氛不相合拍"；从作者在"文革"中所受的煎熬到"文革"后对人生的思考；从自己的困顿联想到孩子的天真烂漫；从家庭到社会，从生活到政治；从梵高写到自己——梵高的《向日葵》说出了本文作者"未能一表的心思"。

作者在《向日葵》里所说的都是真心话。他坦诚而又委婉地表露自己的心境："人的一生尽管有多少波涛起伏，对生活的热爱却难能泯灭。"梵高曾"尝到人世更大的孤凄"，但他"也梦想欢欣"。这篇文章虽然文字平淡，但因作者以其真诚的心描写真实的事，并由此引发对人生和艺术的诸多思考，而且多是真知灼见，所以读来感人。

在对生活进行思考和对艺术进行解读时，作者的心情是复杂的，但他的思绪是清晰的。深入理解作者的思想和感情，领会作者行文叙事的风格，这对译者在翻译时发现和传达文章的诗意很重要。因此，在动手翻译之前和在实际翻译的过程中，揣摩作者未曾直叙的内心感受非常重要。

以上所说是属于理解方面的事情，现就几个例子略加讨论。

［原文］　如今归为私人所有，总有种今后不复再能为人们欣赏的遗憾。我虽无缘亲见此画，但我觉得名画有若美人，美人而有所属，不免是件憾事。

［译文］　Now, having fallen into some private collection, it would not be available for the public to appreciate any more. **What a pity!** I had never had the good luck to see the original but, to me, a masterpiece is like a beauty and when the beauty is claimed by someone else **you feel deprived of your access to her**.

在这两句话里，作者先是说"遗憾"，后又说"憾事"，意思无大差别。作者虽然重复意思相近的词语，但其所表达的情感有程度上的不同。前面的"遗憾"用一个独立的感叹句"What a pity!"译出；后面的"憾事"比前面的"遗憾"情感色彩更重些。作者将梵高的《向日葵》比作美人，当他钟爱的"美人""有所属"时，感情上的反应要比一般意义上的"憾事"强烈。因此将其译成 you feel deprived of your access to her，这样译也许是可以接受的。

[原文] 我记得那一天我走过这家农家时，篱笆里孩子们正在争夺丰收的果实，一片笑声里夹着尖叫；我也想到了我远在北国的女儿，她现在如果就夹杂在这群孩子的喧哗中，该多幸福！但如果她看见自己的父亲，衣衫褴褛，推着沉重的粪车，她又作何感想？

[译文] When I passed the farmer's hut that day, I heard some kids laughing and screaming inside the fence, each trying to get a fair share of the seeds from the crops. I then thought of my daughter in the far north. How excited she would be if she were among the kids, making such noises with them. However, if she had seen her own dad pushing the heavy dung-cart in his shabby clothes as they were, **how would that have made her feel**?

作者看见农家的孩子而想起自己远在异地的女儿，但若女儿真的来到身边，看见自己狼狈的样子，她会作何感想呢？作者触景生情，情感的波动真切而自然。最后一句"她又作何感想？"译成"…how would that have made her feel?"，强调是情感上的反应，特别是最后三个字，作为句子的结尾，在音节上重—轻—重的排列，读起来有力量。

[原文] 人的一生尽管有多少波涛起伏，对生活的热爱却难能泯灭。阳光的金色不断出现在我的眼前，这原是梵高的《向日葵》说出了我未能一表的心思。

[译文] Though one has ups and downs to face down the road, his love for life is hard to fade away. That the golden color of the sunshine keeps popping up before my eyes is an indication that van Gogh's *Sunflowers* voices the feelings I have been unable to express myself.

　　结尾的这几句话很富有诗意。虽然经历了很多坎坷，对生活的爱却不曾泯灭；眼前仍然是阳光的金色。因为梵高虽然曾"尝到人世更大的孤凄"，但他"也梦想欢欣"；《向日葵》里"耀眼的黄色"映着作者眼前的金色，作者和画家是心灵相通的。这就是为什么他特别"钟爱"《向日葵》的原因。最后一句的译文用一个主语从句开始，再用一个同位语从句译出此文最要紧的一句话，两个 that 引导两个长度均衡的从句，有委婉、含蓄的效果。

　　英国《企鹅丛书》古典文学主编瑞奥（E. V. Rieu）在其所译的荷马史诗《奥德赛》的序言中说：

　　我认为，在荷马的作品中，内容与形式是紧密结合，不可分割的。事实上，所有伟大作家的作品莫不如此。因此，在英语散文写作方式允许的范围内，我不仅一直在努力传达荷马说了什么，而且试图传达出他是怎样说的……为了在译文中保留原作的某种相似的效果，我常常发现我必须——事实上，作为一名译者，我也有责任——放弃，或改变原作的某些语言特性和句法结构。太过忠实往往达不到原作自身的目的；如果我们将荷马作品直接转换成英语词汇，那么原作的意义和风格都将不复存在。

（与温秀颖合写）

19

胡二茄子

钟灵（1921—2007），漫画家，画家，在艺术上有多方面才能。《胡二茄子》选自《天津日报》，语言诚挚。

人到了老年，会有一种似乎奇怪又不奇怪的现象：即发生在昨天的事，倒会忘得一干二净；而几十年前对自己印象极深的事情，却像是昨天刚发生一样，记得一清二楚。

我对于我的中学美术老师胡纯浦先生的怀念，就是这样。

1933 年夏，我考入了山东济南的教会学校齐鲁中学（现在更名济南第五中学）。这是一所设备和师资水平较高、学费比较昂贵、在全市知名度也较高的中学，尤其是非常重视英语，高中毕业之后，高才生可能被保送美国深造。我的入学考试，因为不考英语（那时的小学，普遍没有英语课），在近千名考生中，只录取五十名，我居然考中了第三名。

入学之后，一年下来，我的各门功课就相差太悬殊了！语文（当时叫国文）全班第一；美术（当时叫图画）全班第一；而英语（当时叫英文）全班倒数第一；其他功课不过中上而已。我最喜爱的是图画课，老师是胡纯浦先生，当时是一位三十多岁的青年画家，我猜想他排行老二，脑瓜长得有点像茄子，就得了一个颇为不雅的绰号："胡二茄子"。

　　作为一个十二三岁的初中生，爱玩爱闹，我的顽皮程度，可能也是全班第一。当我得知胡先生这一绰号后，在一次上图画课之前，就在黑板上画了一把茶壶和两个茄子，同学们都看懂了这是"壶（胡）二茄子"的形象化，大家哄然大笑，我也十分得意这幅"大作"，并没有觉得是对老师的不尊重，是可耻的。这时，突然笑声停止了，一声"起立"，我知道这是胡老师进来了，大祸就要临头了，便手忙脚乱拿板擦要把我的"罪证"擦掉。胡老师发话了："不要擦！"我尴尬地退在墙角，不敢回自己的座位。胡先生背着手，似乎很有兴趣地"欣赏"这幅作品。全班同学鸦雀无声，空气好像凝固了，大家等待着这出戏的"高潮"。

　　"钟灵，回到你的座位上去！"我一步一挪地回到自己的座位，仍然站着等待训斥。胡先生却走过来按了一下我的肩膀说："坐下吧。"接着开始讲课："作画要意在笔先，首先要立意，就是要有明确的意图，然后再考虑怎样用形象来表现它，完成它。当然最好是诗意，你们现在还不懂诗，也不知道什么叫诗意，我建议你们多读一些优秀的诗词，慢慢体会诗词的内容和含义，使自己的画富有诗意，更有韵味和情趣。钟灵在黑板上画的，当然谈不上什么诗意，但他能把自己的意图形象化，让人看懂他的本意。这是一种漫画的才能，是很可贵的。钟灵要好好努力，发挥这种才能，也许将来会成长为一位漫画家的。不过在构图和比例上、技巧上还不大讲究：茶壶画成正侧面，就显得太板；茄子的摆法太平行，缺乏变化，和茶壶相比较，也嫌略大；虽然是漫画，也要追求美，图画就是美术嘛……"

胡老师几乎用了半个课时，来分析讲解我这幅恶作剧的画，大家听得很投入，课堂出奇的安静，全班同学都被他的涵养、宽容和对学生的一片爱心震撼了！我则鼻子一酸流下了热泪。

六十多年过去了。这堂图画课却深深印在我的脑海里。现在胡先生已经逝世，但音容笑貌依然如在眼前。他不仅是我的美术老师，更重要的是教会了我怎样做人，怎样有更为广阔的胸襟，和用爱心对待他人和事物。这使我终生享用不尽。

| 译文 |

My Art Teacher Mr. Hu Chunpu
Zhong Ling

When you are getting on in years, you tend to have a feeling that seems rather odd but, in fact, not very much so: What happened to you just a couple of days ago, you clean forget about it, but what happened as long as decades ago that had a sharp impact on you, you remember as clearly as if it had occurred yesterday.

This is how I feel about Mr. Hu Chunpu, my middle school fine art teacher.

In the summer of 1933, after passing the entrance examinations, I was enrolled in Qi-Lu Middle School, a missionary school in Jinan (currently known as Jinan No. 5 Middle School). It had a high reputation in the city, for it was well-equipped with teaching facilities and well-staffed with highly qualified faculties, but its tuition fee was also high. Another thing for which the school was distinguished was that it attached great importance to English as a subject; the top students, upon graduation, could be arranged to go to the United States for higher education free of charge. As I was not examined on English in the entrance exams (in those days English was not offered at primary schools), I came out the third of the fifty candidates enrolled out of nearly one thousand examinees.

Having studied at the school for one year, I found that my grades had gone far apart: my Chinese (called "national language" then) was top of the class and so was my fine art (called "drawing" at that time); but in English I brought up the rear; in other subjects, I was just above average. However, of all the subjects, I liked fine art best. It was offered by Mr. Hu Chunpu, a young artist in his thirties. He had a nickname *Hu'er Qiezi* that was not a pleasant-sounding nickname. I guessed it was because he was the second son (*er* means two or No. 2 in Chinese) of his family and his head resembled the shape of a *qiezi*—eggplant.

As a twelve-or-thirteen-year-old junior school student, I was naughty you bet, and my naughtiness also topped the class. When I learned that Mr. Hu had such a nickname, I drew a picture on the blackboard of a teapot (teapot in Chinese is a homophone of his surname Hu) and two eggplants. When the class came to see the innuendo of the picture, they burst into laughter. I was naturally proud of my "masterpiece", without the slightest idea that it was a nasty insult to him. Suddenly the laughter stopped. When our monitor called on the class to stand up, I knew Mr. Hu was already in and disaster was to befall me. In great haste I snatched up the chalk eraser to remove the evidence of my "crime" but Mr. Hu said, "No, leave it there!"

Embarrassed, I stepped aside to the corner, not daring to go back to my seat. Mr. Hu, with his hands resting at his back, seemed to be "appreciating" the picture with great interest. The classroom was dead quiet and the air seemed to have frozen. Everybody was waiting for the "climax" of the "drama" to begin.

"Zhong Ling, go back to your seat!" I shuffled back to my seat and stood there, expecting a good dressing down from him. But Mr. Hu came over and tapped my shoulder and said, "Sit down, please." And then he began his lecture. "In drawing, the artist need have a clear idea of what to express before he starts to draw. By which I mean he should be clear about his intent and then think about how to represent it through an image—a poetic image, of course, if he can manage it. However, at this stage, you do not know much about poetry, less about how to be poetic in drawing. I suggest you read some good poetry, try to understand what it is about and its poetic implications so that you can make your drawings poetic and appealing to the viewer's aesthetic taste. The picture Zhong Ling has drawn on the board is not very poetic, I guess, but he can express his ideas and make himself understood through the image. He really has some stuff of a caricaturist in him and it is something commendable. Zhong Ling, I hope you will make every effort to develop this gift of yours and, some day, you might become an artist. However, the picture is still lacking in composition, proportion and technique. The teapot is drawn with its side facing the front and that makes it a bit rigid; the two eggplants, placed parallel to each other, are a bit dull to look at. Besides, they are too big in proportion to the teapot. Although it is a caricature, it also calls for beauty, because drawing, after all, is an art of beauty..."

Mr. Hu spent nearly half an hour talking about this mischievous work of mine. The classroom was extremely quiet, and the students, listening attentively, were moved by his tolerance, broad-mindedness, and his love for his students. Overcome by a sense of guilt, I felt tears streaming down my cheeks.

Sixty-odd years have passed, and what happened in this drawing class is deeply engraved on my memory. Though Mr. Hu is no longer around, his smiles are still vivid in my mind's eye and his voice still ringing in my ears. Not only was he my fine art teacher, he had also taught me how to live my life and treat others with love and large-heartedness. This, I believe, will guide me down the road for the rest of my life.

| 翻译提示 |

《胡二茄子》是画家钟灵回忆中学时代美术老师的一篇散文，文章写得生动感人，读后留下难忘的印象。

平淡的文字里含着浓郁的感情，是这篇文章的一个突出特点。英译文在这一点上把握得很准确，文字纯正朴实，贴近生活，很好地再现了原文的特色。

一、透过表面意义，看到文字的"精神"

汉英两种语言分属两个不同的文化，其思维逻辑和表达方式都有明显的区别。翻译时如果拘泥于译出语的字面意义，往往不能体现译入语文字的特征，文学翻译忌讳这一点。有些汉语作品译成英语时常常失色，这是一个主要原因。这篇文章的译者既能准确理解原文的意思和语言结构特点，又能根据译入语的语义结构，对措辞和句子做适当的调整，从而用译入语的恰当语义结构（semantic structure）译出了原文的内涵和精神。

[原文] 人到了老年，会有一种似乎奇怪又不奇怪的现象……

[译文] When you are **getting on in years**, you **tend to** have a **feeling** that seems rather odd but, in fact, not very much so...

[原文] 胡先生背着手，似乎很有兴趣地"欣赏"这幅作品。

[译文] Mr. Hu, with his hands resting at his back, seemed to be "appreciating" the picture with great interest.

[原文] 钟灵在黑板上画的，当然谈不上什么诗意，但他能把自己的意图形象化，让人看懂他的本意。这是一种漫画的才能，是很可贵的。钟灵要好好努力，发挥这种才能，也许将来会成长为一位漫画家的。不过在构图和比例上、技巧上还不大讲究……

[译文] He really has some **stuff** of a caricaturist in him and it is something commendable. Zhong Ling, I hope you will make every effort to develop this **gift** of yours and, some day, you might become an artist. However, the picture is still **lacking in** composition, proportion and technique.

　　第一例中的"人到了老年"以现在进行时译成了 getting on in years，不但说明"人到了老年"是一个渐进过程，也再现了老年人讲述往事时悠悠的口吻，是一个恰当的译例。tend to 和 feeling 依照原文做了巧妙转换，符合说话人的心态，译出了这两个词的内涵。第二例中的 with his hands resting at his back，把老师当时的态度和神情传达了出来，形象而生动。第三例的原文中出现了两个

"才能"，虽然是同样的一个词，但含意有轻重之别，译者敏感地捕捉到其微妙的差别，分别译为 stuff 和 gift，准确地再现了说话人的本意；而后面的 lacking in 则把原文较为模糊的说法确定在一个方向上。

二、熟谙英汉两种语言，译文浑然一体

熟悉英汉两种语言是做好双语转换的前提。理解原文，再把它转换成另一种语言，让以译入语为母语的人接受、喜欢，这需要一定的艺术才能。《胡二茄子》的英译文不论是句与句之间、句与篇之间语义的相容（semantic compatibility），还是全部语篇语义结构的整体性（semantic integrity），都处理得很得体，读起来给人一种浑然一体的感觉。

汉语文学作品多以意象取胜，这是一个传统。《胡二茄子》作为汉语文章的标题很妙，让人产生联想，引人去读全文，但在英语中这个标题不易使读者产生同样的联想，处理不当还会使文章有不敬之嫌。译者统观全文把它译成 My Art Teacher Mr. Hu Chunpu，颇得原文要旨，又符合英语表达习惯。

再看文中其他例句：

[原文] 入学之后，一年下来，我的各门功课就相差太悬殊了！语文（当时叫国文）全班第一；美术（当时叫图画）全班第一；而英语（当时叫英文）全班倒数第一……作为一个十二三岁的初中生，爱玩爱闹，我的顽皮程度，可能也是全班第一。

[译文] Having studied at the school for one year, I found that my grades had gone far apart: my Chinese (called "national language" then) was top of the class and so was my fine art (called "drawing" at that time); but in English I **brought up the rear**; in other subjects, I was just above average… As a twelve-or-thirteen-year-old junior school student, I was naughty **you bet**, and my naughtiness also **topped** the class.

［原文］ 我建议你们多读一些优秀的诗词，慢慢体会诗词的内容和含义，使自己的画富有诗意，更有韵味和情趣。钟灵在黑板上画的，当然谈不上什么诗意，但他能把自己的意图形象化，让人看懂他的本意。

［译文］ I suggest you read some good poetry, try to understand what it is about and its poetic implications so that you can **make your drawings poetic and appealing to the viewer's aesthetic taste**. The picture Zhong Ling has drawn on the board is not very poetic, **I guess**, but he can express his ideas and make himself understood through the image.

　　第一例讲主人公入学后的学习和其他有关情况，出现四个"第一"，前两个"第一"所讲意义一致，其余的则各不相同。译者把前两个统一译为 top，把"倒数第一"译成 brought up the rear，而"顽皮第一"译成动词 topped；这样一来，第一个"第一"与后两个"第一"分别形成反义与同义的互文关系，文字简约练达，语义相辅相成，其妙处超出文字之外。而在讲"自己"顽皮时，译者巧妙地加了 you bet，惟妙惟肖地刻画出当年那个少年顽皮的形象。第二例讲画画，老师建议学生读诗，个中词句是翻译的难点之一，尤其"使自己的画……更有韵味和情趣"，在汉语中"韵味和情趣"常被看作是"只可意会"之类，译成英语时常有不同的处理方式。译者根据自己的领会，将其译成如第二例黑体部分所示，十分恰当。I guess 相当于原文中的"当然"，以十分口语化的英语道出胡老师以平常的心态讲评画作，与其既教书又育人的高尚品格完全一致。最后，此篇英译文开头和结尾的翻译，不论是从形式上，还是从文章的初衷上看，都紧密照应。开头回忆很久以前发生的一件事至今记忆犹新，过渡到"我对于我的中学美术老师胡纯浦先生的怀念，就是这样"。"This is how I feel about Mr. Hu Chunpu, my middle school fine art teacher."。最后说"教会了我怎样做人，怎样有更为广阔的胸襟，和用爱心对待他人和事物。这使我终生享用不尽"。"Not only was he my fine art teacher, he had also taught me how to live my life and treat others with love and large-heartedness. This, I believe, will guide me down the road for the rest of my life."。充分显示出译者对文章整体结构的宏观控制能力。

总的来说，《胡二茄子》的英译文深得原文精髓，译文自然流畅，在文章深层意义上完整地再现了原文的神韵，是散文汉译英一个较好的作品。

（丁连普）

20

出生在天津的美国著名作家

周骥良（1921—），天津作家，著有长篇小说《我们在地下作战》，长篇传记小说《吉鸿昌》等。《出生在天津的美国著名作家》选自《天津日报》，语言平实。

岁月悠悠。一晃也是如云如烟的往事了。1981 年秋，天津作家协会刚刚恢复工作，曾任美国作家联盟主席的约翰·赫赛到天津来了。他是自费来中国旅游，又是特地来重温故乡之梦的。

天津怎么是赫赛的故乡呢？原来他父亲是美国传教士，曾任天津基督教青年会干事多年；他母亲应南开中学邀请到南开中学任英语教师。随他来的翻译多说了几句，说他母亲教出了一位世界知名的人物，那就是周恩来。说他曾经玩笑地说，他是在母亲的肚皮里就已经认识这位伟大的人物了。他 1914 年出生在天津，11 岁离开天津，回到美国。但天津一直留在他的心头，1939 年和 1946 年都来重温过故乡之梦，这次是第三次了。

赫赛这次重温故乡之梦，做了一定的准备。随他来的翻译又多说了几句，说他在北京请人为他译读了天津作家的一些作品，对孙犁的《荷花淀》与方纪的《来访者》评价很高，这就看出他对人生和现实的态度了。

　　转天，我应邀到他房间去长谈。他把微型录音机放在茶几上，要把我的原话和翻译的译语都留下来。他要我介绍唐山大地震给天津带来的灾情，又要我介绍天津作家的情况，说那两次重返故乡，他都没听说过天津也有作家，特别是听到作家写作不仅拿稿费而且月月有薪金时，仿佛是一大发现，惊奇得在笔记本上做了记录。我也顺势提出一问，他又是怎么靠稿费维持生活的。他说他在作家身份之外还兼具记者与教授的两种身份。这样既保证了生活的收入，又丰富了创作的源泉，也开拓了学识的领域。他的许多小说都是从记者的报告文学中升华出来的，还有一些作品是在教学中酝酿成熟的。我觉得他的经验还是很宝贵的，为他铺平了现实主义的创作道路，是在雄厚的现实基础上撑开他的丰富的想象力。他的成名作《阿丹诺镇的钟》写了在美军占领下西西里岛的农民的困苦生活，又一惊世之作《广岛》写了在原子弹爆炸之后的幸存者挣扎的画面，又一长篇《大墙》写了华沙犹太人反纳粹起义失败悲惨绝境。这些丰硕成果都是他从记者到作家之路上得来的。

　　赫赛重温故乡之梦自然重点仍在寻访他在新华路230号的故居。幸好小楼依旧，只是楼上楼下整整塞了七户人家。人人都笑脸相迎，任他在父母生前的客厅、书房、住室、琴室、餐厅看遍巡遍。有几家主人还请他坐下来喝茶，一切都是那么突然而又自然。赫赛脸上漾着异样的亮光，说没想到家家户户都这么好客。这些好客的人是过去不能住洋楼的人，现在住进来了；还说，这在他童年记忆中是没有的，家家都有自行车，而且有那么多女人骑自行车。

　　赫赛的重温故乡之梦结束了。当我在车厢和他话别时，他满怀激情地说，将把所见所闻以连载的方式留下来。果然，他回美国后发表了《故乡之行》的专栏。赫赛本想再来天津的，遗憾的是被癌症夺去了生命，没能看到改革开放给他的故乡带来的翻天覆地的变化，也没能使他的《故乡之行》留下续集。

| 译文 |

An American Writer Who Was Born in Tianjin
Zhou Jiliang

How time flies! It has been gone like smoke and clouds. In the autumn of 1981 when Tianjin Writers' Association had just resumed its normal function in the wake of the Cultural Revolution, Mr. John Hersey, Ex-Chairman of American Writers' Federation, visited Tianjin. He had come to China as a tourist and made a point of revisiting his former home there.

How come Tianjin was Hersey's hometown? What happened was that his father, a missionary from America, was a secretary to the Tianjin YMCA for many years and his mother, at the request of Nankai School, taught English to its students. His interpreter offered a few humorous remarks that at Nankai School his mother had taught a student that later became a world-known figure and that student was Zhou Enlai. He added that Hersey had once said half jokingly that he had known this great figure when he was still in his mother's womb. He was born in Tianjin in 1904 and left for America at the age of 11. But the city had ever been in his mind. He had visited Tianjin twice earlier, the first time in 1939 and the second in 1946, and this was his third visit.

Hersey was well prepared for this visit. His interpreter again offered some extra information that, while in Beijing, he had asked someone to translate and read to him in English some works by Tianjin writers and he had a high opinion of *The Lotus Lake* by Sun Li and *The Visitor* by Fang Ji, and that gave us a glimpse of his attitude toward life and how he looked at social realities.

The next day I was invited to the hotel where he stayed and we had a long talk in his room. He put his mini recorder on the tea table, to take down what I was going to say and its translation as well. He began by asking how Tianjin had been affected by the Tangshan earthquake and then he said he would like to be furnished with some information about Tianjin writers because, on his earlier visits, it had never occurred to him that there was any writer in this city. When he learned that writers in China were paid regular salaries in addition to contribution fees, he was amazed and put it down in his notebook as if it was a great discovery. Picking up the topic from where he left off I asked how he had managed to make a living by writing and he said he was concurrently employed as a journalist for a newspaper and a professor at a university. His employment in the two occupations not only ensured sufficient incomes for a living, but also provided him with materials for creative writing and widened the range of his learning. Some of his novels were developed on the reportage he had written as a journalist and others were conceived while he was teaching at university. This, I believe, was a rewarding practice which had actually helped to develop his creative writing techniques and his luxuriant imagination growing out of the rich soil of social realities. *A Bell for Adano* (1944), the novel that established him as a novelist, depicts the life of the farmers in a Sicilian village under the U.S. forces. *Hiroshima* (1946), his another remarkable book is about how the survivors of the atom bombs desperately struggled for life. *The Wall* (1950), his another novel, is about the ill-fated uprising of the Jews in Warsaw's ghetto against the Nazis. All these great works were written along the road from a journalist to a writer.

His trip to Tianjin was highlighted by his visit to his former residence at 230, Xinhua Road. Fortunately the small building was pretty much the same as it had been except that it was now crammed with seven households. The friendly residents gave him a warm welcome, letting him see the rooms, from the former sitting-room, the study, the bedroom, the piano-room to the dining-room, used by his parents when they lived there. Some of the hosts offered him tea. He was not prepared for such hospitality, but he found it was all real and inartificial. His face lit up with a radiant smile and said that in the past these hospitable folks could not afford to live in buildings like this but now they were right there. He also commented that every household had bikes and he found so many women riding them and it was not part of the memory of his childhood days.

When his visit was over and I got on board the train to say good-bye, he said, excitedly, that he was going to write, in the form of a series, about what he had seen and heard in Tianjin. Back to the United States, he set about writing a special column titled *A Journey Home*, as he had planned, in a special column. In fact he was planning to return to Tianjin for more visits but, falling victim to cancer, he was unable to come and see the changes that had been taking place in his hometown since the reform and, consequently, unable to write more to follow up his series of *A Journey Home*.

| 翻 译 提 示 |

《出生在天津的美国著名作家》属于叙事体短篇散文，全文只有 31 句。作者以通俗简朴的语言，记述了美国作家联盟前主席约翰·赫赛来天津寻访故土的经历。译者力求保持原作娓娓叙事的朴素风格，同时充分考虑到中英两种语言各自的特点，有些句子比照译语行文习惯做了适度的剪裁，另外一些则依据译语表达习惯调整了语序。整个译文读来流畅自然，平易质朴，做到了剪裁有度、拆合得法、用词精当。

由于中英两种语言在文字及文化层面的差异，加之目的语读者背景知识的不同，译者势必要对原文内容适当剪裁，以保证行文的流畅及译文的可读性，但剪裁的尺度要恰到好处。仅在第一段译文中，便可以看出译者娴熟的剪裁技巧：

［原文］ ……天津作家协会刚刚恢复工作……

［译文］ …when Tianjin Writers' Association had just resumed its normal function in the wake of the Cultural Revolution… （加词）

［原文］ 他是自费来中国旅游……

［译文］ He came to China as a tourist… （减词）

译者意识到英语读者无法体味"刚刚恢复工作"的言外之意，故而增加了 in the wake of the Cultural Revolution（"文化大革命"结束不久）。这种背景知识方面的释义性增补是允许的，也是必要的。在第二例中，译者将"自费"（at his own expense）略去不译是有充足理由的，如果照实译出，不仅会破坏行文的自然流畅，使英语读者感到突兀，而且在信息上实属多余，因为按照常理，旅游是个人的事，当然应自费。可见，"自费"的含义已隐含于 tourist 一词中。此外，英语读者并不像我们那样过分强调"自费"与"公费"的差别。译文适度剪裁的例子还有几处，比如第二段将"随他来的翻译"径直译为 his interpreter，而不是 the interpreter who accompanied him，第四段在作家的每部作品后加上括号标明了出版年代。这些做法都是为了照顾译文读者的阅读习惯、思维特征或顺应英语的表达习惯。

汉语散文的特点是形散而神聚，但英语散文讲求行文紧凑严谨。为保证译文的可读性，译者必须在紧扣原意的前提下，将若干汉语小句的意思融汇综合，选择英语中最恰当的句型与结构，实现句型与意义的顺利转换。从翻译的技巧来看，译者在转换融合方面处理得当。例如，原文第四段"他要我介绍唐山大地震……"一句，共包括七个分句，而主语"他"只出现两次。译者灵活地将原句拆为两句，he（包括 him）在译文中虽出现九次之多，但读来自然流畅，层次分明，毫无拖泥带水之感：

He began by asking how Tianjin had been affected by the Tangshan earthquake and then he said he would like to be furnished with some information about Tianjin writers because, on his earlier visits, it had never occurred to him that there was any writer in this city. When he learned that writers in China were paid regular salaries in addition to contribution fees, he was amazed and put it down in his notebook as if it was a great discovery.

至于文中频频使用的同位语（如 Ex-Chairman of American Writers' Association，a missionary from America）、各种修饰性状语

（如 excitedly，separately，back to the United States，falling victim to cancer），不仅丰富了译文表达方式，提高了可读性，而且增加了文章的韵律美和修辞美。

在选词上是否精当地道，这是衡量散文翻译优劣的重要尺度之一。译者只有在发挥译文优势、遵从目的语表达习惯的基础上，才能找出最佳对等语，而这种能力源于大量的阅读和写作实践以及对两种语言感受能力的长期培养。请注意下面几个字句片段的处理：

［原文］……又是**特地**来重温故乡之梦的。
［译文］…and **made a point of** revisiting his former home there.

［原文］……小楼依旧，**只是**……
［译文］…the small building was pretty much the same as it had been **except that**…

［原文］这些好客的人是过去**不能**住洋楼的人……
［译文］…in the past these hospitable folks **could not afford to** live in buildings like this…

［原文］我也**顺势**提出一问……
［译文］**Picking up the topic from where he left off** I asked…

［原文］重温故乡之梦自然**重点仍在寻访**……
［译文］His trip to Tianjin **was highlighted by** his visit…

［原文］……这在**他童年记忆中是没有的**……
［译文］…it was **not part of the memory of his childhood days**.

通读全文，好的译句比比皆是，整篇文章一气呵成，如行云流水，无斧凿痕迹。归根结底，这种效果源于对原文深刻入微的把握，对译语淋漓尽致的发挥，显示出翻译家的艺术修养。这是一篇较好的译文。

（马红军）